COME TO DUST

By
Bracken MacLeod

Trepidatio Publishing

TREPIDATIO
PUBLISHING

Trepidatio books may be ordered through booksellers or by contacting:

Trepidatio Publishing an imprint of JournalStone

www.trepidatio.com

The views expressed in this work are solely those of the authors and do not necessarily reflect the views of the publisher, and the publisher hereby disclaims any responsibility for them.

ISBN: 978-1-945373-66-4   (sc)
ISBN: 978-1-945373-67-1   (ebook)

JournalStone rev. date: June 23, 2017

Library of Congress Control Number: 2017937092

Printed in the United States of America
1st JournalStone Edition
Originally Published by Maelstrom Press

Cover Art & Design: 99designs – Mastah Killah 187
Images: http://mercurycode.deviantart.com/art/Rust-texture-IX-389490690 and https://creativemarket.com/DesignSomething/18560-10-Vintage-Overlay-Textures-Mock-up?u=parrot

Edited by: Sean Leonard

For BOB BOOTH,

sleep well, Papa Necon

COME TO DUST

Let us beware of saying that death is the opposite of life. The living being is only a species of the dead, and a very rare species.
— Friedrich Nietzsche, *The Gay Science*

Golden lads and girls all must,
As chimney-sweepers, come to dust.

— William Shakespeare, *Cymbeline*

Children begin by loving their parents. After a time, they judge them. Rarely, if ever, do they forgive them.
— *Oscar Wilde, A Woman of No Importance, Act II*

Prologue: Scenes from an Ending

The cool earth of the grave in front of them was the only place the August heat couldn't penetrate, but no one who would benefit from the shade would be going down into it. A cemetery employee discretely released the handbrake on the lowering straps and the half-sized pink box started to descend slowly. From a small wireless speaker, the bagpipe strains of "Amazing Grace" began to play, drowning out the soft sounds of the well-oiled ratchet gears. It couldn't compete with the soft weeping of the girl's mother. Although green AstroTurf had been draped down to cover the bare earth sides of the hole, there was no imaginable way to disguise the fact that they were lowering a child into a grave. There was nothing loud enough to dispel the silence of a dead child.

The mourners slowly dispersed, each one offering their final condolences to the woman who remained seated. Her veil obscured the tears streaking her face, but still, she looked down, hiding her grief from friends and family. So many had asked how they could help, but there was nothing any of them could do for her. Her mother sat beside her, an arm around her shoulders, whispering comfort in her ear as if she was still six and could be consoled with gentle shushing. Laura wanted to throw that god damned arm off her shoulder and scream. She wanted to stand and scream. She wanted to scream at her mother and the priest for their platitudes and assurances that there was a plan, she just wasn't privy to it. She wanted to yell at her absentee ex-husband standing near the road already with his friends, smoking and solemnly shaking hands as if he wasn't glad to be relieved of his child-support obligations. She wanted to scream and scream and scream. And, instead, she held it in. A good New England woman who wouldn't burden anyone else with her pain. She'd hold it in and push it down until she was home again, alone in a house full of toys and Sesame Street DVDs and silence so painful. She'd hold it all in, and curse the sky for not darkening on the day of her only child's funeral and the earth for not rejecting a body so small and unfinished. She'd curse all of creation for abandoning her baby to die under the car of someone cutting through her street to beat the light. Most of all, she'd curse herself for turning away in that moment to look at her cell phone as her child rode her tricycle from the driveway out into the street. Staring at a picture of a baby fox with a cute saying she couldn't remember now, but oh, how that picture was burned in her mind. It was there like a spot in her eyes after a camera flash along with the sounds of rubber screeching on asphalt and metal grinding on metal that would never leave her ears. And she was still smiling when she turned around, unaware of what was happening, because it was all over before her mind could grasp that she was witnessing the single most horrible thing it could conceive.

As the last of her well-wishers departed, the funeral director approached and held out a hand to help her up. She found it in herself to stand, but that took the last of her strength and she was unable to move another step. With him holding one arm and her mother on the other, they turned her away from her child, and led her away. She didn't want to leave. She never wanted to leave. Instead, she imagined herself crawling into the hole along with Cherie and letting the men standing in the distance with their shovels and the backhoe cover them over. The funeral director told her how lovely the service was, and assured her again how terribly he felt for her. She knew that couldn't possibly be true. His job was grief and despair and he saw it all day, every day. He had to feel as blasé about other people's grief as she was about photographing people's weddings. *How could seeing people on the happiest day of their lives ever get old?* She'd asked herself. She learned. It got old the way anything that was work got old. Her pain was just another day on the job for him. Still, she let him do his job and nodded and accepted his sympathy as if it was a real thing he felt, and something she wanted to receive. And together they walked away.

His skinny blond assistant collected the Bluetooth speaker and stuffed it in her bag before following along. Only the sounds of the cemetery remained. Birds and the distant sound of traffic beyond the wall. And a light scratching she knew had to be the sounds of shovels and respectful men working. It was not the sound of a child trying to get out of a box before it was covered with earth. That would be a horrible sound. More horrible than the sound of a car hitting a child. More horrible than anything she could imagine.

Yes. That was what the scratching was.

She looked over her shoulder to see the cemetery employees still standing in the distance, waiting for everyone to go before beginning their work. The funeral director helped her into the car and her mother crawled in after her. And all Laura wanted to do was rush back to the gravesite and scream, *Let her out! For God's sake, let her out; she's not dead. My baby is alive!* But that was impossible. Her broken little girl's body had been cut, drained, sewn, and embalmed. There was no life in her. There was no panicked child in a box desperate to get out, crying for her mommy. Of course there wasn't. It was monstrous to even think it.

The door closed and she couldn't hear the scratching any more.

Part One: Sophie's Death

September

1

Mitch dodged out of the way as the woman pushed her carriage into the space he'd been occupying. She shoved forward, guiding the half-sized shopping cart with one hand while she held her iPhone against her cheek with the other, declaring, "I got right up in that little bitch's face and said, 'I don't want to hear it!'" She grabbed the carton of cubed pineapple he'd had his eye on, plopped it into the carriage, and moved on without acknowledging she'd barged in front of him like he was invisible. He'd carefully nurtured that invisibility and perfected it. He had mousy brown hair, cut short but not shaved, stubble on his chin, but no beard. He wore a pair of thick-framed glasses (with an actual prescription in the lenses), and a plain black T-shirt and gray chinos. Only his shoes were an indulgence: Oxblood red Doc Marten 1460s. They were expensive, but he worked on his feet and didn't own a car. He needed boots that were comfortable and durable.

Mitch grabbed the container of pineapple below the one he'd intended to buy and set it in his basket. Sophie would squeal when he showed her what he got. A man wearing an apron stepped up next to him and started straightening the organic strawberries. Mitch caught a glimpse of heavy black tattooed letters on his forearm reading "PRIDE" and backed away, looking around for the quickest way out of the produce section, maybe even out of the store. He might have misjudged how badly he wanted organic pineapple. Then again, he didn't actually want organic anything. He preferred shopping at Star Market where the aisles were wider and no one came close to him.

The guy looked over and said, "Anything I can help you find?" Mitch shook his head mutely. The man went back to work and Mitch saw the companion word, "VEGAN," inked on his other forearm. He let out a small sigh and tried to tell himself not to panic. *You'll be fine, man. Just get your stuff and get out.*

He sped through the rest of the store, snatching a bag of spicy hot blue corn chips and a jar of chutney salsa. One treat for Sophie, and one for him. He grabbed a few mini-scones for breakfast and made his way toward the checkout.

Scanning the lines, he found the one he wanted and queued up. A middle-aged man in an apron called out from two lanes over, "Next in line!" Mitch turned to invite the person behind him to go on ahead, but plenty of people who weren't in a position even remotely resembling "next" descended on the checker. He stayed put, happy to wait. When it was his turn, he unloaded his scant groceries onto the belt and slipped the plastic basket around the side, out of the way. The woman behind the register smiled with cheerful recognition.

She was Mitch's opposite. Bright and noticeable, with a shining nose ring and fuscia streaks accenting a loose afro she parted on the side. Tattoos snaked down her dark arms, ending in a lotus flower inked on the back of the hand she used to check his things through. She smiled as big as anyone he'd ever seen. It was infectious. He smiled back, feeling stupid and mute and all of the things he didn't want to be in front of her. In this moment, standing in exactly that spot, he wanted to shed his carefully cultivated invisibility and be seen. Specifically, he wanted to be seen by her.

"You don't have much today," she said.

He looked at the single bagful of items he'd picked out and shrugged. He couldn't actually afford to shop in her store, but didn't want to admit to it. "Just a few necessities."

She blinked and he felt like winking out of existence in that brief time she wasn't seeing him. But she opened her eyes and looked directly at him. She swiped his pineapple over the scanner and held it up. "Yeah? Necessities?"

"Stocking up for the... Pineappocalypse." Blood rushed into his face and although the store was air conditioned, he felt like he was standing outside in the sun. Sweat beaded up on his forehead, but kept his arms at his sides instead of brushing it away. *Stay cool,* he told himself, the voice in his head sounding like it was about ready to run and leave him standing there alone.

"How forward thinking of you. I rarely plan ahead for fruit-based catastrophe."

He brushed his fingernails on his shirt and said, "Yeah, I'm a surf-vivalist. I've got a whole stockpile of Mai Tai ingredients and sunblock. You know. When global warming makes the whole world the beach, I'm totally ready."

She laughed and finished bagging his things. He stood staring at her, a stupid smile on his face, while she repeated his total a second time and he realized he'd blown it again. His time with her was nearly over and, while he'd pushed himself to be funny and charming, he hadn't worked up the nerve to do more than joke around. He'd have to submit to shopping here again. He pulled his only twenty out of his wallet and handed it over. She took it and handed him back less money that he'd hoped.

"I've never had a Mai Tai. Are they any good?"

"What?"

"Mai Tais. Surfaggeddon or whatever."

He laughed. "Oh, that. The Pineappocalypse. I actually don't know. I'm more of a beer drinker."

Her back straightened and she grew an inch behind the register. "I like a really dank IPA. I know where we can go get one if you ever get around to asking me out."

A lump caught in Mitch's throat and he choked out, "Would you... like to... go out sometime?"

"Sure. If you tell me your name."

The heat surged back into Mitch's face and he stammered out, "Mitch. Mitch LeRoux."

"Is that short for Mitchell?"

The man standing next in line was beginning to look annoyed and shifted from foot to foot as Mitch introduced himself. He cleared his throat loudly, but Mitch didn't care if the guy was upset. He'd been shopping in this hellscape of a store for weeks trying to build up the nerve to ask her on a date, and now it was happening. He'd gladly take a beating if it meant getting her number.

"It's a nickname. My name's... Michel."

"Hi, Michel," she said, putting the emphasis on the second syllable, mee-SHEL, like she heard the name every day. "I'm Liana. What's your number?" His heart dropped at the thought that she wasn't going to give him *her* number. She wasn't interested, but let the game get out of hand.

"You're not going to give me yours?"

"I will. But I want to make sure we make this date, and it's taken you forever to work up the nerve to talk to me in this line. I don't have time to wait while you find the courage to call." Mitch smiled and rattled off his number. She wrote it down, tore the piece of paper in half and handed him back hers.

"I'll talk to you later, Mitch, a.k.a. Michel." She winked, and afterward he had no recollection of leaving the store and going outside.

2

The pavement seemed a yard beneath his feet as Mitch floated along the sidewalk, his thoughts swirling around alternate scenarios the future might include. He imagined himself on a date with Liana, on a second, and a third. He imagined touching her skin and tasting her breath, what her hair smelled like, what her body felt like. He wasn't superstitious but still he often forced himself not to imagine good outcomes. Although he knew it was nonsense, he worried that if he pictured any desired experience too well in his mind, he'd never get to realize it in the real world. But not today. Today, he let himself fantasize about getting close to someone. He dreamed about letting down his guard, just a little.

Turning the corner by sense memory more than intention, he barely noticed his surroundings until he reached the house. Heading up the driveway, he cleared the clouds from his head and tried to bring himself back down to earth. That he'd gotten her number had him feeling high, but he needed to be *present* now. The time for living in the dream had passed, and he had responsibilities.

He climbed the steps around the side of the house, and let himself in. Taking off his shoes, he crept to the door under the staircase and listened. He pushed it open and slipped quietly downstairs. Mitch had to stoop in the low-ceilinged basement. Peeking around the corner, he saw the children getting cleaned up after lunch. He crept into the room and tapped the little brown-haired girl on the shoulder. She spun around, smiled and shouted, "Yunka!" She jumped at Mitch, and he caught her, the shopping bag banging against his ribs as he lifted her up in a hug. The women at the changing table turned and smiled. One waved. The other said, "Someone's happy to see you, Michel."

Mitch had never wanted kids of his own. He felt too damaged by his own upbringing for that. When his niece, Sophie, was born, something in him changed—a small piece of that resistance broke, and he doted on her and did all the things that the man who'd donated half her DNA never did. At the end of the day, though, he would go home to his apartment, and resume his solitary life. Every few weekends, he'd take the girl for a couple of days while his sister, Violette, went to listen to her new hippie jam band drummer boyfriend lose the tempo. And then one weekend, she declared she was going on the road, and left him with the girl and a power of attorney. He'd never wanted kids of his own, but now that he had one, he was dead set not to screw it up.

He smiled. "And I'm happy to see Sophie." He looked the girl in the face and asked, "Did you have a good day today?" She nodded and replied with an "Uh-huh."

The woman who'd greeted him finished fastening the other child's diaper, stood him up on the changing table and pulled his pants up. "Sophie *always* has a good day," she said over her shoulder. "She is a perfect child."

"I *don't* believe it!" he said. "Are you sure you're *my* Sophie? You're a changeling, aren't you!"

"Nooooooo! I'm Sophie," the girl insisted. She giggled at the suggestion she wasn't the same child he'd dropped off that morning.

He sidled over to the day care operator, Khadija, and pulled a check from his shirt pocket. "I'm sorry it's late. Thanks for being so patient."

She smiled. Mitch always wanted to mention how much she looked like the supermodel Iman, but he figured the compliment wouldn't be appropriate. Her hijab and modest but practical clothes told him that he should keep his thoughts on her appearance to himself—even if he merely wanted to be complimentary. Sophie's grandmother would have been scandalized to know that Mitch had placed her in a residential day care run by a Somali Muslim woman, but he knew there wasn't anywhere better. Khadija was amazing with the kids— it was obvious she honestly loved them—and her own children were the politest, best behaved kids he'd ever met. He could do a hell of a lot worse for much more money than she charged.

"Thank you, Michel," she said. "I know you're always good for it." She squeezed his hand and turned to write a receipt for him. He didn't need one, but she did it every time anyway.

Her assistant helped the child she'd been getting cleaned up off the table and turned to Mitch. She grinned at him and grabbed a piece of paper from the table. A bit of glitter fell off as she held it out to Sophie. "Do you want to show your uncle what you drew today?" Sophie pushed and scrambled to get out of Mitch's arms so suddenly he almost dropped her. She landed like a gymnast and bounded over to grab her picture. She spun around with it and held it up, more glitter casting off in the air like faerie dust.

"It's a castle!" she said.

"A princess castle?"

"No, silly. Bampire!"

Mitch straightened up, the top of his head brushing the ceiling. Khadija and Samira smiled at him knowingly. "The

Count. On Sesame Street. He's a vampire. I don't let her watch—"

Khadija handed him his receipt and laughed. "She's a very special child, Michel. Whatever you are doing, keep doing it." He grinned and mutely accepted her compliment. Whatever he was doing, he was barely hanging on. He suspected at least half, or more, of her happiness and well adjustment was due to Khadija. He thanked her, and asked Sophie if she was ready to go.

"No. Wanna stay and play."

"But we've got to get home." He pulled the shopping bag around and opened it up. "We've got to get this pineapple in the fridge."

"Can I have some now?" she shouted.

"At home. Can you say, 'see you Monday'?"

She turned and waved at the women. "See you Monday!" She ran over and gave each of them a hug. Mitch said his goodbyes and led her upstairs. They slipped into their shoes and out the door. Outside, he wished he had a car with air conditioning. The walk home was going to be long with her little legs. She was already sweating, and her badly cut bangs were plastered to her forehead.

"Carry me," she said, raising her arms.

"We're not even out of the driveway."

"Carry me. Pleeeeeease!" He couldn't say no to her. Although he could barely breathe in the humidity and he smelled like B.O. and spilt espresso, he hefted her up and started toward home. She lay her head on his shoulder and traced the company logo on his shirt with a tiny finger while they walked. As hot and sticky and stinky as it was, he loved these moments, and "accidentally" took a wrong turn so the walk took just a little longer.

Not once along the way home did he think about Liana or the future. That exact moment was all that mattered.

3

At the end of her shift, Liana went to the employee locker room to change out of her smock and company T-shirt. Although she took her uniform home with her every night, she didn't like to go out looking like she was coming from work. She pulled a snug Les Discrets shirt over her head and shut her locker. A coworker stuck her head into the room and said, "Hey, Li. Mike wants to see you before you go." Liana spun the dial on her locker and asked if he said what it was about. The girl from the customer service desk shrugged and grunted a "Huh uh." Liana slung her bag over her shoulder and made her way to the manager's office.

Inside, Mike sat at his micro-desk, piled high with papers and odds and ends from around the store. He looked up from what he was doing and waved her in. "Have a seat." He gestured toward a metal folding chair opposite him, also stacked with papers. Liana smirked and stood. It was a running joke that he invited everyone to sit in a chair that no one had actually sat upon for years. It was rumored, the first person to actually have the guts to move the papers and take a seat would be the Once and Future King of Wholesome Market. To date, no one had ever heard the strains of "Carmina Burana" coming from the vicinity of Mr. Niles' office.

"What's up, boss?" Liana said.

He leaned back and raised an eyebrow. "I had a very irate customer come in today to complain about you. He said you were rude and didn't seem interested in doing your job as much as flirting with boys."

"He said that? 'Flirting with boys'?"

Mike nodded his head. "Indeed he did. He was very concerned with the level of attention you devoted to 'recreation,' while 'manning the till,' as he also put it. He was very tightly wound. Said you didn't seem up to the responsibility of handling people's money and that he didn't feel comfortable letting you ring him through. This last observation he based on your appearance, incidentally, not your social interests. He was concerned you might frighten..." He waved a hand in the air dismissively. "I don't know. I stopped listening at that point. I assured him that I would speak with you about your performance just so he'd fuck off out of my office. He smelled like bologna."

"Okaaaay."

"So, was he cute?"

"What do you mean, 'cute'? If he came in here to complain, you saw him."

"No, no. The guy you were flirting with."

Liana chuckled and nodded. "Oh, him. Yuuup. You know I don't give my number to lamers."

Mike closed a file on his desk and stood. "Glad to hear it. Now, do you know what you did wrong here today?"

"I didn't ask the cute guy if he had a cute brother for you?"

Mike pointed a finger at her and said, "Exactly! Next time, think of me. I sit in this little box all day and barely get to meet anybody, except douchebags like that guy. You're not the only gal around here who has needs." He wagged a finger at her in mock scorn. "Well, I guess that's that then. We've spoken; you are officially admonish-ed. See you tomorrow."

Liana tilted her head to the side. She knew she could count on Mike to have her back. When the aging hippies who shopped in their store got upset that she wasn't dressed in a paisley crepe dress and stinking of patchouli, he always defended her. More than that though, Mike had been her guardian angel ever since rescuing her from a pair of popped collar and beach muscle bros who thought they saw Satan walking down the street and felt it was time to do the Lord's work. Or what they thought was the Lord's work, anyway. Mike came across her lying in the street after the pair had worked her over with an ax handle and work boots. He helped her into his car and took her to the emergency room. Her attackers had done a number on her face and ribs, and broken one of her arms. She said she hadn't had the chance to even put up a fight. They hit her from behind with a bottle. She had no health insurance. Mike worked some kind of magic, hiring her at the grocery store while she was still in the hospital and backdating her paperwork. He might not have saved her from the beating, but she felt in every way she could imagine that he had saved her life. And he was still defending her, if for no other reason than that he knew when to send the elevator back down to help other people who were where he had once been.

"Ciao, boss!" Liana waggled her fingers and blew him a kiss. She wandered out of the store into the sun.

● ● ●

Feeling blissed out on take-out tikka masala and red wine, she reclined on the sofa reading the new barrio noir by Gabino Iglesias while King Woman's singer howled from her record player speakers like the lovechild of Glenn Danzig and P.J. Harvey. In the middle of her near-Zen chill, she almost missed the sound of her cell phone ringing on the kitchen counter. She considered letting it go to voicemail until she recalled the cute, funny guy she'd given her number to that afternoon. He'd been coming to her store for weeks just to talk to her. She could tell by the odd assortment of things he always bought—no one needed that much chutney salsa and lime mango shave butter—and she'd been waiting nearly as long for him to ask for her number. She stumbled off the sofa toward the kitchen counter to answer the call before the robot woman who lived in her phone answered and got to him first. "Keep away from him, you bitch!"

She snatched the phone off the counter and almost swiped the screen in the wrong direction, sending him right into the clutches of her virtual competition. She answered and said, "Hello?" trying to control her sudden breathless excitement.

"Uh, hi. This is Mitch LeRoux... We talked today at—"

"Hey, Michel. What took you so long to call?" Liana glanced up at the clock on her microwave. It had been almost nine hours since she gave him her number. He was right in the zone between not wanting to seem desperate and unable to wait. That made her heart flutter a little. She'd almost phoned him twice since getting home, but chose instead to give it a full day to see if he called first. She was relieved he had; it allowed her to maintain her mystery for a little while longer.

"I actually thought I'd get your voicemail. I figured... I don't know."

"That I wouldn't be a lame-o homebody?"

"That's not what I meant!"

She laughed. "It's okay. That's pretty much what I am, despite appearances. I hope that's not a disappointment."

"Not at all. It's pretty much who I am too."

"We're two boring peas in a pod. Perfect couple!" She held her breath waiting for him to reply, feeling certain she'd taken the banter a step too far and entered the realm of overly attached crazy-person in record time. She might as well have told him she downloaded his picture off the store's security cam so she could make it her new phone wallpaper. *He's totally not going to think you'll murder him in his sleep so he can be yours forever!*

"Ha! Should we pick a wedding date, or go on a first date?"

She let out the breath she was holding and laughed. "Let's start slow. Maybe we can just go to a few open houses."

"Perfect. You want to get dinner first?"

The heroic quantity of lamb she'd already eaten made a dinner invitation sound less appealing than running off to a justice of the peace with a complete stranger, but she understood that eventually, yes, she would feel hunger again. Best to plan ahead for such occasions. "Sounds good to me."

"You want to meet in Kendall? There's a couple of new places that have opened there with tremendous beer menus."

She hesitated, wanting to make a joke about being swept off her feet on a white horse. But then it occurred to her, that in all the times she'd watched Michel leave her store, she'd never once seen him walk out to the parking lot to get in a car. He always headed over the overpass in front of her store toward what she realized now was the bus stop. Normally, Liana didn't care whether her humor, appearance, or opinions were off putting. It was how she survived in the liminal space between the different cultures she straddled. But once in a while, she met someone she didn't want to have to make scale her walls to prove himself. On occasion, she wanted to be approachable and easy to like.

"Tell you what," she said. "I'll pick *you* up day after tomorrow at seven. I got a couple of advance tickets to a sneak preview of that new witch movie. Sound good?"

"Sounds great," he said. Although he sounded enthusiastic about the date and the movie, when he gave her his address it was halting, and he seemed guarded. Liana didn't wonder why she went on a lot of first dates, but not as many second or third. She liked being in the driver's seat. Had as long as she'd been able to reach the pedals both figuratively and literally. A lot of guys were put off by that. It was something she was used to. But this guy seemed different. She hoped Mitch could handle someone who liked to stand beside, not behind. She really liked him so far.

She hung up the phone and proceeded to stare at the same paragraph in her book for forty minutes because she was day dreaming about the night after next.

4

Mitch peeked out the window at the car that had pulled up in front of his place. He had no sense of cars. To him, they were all the same, except for the ones that were built to stand out, and even then, he only knew them by appearance, not performance or spec. He couldn't tell what the difference under the hood was between something that had a V8 versus a Hemi—he wasn't even sure what a Hemi was, although he knew the word referred somehow to engines—but when Liana parked hers, somehow the car seemed appropriate. It looked like an extension of her personal style more than just a thing to get from point A to point B. He couldn't place it other than to say it was mid-sized and classic looking, if a little road weary, like she'd driven it out of a black and white movie set in the desert. Then she stepped out, and he lost his breath. She wore a tight black scoop neck shirt, matching jeans, and tall black boots. If she'd had lighter skin and a Betty Page hairdo instead of her bouncy afro, she'd be a dead ringer for Tura Satana. She looked like she didn't just own the car she'd pulled up in, but the whole street, and maybe every other god damn thing on it too. She strode up the walk, and he disappeared from the window to answer the door before she could ring the bell. If it seemed anxious, too bad. To hell with posturing. He hadn't felt this excited and anxious since the parole board said "Yes."

His heart beat fast and his guts were in a clench. His pulse was racing because of the girl at the door, but his nerves were driven by the one playing behind him on the floor. Although she went to day care, he hadn't ever left Sophie alone with a sitter at night. Khadija wasn't available to watch her, so he'd asked the girl next door, Meghan. She wasn't ideal, but her mother, Faye, kept telling him that she was available to sit, explaining that she did it all the time for other kids, and offering him references. He'd never taken her up on it because he *was* actually a homebody, like he'd joked on the phone with Liana. Not being networked into a mommy's group or the public schools yet, he had no idea how to go about finding another sitter. Sophie would be fine, he told himself. *For Christ's sake, Meg lives next door. She's not a stranger.* She was only fifteen and he'd seen her more than once behaving irresponsibly with her friends, but that was what fifteen-year-old girls did, right? He tried to dial his anxiety down as he opened the door. Chances were fifty-fifty that once Liana saw Sophie, and he explained that he was more or less a single parent, their date would end right there on the doorstep. *There is no "more or less." You* are *a single parent,* he told himself. Mitch didn't intend to be dishonest about his obligations, but he wanted to start on his best foot before laying out all the obstacles to his being in a relationship. Maybe once he told her he was an ex-con, she'd forget all about him being responsible for a kid.

He opened the door. She said, "Sorry, I'm early," before he was able to invite her in.

"It's all good. I just need to get my shoes on. Come on in." He stepped aside, revealing the four-year-old on the floor surrounded by her off-brand interlocking blocks. She wanted Legos, but they were too expensive, so he gave her what he could and hoped she'd be happy with second best. Of course, she was. At this point in her life, close was good enough.

"Who's *this*?" Liana asked.

"Liana, meet Sophie. She's my niece." *My world.*

"Your niece? Did I just screw up? Is this the right night?"

"No, no. You didn't mess anything up. We have a date tonight. Sophie is my niece, but... she lives with me. The babysitter's in the kitchen getting dinner ready. I'm sorry I didn't tell you before. If you want to go to the movie without me—"

Liana put a hand on his chest and shoved gently. Instead of taking the escape hatch he'd opened, she closed the door behind her and got down on her knees on the ratty carpet next to the girl and cooed to her about her hair.

"I like yours too. It's like mine," Sophie said, pulling at one of her own curls. "Build a pyramid," Sophie commanded, holding out a handful of blocks. Liana smiled at the precociousness of a four-year-old who demanded pyramids like a miniature Nile queen. Without complaint, she started stacking, and even though she couldn't get the tribute to the toddler's magnificence more than a second layer high before Sophie dashed it to pieces with a little hand, she kept trying, the both of them laughing. She played and when the sitter came back with dinner, Liana gave the child a big hug and said, "We'll see you later, hon."

Mitch was definitely in love.

• • •

In the car on the way to dinner, she never asked about the girl's absent mother. She didn't comment on the state of the apartment—littered with the debris of a young girl at play and semi-neglected by a man who worked full-time, parented the rest of the day, and was too tired to pick up every night. Instead, she told him about her own niece who was going to be starting middle school in the fall. She talked about how important family was, and that she respected a man who stepped up for his blood, even if she wasn't his. "Not enough brothers take responsibility."

"I'm not sure I qualify as a brother." He held out his arm showing the blue veins visible under his pale skin.

She feigned shock. "Whaaaat?" Backhanding him playfully again in the chest, she said, "You know what I mean." He wished she'd touch him again, even if it was just to hit him.

Dinner at the taqueria was good. The movie was better. Scary in all the right places. And she grabbed his arm at the big reveal at the end, sending his stomach tumbling again with anxious pleasure. He hadn't felt this way on a date since he was fourteen and thought he was a high roller because he'd paid for his date's dinner *and* subway fare. Walking out of the theater, he reached over and slipped his hand into hers. And she didn't pull away. In fact, she held on and gave his hand a squeeze. He thought about how nice that felt. About the long loud nights in MCI Concord, lying in his bunk staring at the cinder block ceiling, unable to sleep, and listening to someone yelling just to be yelling. Listening to the snoring coming from the bunk three feet below, and still feeling perfectly alone, as if the years ahead were an insurmountable gulf of time and he'd never feel the affectionate touch of another human being again. Something as simple as holding hands with an adult woman made him want to cry and thank the universe for pulling him out of the hole into which he'd thrown himself. Of course, the universe had done no such thing. It cared about him as much as it cared about a speck of dust floating in the void forever. Which was to say, not at all. Still, he felt grateful for the chance to hold a hand.

"I suppose we ought to go relieve the sitter," she said. He didn't want to admit it, but it was time. Liana was nice, smart, and attractive. Best of all, she seemed to have had as good a time on their date as he had. Still, it was time to wrap the evening up and head home. He was butting up against the amount of money he could afford for a night out, even accounting for the free movie tickets and Liana driving instead of taking a cab or the train. While Sophie had been out of his thoughts during much of dinner, she was in them increasingly at the movie. He'd tried not to be obvious about checking his cell phone for messages from Meghan. When he'd pulled the door shut behind them on the way out, Sophie was crying and begging him to stay. It tore at him to go, but he did it. He remembered her doing the same thing the first few times he'd dropped her at daycare, despite their elaborate parting ritual that included a hug, kisses, high-fives, fist bumps, and a tickle. She'd eventually come to love day care and stopped crying every time he left her there. But he hadn't spent an entire night away from his niece since his sister had abandoned them both. He'd gotten the knack of her day to day needs quickly (he *had* to), but an evening for himself? That required a further adjustment. Leaving her at home was not the same as taking her to Khadija's, and she was freaked out, asking if he was coming home. Of course, he assured her, he was. But still, she cried. She made both him and Liana promise to come in and say goodnight to her when they got back.

He looked down at his hands and huffed out a half-hearted laugh. "So, that was... awesome." Liana reached over and put a hand on top of his, he felt his chest tighten and breathing became a little harder. Dating wasn't quite like riding a bike. His confidence was atrophied and his concern for Sophie kept him distracted and wobbly.

"I had a good time too," she said.

He turned his hand over, expecting her to pull away. Instead, she laced her fingers with his and said, "So, can I come in and give Sophie a kiss good night like I promised?" It was after eleven and if Sophie wasn't asleep, Mitch knew he'd never be able to get her up in time in the morning. Still, he loved the idea of bringing Liana in to check on the girl. Keeping promises was important.

"I could fix you a cup of coffee," he said, stuttering over "cuppacoffee." "It's kind of my thing. Coffee." She laughed and turned the ignition off. The car's engine pinged and clacked a little before settling down. Like his heart.

"I just bet. I'd love some, if it's not a trouble."

"Trouble? I can practically brew it in my sleep." He wasn't lying. He was a barista at the flagship Brogdon & Palmer Coffee Roasters Café across town and more often than not, he dreamed about work.

Mitch waited for her on the walk, while Liana circled around the car. She slipped her hand in his as they walked up the cracked pathway to the front door, and he almost tripped over his own feet. *Jesus, man. You're twenty-eight, not eighteen. Stop being so squirrelly!* That was easier said than done, however. He had as clear an intention of making a cup of coffee as she had of drinking one. And the thought of what just might happen if he didn't screw it up was twisting his insides like a wet washrag.

Pausing at the door, he looked in her face, searching for reassurance—a sign he wasn't misinterpreting some innocent intention and the evening was about to go horribly wrong. She smiled again. A couple of light wrinkles formed at the corners of her eyes. Her brown irises were so dark they looked almost black in the starlight. She was younger than him, but not much. Still, she had character in her face, a few laugh lines that suggested evidence of a rough youth. Something else they had in common. She leaned in and kissed him on the mouth, her tongue probing lightly at his lips. Her kiss was warm and tasted like wax. She was naturally gorgeous and wore more makeup than she needed, but how she adorned herself wasn't his business. She did what she did to feel like herself. He knew how to look through the armor people put on. Wearing such a heavy suit of his own gave him insight.

Her tongue darted into his mouth and he tasted her breath. She'd chewed Altoids compulsively during their date. He squeezed her hand and she squeezed back. Her middle finger rubbing against his palm. His pants fit a little more snugly. Pulling away, she delicately wiped at a small, glistening line beneath her lower lip. Embarrassment burned in his mind as he realized he was salivating like a St. Bernard. "You have your keys?" she asked when he didn't move to open the door. He fumbled in his pocket, trying not to draw attention to his throbbing crotch, and unlocked the deadbolt.

Inside, Meghan's mother, Faye, stood in the middle of the living room holding a bottle of beer, swaying on her feet slightly. He lost his erection. Despite the pungent odor of smoke that clung to Faye's skin and clothes, the air around her also smelled like she'd had more than a few bottles. "Where's Meghan?" he asked, trying not to lose his temper and shout before knowing all the facts. Keeping it together was also new to him. He was getting better at defusing confrontation, but still, his first impulse was always to protect himself and what was his. And he only knew how to do that by balling up his fists. He took a breath like his mandated anger management counselor had taught him and asked his question again, only slightly more forcefully.

"Huh? Oh, Sophie? She'sh fine," the old woman said. "Wen' right ta bed at eight like you said so to do."

"No. Meghan. *Your* daughter. She's the one who's supposed to be here taking care of Sophie." Mitch felt regret creeping into his guts. How could he have been so wrong? So irresponsible? The old woman was a wretched soak, and her daughter... she was nowhere to be found. He looked at Liana, silently giving her permission to slip out and head home. She shrugged and stepped into the kitchen archway to wait.

Faye turned and said, "She had a... some... I took over becaush she hadda thing she forgot."

He pushed past her and went to check on his niece. Peering over the crib with the light from the hallway spilling into the room, he saw her lying on her side, sleeping. He tried to take a breath and calm down. But he still felt like he might be sick. *Everything's okay. She put Sophie to bed and* then *got drunk. Sophie's okay. It's not a crisis. Be cool.*

He composed himself and returned to the living room. Passing between the women who were staring at each other with a low simmering hostility, he yanked open the front door and through gritted teeth told Faye to, "Get. Out." Faye took a few awkward staggering steps to the door and stopped, holding out her hand for payment. He wanted to yell and shove her out into the night, slam the door, and yell some more. Instead, he held it together. Despite his attempts to assuage his anger by reasoning that since she'd raised her own daughter, she could probably handle a single night with Sophie, regret and anger and shame fought for dominance over his emotions. This was *his* fuck up. He should have postponed the date until he could have gotten

Khadija or vetted a real sitter. He had to own this failure. He withdrew his wallet and silently counted out the last of his cash. No tip. Faye took it with a sun-withered hand that stank like cigarettes and spilled beer. She smiled at him crookedly, glanced over at Liana, and winked before staggering out of the house. He watched her walk down the path, turn and nearly miss the gate that led into her own front yard.

Mitch's head dropped and he turned to say good night to Liana and show her out to her car. *I'll just tell her that it was nice, but I need to get some sleep and...*

She was gone.

He closed the front door and peeked into the back to see if she'd ducked into the kitchen or gone to the bathroom. Instead, he found her in Sophie's room standing over the crib. He walked up beside her, reached down and brushed some of the hair out of his niece's face. He rested his hand on her shoulder, feeling her warmth. She didn't stir.

"I'm sorry about that," she whispered.

"It's my fault for not finding a better sitter."

"Everything seems all right, though." The hand on the small of his back felt like an electric charge. It moved the pit from his stomach up into his throat.

"Yeah. I suppose she's good," he said. "You know, I really need to—" Liana turned him around and gently kissed him again, this time rubbing her hands up over his chest and shoulders and around the back of his neck. She held his head and kissed him, and he felt like the whole world was floating away.

She pulled away and said, "Everything's all right. Let her sleep." Stepping back, she took his hand, leading him out of the child's room. He followed as she pulled him into the other bedroom. She didn't blink at the way it was appointed like a young woman's room, with a flowered duvet and a stack of decorative pillows and stuffed animals thrown onto the floor. She pulled him over to the bed and sat down on the edge of it. "Now, about that coffee," she said, undoing his belt.

5

Morning came as it always did: unwelcome and intruding on his rest like a house guest who wakes up too early and fumbles around noisily, not knowing where anything is. Mitch rolled over and looked at the clock, wondering if he could get a few more minutes rest before Sophie began summoning him from her crib. "Get out now? Out now?" she would call until he got up and wearily rescued her from her pink Ikea prison.

The clock read 10:00 a.m.

Mitch sat bolt upright. It was hours past when they normally had to get up. He jumped out of bed and scrambled for the door forgetting that he wasn't wearing his pajama pants. He wasn't wearing anything. He looked back at the bed, remembering the night before, looking for Liana. She was gone. On her pillow was a piece of notepaper folded in half. He snatched his cast-off boxers up off the floor and slipped into them while flipping open the note.

Thanks for a great time last night. Sorry to sneak out. Didn't want to confuse Soph. CALL ME!!!

He smiled and dropped the note back on the pillow, intending to come back throughout the day and read it again and again. Maybe he'd carry it with him when he went to work. Work. Ten o'clock! He was so terribly late for work.

"Sophie! Sophie! It's time to get up, sweetheart." He sing-songed as he walked into her room. She was still lying on the side she had been the night before. "Sweetie. Come on. We're late. It's time to go to play with kids." He shook her shoulder gently, expecting the girl to groan and launch into her normal slept-too-long crankiness. Instead, she did nothing.

Mitch bent down and rolled her over onto her back. Panic seized him, holding him in place like a leg caught in a bear trap. "Come on, Sophie! Wake up. Oh god, wake up, please!" His vision narrowed down to a slender tunnel. His breathing quickened in pace with his heartbeat and he felt sick. She didn't move.

He ran back to the other bedroom to phone for help. The dead receiver sat in his hands silently reminding him that they'd shut off the service for non-payment two months earlier. He ripped his cellphone out of the jeans he'd been wearing the night before and tried to wake it. The blank screen refused to respond. Dead battery. "Fuck! Shit! Fuck!"

The sun blasted his sleep-weary eyes as he flung open the front door. The world outside moved as though nothing was wrong. People drove by in their cars, honking at perceived slights only they could see. Across the street, a bus pulled away from the stop in front of the shuttered Blockbuster Video store. The riders aboard stared down at their phones and books, earphones in pumping out the soundtrack for their travels and blocking the rest of the world. His cries, muffled in the noise of the city. He scanned the neighbors' houses. The Melendez's truck was gone. It was *always* gone. Carla and Hector worked like machines and were off before sunrise. Breaking free of the paralyzing normality of the morning, he ran toward the only other neighbor he knew. He ran to Faye's house.

He banged on the door and shouted for her to open up, to help him, to call an ambulance. "Sophie won't wake up," he screamed. Faye didn't come to the door. He looked down the driveway and saw her car was also gone. He tried the knob, but the door was locked. Mitch kicked against the jamb, but the door didn't budge. It would take more work and time to break the molding holding the deadbolt firm, and even then, he wasn't sure if it would give, this being the real world and not some fantasy movie where door frames were made of balsa. He ran around the rear of the house. Although the kitchen door on the back deck had a sturdy deadbolt installed in it as well, the lock only provided the illusion of security. He picked up a potted plant from the rotting deck railing and threw it at the window pane in the top half of the door. The pot exploded as it shattered the window, raining dirt, terracotta, and glass on the filthy kitchen floor. He waited a half-second, expecting to hear a shout of "What the fuck?" from Faye. When it didn't come, he reached in as carefully as his panic allowed and unlocked the bolt.

Although he stepped cautiously as he could around the pot shards and broken window glass, he felt a piece of something jab and slide up into the ball of his foot. He suppressed the instinct to scream and drop to the floor to tend his wound. Instead, he pulled the shard out, throwing it into a far corner where it broke against the wall. Then, with strides as long as he could manage, he lunged clear of the debris and headed for the living room to look for the telephone leaving a trail of crimson footprints behind. Twice, he almost slipped in his own blood on the linoleum until reaching the worn rugs thrown down on the rough and ruined hardwood floors.

The smell in the front room choked him. Faye's house stank like a bad fridge filled with cat shit and used ashtrays. He found the phone on the wall by the hallway to the bathroom and yanked the handset off its cradle. A dial tone never sounded so good. He punched three numbers and waited.

"Nine one one, what is your emergency?" The woman's voice on the other end was calm and efficient. It belied the nature of the conversation he was about to have and unsettled him. *How can she be calm? How can she sound like nothing is happening?* His mouth dropped open, but his throat and lungs and lips all refused to comply with his racing mind. He choked out a weak, half-strangled cry for help. "I'm sorry, Ma'am," the dispatcher said. "You're going to have to speak up. What is your emergency?"

And then it came. He gave voice to the terror, invoking the worst fear he could imagine, giving it life by speaking its name.

"It's Sophie! She won't wake up! I tried getting her out of bed but she won't open her eyes! Please help!"

"Calm down. I'm sending an ambulance. How old is Sophia?"

"Sophie. She's only four. Please help us!" Tears spilled down his face and he wanted more than anything else in the world to hang up the phone and go back to the girl's room. He *needed* to go back. She was alone in the house and needed him. He knew she had to be awake now, after all that noise, and frightened. He had to get back to her.

"Okay. Tell me your name."

"My name? Mitch LeRoux. I live at 325 Rutledge Ave. on the first floor. Please come now!"

"Are you the girl's father?" the dispatcher asked.

Time stopped.

He'd told no one about his sister or his niece, knowing as soon as he did, DCF would get involved and he'd lose her too. The state would stop sending their Section Eight vouchers and refilling the EBT card and they'd take her. Everything that kept them together and alive would be yanked out from under them. He could lie, like he'd done for the last year and say her mother wasn't available. She was at work—he was baby-sitting—she was visiting a friend. But they'd find out. He'd lose his niece and let down the very last person who depended upon him before she was even old enough to know how he'd failed her.

All that mattered was Sophie. They had to help Sophie. He could figure everything else out later. "It's just me and Sophie," he said, knowing that admitting it was the beginning of the end.

He needed her as much as she needed him.

6

While the medical team wheeled Sophie up to the Pediatric ICU, the admitting nurse urged Mitch to wait out in the lobby with everyone else. Feeling shell-shocked, he did what he was told. The Emergency Department was full of people quietly waiting to hear their names called. They sat with hands wrapped in blood-soaked dish towels, with limbs cradled and bent at strange angles. They sat holding on to each other, seeking comfort in familiar and tender touch. Most were silent but a couple spoke softly to one another, and one woman—a mother—cradled her little girl's head as the child lay in her lap, a compress stuck to her foot where it was sliced open. The child whimpered, and her mother shushed and cooed at her, assuring her it would be all right. Everything was going to be just fine.

He rubbed his palms over his eyes, trying to hide his fearful tears. He was forced to look up when a nurse holding a clipboard asked where his shoes were. Mitch looked down at his own feet, bare except for the quick bandage job the EMT had given him in the ambulance as they rode to the hospital. In his rush to get out of the house and into the ambulance, he'd grabbed a T-shirt and the jeans he wore the night before off the floor, but missed his shoes. He told the nurse he'd left them home, and asked about Sophie. She said she'd check on the girl. In the meantime, she'd try to scrounge up something for him to put on his feet. "It's a hospital," she said as if he was only now realizing where he sat. She came back a few minutes later with a set of green paper booties made to slip over a person's shoes. He pulled them on, pretending they were his favorite winter comfy socks and not crinkly paper.

After four and a half hours, everyone else in the waiting room had cycled through triage and on to treatment rooms. Everyone except Mitch. He sat in the same seat watching the same clock above the same receptionist typing on her computer. He'd gotten up a couple of times to ask about Sophie. She told him that she didn't know; he'd just have to be patient. She gave him paperwork to fill out. He completed it as best as he could, but only knew the answers to the most mundane portions of the form: names, birthdates, addresses. He imagined that Sophie's health history—wellness checks, her pediatrician, if she had one—was all recorded under his sister's social security number, which he didn't have committed to memory. The information regarding her Children's Health Insurance Program enrollment was back at their house. There was so much he didn't know. So much he was failing at.

Then, through doors marked "HOSPITAL STAFF ONLY. NO ADMITTANCE! a trio of men emerged. Two wore similar tan raincoats and charcoal colored suits. Both white. Both middle-aged. One blond and the other with thinning brown hair. A mostly-matched pair. Ahead of them, a doctor in a white coat raised a hand to summon the nurse from behind the admissions counter. Mitch wanted to jump up and race her to the group so he could ask the doctor about Sophie before the man could brush him off or disappear through the doors again without updating him. The look of the men flanking the doctor kept Mitch rooted to his seat, however. Nothing about them was inviting and whatever they were doing here, Mitch wanted no part of it. He recognized them for what they were.

The nurse nodded vigorously as the doctor spoke. She turned and pointed at Mitch. The doctor's wingmen looked past her at him and nodded once. Mitch couldn't read lips, but he could clearly see the doctor say, "Thank you," before he turned to leave. One of the two men handed the doctor a business card before breaking off and heading toward the waiting area. Mitch could hear his grandfather saying, "Look who it is. Frick and Frack!" When he was a kid, he had no idea what that meant other than that it signaled the old man's contempt for authority and usually an altercation in the offing. Grampa was always outwardly contemptuous of authority. The greater the assumed power over him, the more strongly his derision and mocking. It never served him in the long run. Not at home, in jail, with his parole officer, or with the administrators or staff of the nursing home where he died. He bucked hard every time, and they tried to break him. Sure, he died wild, but he'd been whipped his whole life. Mitch felt the same inclination; he always heard that mocking tone of his grandfather's in the back of his mind, rushing up right before the old man's words came spilling out of his mouth. He pushed it down and adopted a different tack. Be respectful, but not effusive. Be nondescript. Blend in. Don't get noticed. Do your time quiet. Rules for survival.

Except here he was, being noticed. The two men stopped in front of him. The blond was slightly taller than the other one. He was a good looking guy, solidly built with a cauliflower ear and a slight cant to his jaw that said "boxer." Like Mitch. The other one wasn't as handsome, but looked nicer, slimmer and without any odd damage to his face. His hairline was receding, but he wore it well, like he wasn't fighting with his recessive genes. "Are you Michel LeRoux?" the shorter one asked, using his legal name, and pronouncing it incorrectly, like the angel he wasn't.

"Yes, sir," he said. "I go by Mitch."

The shorter man gestured to the chair next to him. "You mind if we have a seat? Maybe a little chat?" Mitch looked at the chairs on either side of him, silently saying "go ahead." Just *imagining* the two men on either side of him made him feel penned in, however. The short one took the seat to his left while his partner remained standing, arms folded. Even worse.

The balding man pulled a billfold out of the inside pocket of his suit and flipped it open for Mitch to see. Above a heavy-looking gold badge, his unsmiling face peered out of a small square beside a bunch of text, too small to read without taking it in hand. Mitch knew better than to touch it. The badge was a totem—a symbol of the power of the state—the power that was assembled in front of him right at that moment. Touching it would burn him.

"I'm Detective John Braddock. This is my partner, Detective Bill Dixon. We were hoping you could answer some questions for us."

Mitch's stomach felt emptier than it ever had in his life. He folded his arms over it and pressed down, trying to keep it from aching or collapsing in on itself. "What about?"

"The child you accompanied here—Sophie—where is her mother? Have you tried to get in touch with her to let her know her kid's in the hospital?" Dixon asked. He'd never bothered to flash his credentials. He just stood there with his arms crossed, mirroring Mitch. He didn't look like he was trying to hold himself together the way Mitch was, though. He resembled a sliding trap wall glacially closing in to crush him. Mitch shook his head.

"Why not?" When he didn't answer, Braddock continued conspiratorially. "Look, Mitch, we're here to help. Bill and me, we need to know everything there is to know about what happened in the last twenty-four hours if we're going to do that. We're not trying to trick you, okay? We just want to make sure we have all the facts straight."

Dixon leaned in. Mitch could feel his presence pushing against him. The man's fundamental essence was threatening. "Don't try to protect her. Not after what she did to that little girl. Where's Violette LeRoux now? We need to speak to her."

Violette LeRoux. The sound of it stunned him. It sounded alien, like a sour musical note. Something that wasn't supposed to be hanging there in the air. She was just Violette—Mama to Sophie—until she wasn't anyone to either of them anymore. Just a ghost who'd left them alone in a house whose every room cruelly pointed out her absence. Mitch shook his head again. He knew better than to say anything. No matter how friendly or innocent any question from a cop seemed, he'd learned the hard way that they weren't there to help him. The day he'd feared would come was at hand. He was losing everything. He realized that since they called him by the name on his driver's license, they already knew everything they needed to about his past. Even if they didn't, it wouldn't take more than a few minutes to uncover who he really was. It was all on that application for their food assistance and Sophie's CHIP coverage. He didn't care about the past; the present was all that mattered. Maybe, if he came clean, they'd let him up to see his niece.

"When can I see her?" he asked.

The detectives ignored his question. "Where's the girl's mother?"

"Violette asked me to come over and help out for a while. She said she needed to get away and have some time alone. So... I've been staying over."

"How long ago was that?" Dixon asked.

Mitch's head dropped. "August."

The detectives shared a glance and Braddock pulled out a notebook and began writing. "A month ago?"

"Thirteen... months ago."

It was the detectives' turn to look shocked. Braddock leaned back, a look of honest surprise washing across his face before being replaced by the stoic cop expression that his partner unfailingly wore. "And you're her legal guardian?" Braddock asked. "Appointed by the court?"

"I have a power of attorney. Violette said she was just going away for a little while, so I came over and she handed me the paper—in case anything happened—and said she'd be back. It's just been me and Sophie since then." So far the document had allowed him to enroll the girl in day care and keep her social benefits coming in. Violette had sprung the power of attorney on him and he hadn't questioned it because he loved Sophie and didn't want to see her in the system. He figured it was just his sister being dramatic, like she so often was. She was going to split for a couple of weeks and when she came back, he'd go home and resume his normal life. He later learned it was an uncommon moment of forethought and planning ahead for her. She never meant to come back. Mitch had known that for a while, but only chose to acknowledge it at the present moment.

"So, if it's just the two of you, Mitch," Dixon said. "Why don't *you* tell us what happened last night?" Braddock put a hand on Mitch's forearm. His palm was dry and soft, but there was a promise of power in the man's touch. If he squeezed, Mitch was certain his thin arm would squish out between his fingers like putty. "Just tell us what happened." The focus of the men's intensity seemed to shift. The feeling of being stuck in between two walls closing in intensified.

"I-I went out on a date. I got home, paid the babysitter, and... went to bed. When I woke up, Sophie... Sh-she wouldn't wake up. So I called 9-1-1." Mitch felt about to break. He'd been doing the right thing, getting Sophie up in the morning and off to day care. Fed and to bed at night. His work had suffered. He lost a promotion and was stuck as a barista at the coffee shop instead of assistant manager like his bosses had promised him before Violette took off. That didn't matter, though. Sophie was more important, and as long as she needed him he was there for her, whatever the cost. Until he felt like he needed to have a night off to play. And now she was sick. He imagined drunk Faye feeding the girl something spoiled from the fridge. Giving her food poisoning. Except with food poisoning, she'd wake up. She'd be puking all over the place and crying. No. It was something else. Something he didn't want to imagine.

"That's it, guys. I'm not saying anything else until you tell me how she is. I need to know. Can you get someone to tell *you* how she is? They just keep making me wait here saying someone will come out. But it's been all morning and nobody's told me a god damned thing."

"Michel," Braddock said, using his legal name again—the one he hadn't written on the admission sheet—giving his arm another light squeeze. If it was meant to be calming, it had the opposite effect. "Sophie died. Three hours ago."

"We're from homicide division," Dixon finished.

Mitch's lungs refused to expand. He felt like a ton of dirt had just been shoveled in on top of him. Buried alive in open air, he choked out, "No! How?" He tried to stand. Dixon took a step closer, forcing him back down into the waiting room chair. He spoke through gritted teeth.

"MRI scans suggest a brain hemorrhage. It could have happened from a fall off of something high, but since you never mentioned an accident and the hand-shaped bruises on her arms didn't come from toppling off the sofa we know different. That's what we call, 'non-accidental trauma.' You know what that means?" Dixon didn't wait for an answer. He continued on, voice edged with contempt and barely restrained anger, spitting out the words like they were ashes in his mouth. "We won't know anything for sure until the autopsy."

"Autopsy!"

"But we *will* know. Maybe you want to tell us something else. Tell us the truth about last night."

"That is the truth. I went out on a date. Faye... Mrs. Cantrell and her daughter, Meghan, from next door were watching her. When I got home everything was... fine. I thought it was fine anyway. Sophie was sleeping and Faye was drunk. I sent her home. I... I went to bed and... What are you saying? What did she do?"

"Where'd you go on your date?" Braddock asked. "Who were you with?" His pen hovered above the notepad waiting for the answers.

Mitch struggled to remember the details of the night before, but everything was blank. Dixon's words were clanging in his head like hammers against steel plates ringing and bouncing off of his skull, making it vibrate and ache.

Hand-shaped bruises.

BANG!

Non-accidental trauma.

BANG!

Autopsy.

BANG!

Finally, the fog began to clear. "Liana. Liana Halliday. We went to see *The Witchfinder* at the Savoy Theater." He fished in his pants pocket and pulled out a ticket stub. Braddock reached for it. Mitch pulled back a little before deciding to hand it over. The detective took a long look and then wrote in his notebook some more. Mitch held his hand out to take the stub back, but Braddock didn't seem interested in returning it.

"You went to the nine o'clock show. When did the date end?" Braddock asked.

Mitch struggled against his first instinct to protect Liana's reputation. Chivalry would have to take a back seat. They thought he killed his niece! "This morning, I guess. She stayed the night." He didn't expect either cop to give him an "attaboy" wink and a nod, but he'd hoped for some sort of recognition that it was a believable story. Instead, what he got was the same stone-faced expression that said no matter how much Dixon sounded like he cared, no matter how much Braddock reassuringly touched Mitch's arm, they were doing a job and were *not* on his side. "She left me a note. It's at home."

"And how can we get in touch with Miss Halliday?" Braddock asked.

Mitch had her phone number written down on a piece of cash register paper in his wallet. That was back at the house, along with his shoes. "I don't remember her number. She works at the Wholesome Market on Lear Street."

"I know that one," Braddock said. "It's new right? Used to be a Foodbasket."

"Yeah." He turned and looked directly in the seated detective's eyes, his own blurry with nascent tears. "Please let me see her. I need to see Sophie."

Detective Braddock shook his head, *no.* "Sorry," he said.

"You said you had someone over to watch the girl," Dixon said.

"I told you. My neighbor, Mrs. Cantrell." Mitch felt the sick realization of what had happened slip over reality like a final curtain. He'd come home from his date at first too excited by

Liana inviting herself in and then too furious about Faye being there—drunk—instead of Meghan that he hadn't bothered asking whether Sophie had stopped crying after he left or what and how much of it she'd eaten for dinner. He'd just wanted the old woman to go home and sleep it off. He'd wanted to banish the evidence of his poor decision making before he had to acknowledge it. Neither had he wanted to disturb Sophie's sleep. He knew that doing so would mean getting her a drink of water, maybe reading a book, getting her back to bed with a few whispered songs and cuddles while Liana waited alone in the living room reconsidering "coming in for coffee." Another bad decision.

Faye killed Sophie. And I didn't stop her. I let them in the house!

Another selfish choice for which he deserved to pay.

Braddock consulted his notes. "It was her place you broke into to make the call. Why's that?"

"My cell was dead and we don't have a landline. I needed a phone. Faye wasn't home and I didn't know where else to go."

"And do you know how we could get in touch with Mrs. Cantrell?"

"I just go and ring the bell." *Except when I smash her windows.* A dark realization settled over Mitch's consciousness and he let his shoulders slump and head drop. *Except you probably already tried to talk to her, didn't you? You tried to find her because I broke into her house and you need to investigate that too. But you can't because she's not home. She's not ever coming home because she got drunk and killed Sophie and ran away.*

Mitch let out a loud sob, his weakly maintained composure finally giving way to the weight of reality. He knew from experience, it only takes a single night for the whole world to change. One moment where someone does something you can't control and everything you know shifts, leaving you off balance, disoriented, and looking back at what you had while the world pitches and rolls beneath your feet. Time carries you forward like a cresting wave. The best you can do is brace yourself and hope you don't get crushed when it slams you into the rocks on the shore.

He dropped his face in his hands and met his grief in the dark. "When can I see Sophie?" he whispered through his palms. "Please, let me see her." He looked up, pleading with glassy eyes, face ruddy and wet.

Dixon's expression cracked for the first time since the pair had started talking to him. He knitted his brows and his lips went thin and white. He reached down and put a giant hand on Mitch's shoulder, squeezing softly. Looking in Braddock's eyes, the partners engaged in a moment of silent communication until Braddock finally nodded. Dixon stood up and pulled Mitch gently to his feet. He turned him around and began handcuffing him.

"We'll have more questions for you at the station."

"What? Why? I told you, it was Faye."

"That may be, Mr. LeRoux. But we know who *you* are. That means we have more questions."

That was the final answer. He wouldn't be seeing Sophie again.

Not until her funeral. Maybe not even then.

Maybe not ever.

7

Dixon sat on the table in the interview room while Braddock stood in the doorway watching Mitch being led by a uniformed officer toward the elevators. The closeness of the stark, white room was designed to keep all of the participants involved in a conversation in sight of the camera in the upper corner. Unlike television, no one was standing out of the line of sight with a baton and a phone book waiting to pull the line out of the wall. Tapes with big gaps in the time stamp weren't any good in evidence. The secondary effect of the room was that it was a little bit too much of everything. It was too bright, too cold, too intimate. Most guys couldn't keep up the bad-ass hoodrat rap when they were squinting, shivering, and someone Braddock's size was practically sitting in their lap asking hard questions. Michel LeRoux was no different. Except, he never tried the hoodrat shit. Neither was he quietly defiant like some guys got, making a show of how well they shut up—no snitchin' perfected. Mitch wasn't the average subject they had in the room. By all appearances, he was living like a citizen since being paroled. He'd lied to his P.O. about his address, which was enough to violate his parole and bounce him back to the House of Correction. Other than that failing, everything else about him checked out. They hadn't gotten ahold of the girl to confirm his alibi yet, but his boss, the day care, the receipt for dinner and the movie ticket in his pocket all supported the story he told of how his day progressed. In six hours of questioning, his version of events hadn't changed. On top of that, he was as broken as anyone they'd ever seen in the box. If LeRoux wasn't actually devastated by the girl's death, neither an Oscar nor a Golden Globe were good enough; he deserved to have a whole new award created just for this performance.

Braddock said, "You like him for it?"

"Nope. He's telling the truth." He closed a tan folder with Mitch's criminal history in it, and rubbed his temples. They'd sweat him hard, threatening to VOP him—put him back in jail for violating the conditions of his parole. He'd accepted that idea with a sense of defeated resignation that almost made Braddock feel bad for making the threat in the first place. Aside from petty hits as a teenager for shoplifting and underage consumption, LeRoux only had one other conviction: the one he'd done three years for. Assault with a dangerous weapon. He served three-fifths of his sentence before being paroled, and now he was as mild mannered as Clark Kent. Violating a guy who's been living clean just because he stepped up to take care of his kin would have earned both detectives extra hot pokers in Hell that no amount of contrition could cool.

They walked out of the interview room back to their carrel. Braddock and Dixon's desks were as similar as they were. Cluttered with files and seemingly disorganized, each man knew where everything was on either desk. Other detectives joked that if Braddock thought about beans, Dixon farted, but their cognitive overlap was greater than mere simpatico. Each one of the pair filled in whatever blanks the other missed. They had the highest clear rate in the department. It didn't help them divine facts, though. Neither was psychic and the unknown was as lost to them as it was to any other person.

Dixon slid a file off his desk and opened it. Faye Cantrell's police record was considerably longer than LeRoux's, but aside from a couple of short, month-long slaps on the wrist, she'd never done any real time. She always got a plea, a diversionary program, and a fine. She'd gotten so many bites at the apple, there was only the core left. He'd hoped that the uniforms would have picked her up by now so they could keep their momentum going, but the woman and her kid were in the wind.

And then there was the sister. He wanted a piece of her too. He figured he could nail her with an abandonment charge, and even if it didn't stick, the process of defending against it would serve as some kind of punishment. He might have started to sympathize with Mitch a little at the end of their interrogation, but what he really wanted was justice for Sophie. And there was more than one person responsible for her being in a cooler. The unresolved question was how to hold someone accountable who had actually done her wrong. So far, Mitch was the only one it seemed who'd stepped up for the girl. And he was the only one paying the cost.

Interlude: Scenes from an Awakening

8

The child's tiny body lay naked and pale on the autopsy table under the bright light, a small square of white cloth laid over its groin as a gesture of simple dignity in the face of the unsympathetic setting. The medical examiner in her blue paper gown and plastic face shield was not sentimental, but neither was she heartless, and she hated performing her duties on children. Her services were not meant for them, no matter how many came through her office. Her carefully maintained professional distance was lessened in the presence of a dead child. The size of the body necessitated she draw nearer, look closer, be more attentive. Everything about an infant on the slab demanded her fullest attention, and pulled back the curtain on the fact that almost every last one of us will be intimate with death before we're ready to be. She took a deep breath and prepared to do her job.

She bent over the body to begin work while a small group of somber people in suits stood at the far end of the autopsy theater, observing. She spoke aloud into a tape recorder held beside her face by an assistant. "Subject is a Hispanic male child approximately six years of age. Perimortem trauma to the right parietal bone a centimeter above the squamosal suture is consistent with severe blunt force impact as detailed in the state police incident report involving subject dated September 12, 2017. At first glance, the cause of death appears to be consistent with the terminal event described by witnesses that this child suffered a fall from a significant height, landing laterally on the protrusion of an uneven surface. Medical record and X-ray review, however, revealed signs of antemortem trauma to limbs and torso with evidence of healing. Although no prior head injuries were detailed in the medical history of the subject, deliberate force cannot be ruled out as a possible cause at this..."

The pathologist straightened her back and looked at her assistant. "Excuse me. Please don't bump the table," she said before continuing. "Cannot be ruled out as a possible cause of death at this time. I am going to proceed to make an incision along the..." She stepped back and placed her scalpel on the tray next to the autopsy table. "Are you all right, Glenn? Do you need to take a break?"

The assistant clicked off the tape recorder and lifted his face shield. "I'm fine. What's the problem?"

One of the observers, an assistant district attorney, stepped forward, eyes wide and a hand raised to her mouth. Dr. Downum had known her since she was added to the fatality review team and had grown to like the woman considerably. She was poised to head up the Child Protection Unit of the DA's office and had seen the worst cases there were to see. As a result of the horrors she dealt with on a daily basis, Dr. Downum thought of ADA Wishnevsky as unshockable. "What? What is it?" She leaned in to take a closer look at the subject. Perhaps it was something from the observers' point of view she hadn't noticed.

The child on the table raised his hand to his face and moaned weakly.

Dr. Downum ran to the wall and slapped the emergency alarm button while the rest of the team stood in mute shock. She had no idea whether the antique clarion would work, or if anyone would even respond. What kind of medical emergency could you have in the *morgue*?

9

The smoke from the fire reached up like a black scar marring the cheery blue sky above. Below, a team of firefighters sprayed water into the smoldering remnants of a three-story apartment building while a crowd of onlookers watched in fascination. Having started in the daytime, most of the tenants were at work, leaving twelve living people homeless and without possessions except for what they wore and carried to the office that morning. Two, however, were dead. Myrna, the retiree on the third floor, and her granddaughter, Joy, both succumbing to smoke inhalation before rescue teams could reach them.

The EMT pushed the gurney carrying the girl's body into the back of his ambulance, listening for the clicks of the latches on the floor of the van as they caught and held her bed in place. He both loved and hated his job. He loved the excitement and adrenaline of rushing toward disaster. Being first to race to the aid of people who needed him. Being that person they saw when they thought hope was lost. He loved riding along as his partner weaved through traffic, siren screaming, lives hanging in the balance. Lives *he* saved. But then, there were the ones he couldn't save. They didn't see him as a rescuer or a helper or even at all.

And then there were the kids.

He hated when it was a child. Injured was bad enough. But dead ones made him want to throw his kit in the nearest dumpster and become a librarian or a yoga instructor or something else quiet where he never had to pull another sheet over a baby's face.

He closed the doors of the truck and gave them a tug to make sure they were secure. He slapped on the window to signal that everything was locked down and secure. Neither he nor his partner heard the girl gasp under her sheet as they drove her body to the morgue. It wasn't until she began to cough and cry that they turned on the lights and siren.

10

Pete Vitti had had enough and was hurrying home so he could fix himself an Old Fashioned and relax in front of the television a little before he needed to help Kendra with dinner. The partners had put him through his paces today and all he wanted was to feel the warm spread of whiskey in his belly and perhaps later the warm spread of his fiancée's thighs, if one cocktail didn't become three and leave him a little too relaxed for that. Two drinks was a guarantee, however.

As he pulled onto his street, he almost missed the sight of the dirt-covered child emerging from under his neighbor, Kyle Bailey's, front porch. The incongruity of the image made him take a quick second glance that wrenched his neck and caused him to nearly drive into one of the trees lining the way.

The child clawed and scraped at the lawn, pulling itself out of the small hole broken in the side of the lattice crawlspace siding. Once free, it got up from its hands and knees and began to stagger away. Despite the filth covering him, Pete recognized the kid from the faded posters tacked up all around town. In the nine months that Byron Davidson had been missing, his parents never failed to renew the faded and weather-beaten flyers every two weeks like clockwork. They refused to give up hope that their son was still alive, despite what everyone else in the community thought, but refused to say within earshot of them. He knew that boy's face like he knew his own reflection.

He cursed and stomped on the brakes, narrowly missing the mailbox at the end of his driveway. He scrabbled for his cell phone in the cup holder beside the radio, fumbling against the dash and accidentally cranking the volume on the news report he'd been ignoring. He dialed 9-1-1 and jumped out of his car to intercept the kid before Kyle saw what was happening and came out of his house. *Has Kyle been keeping the kid captive right under our noses? We have him over for drinks on the fucking back patio, for Christ's sake!*

He caught up with the boy as the dispatcher on the phone asked what his emergency was. The smell of the boy up close stopped Pete dead. The child's face sent him running in the opposite direction, crying and screaming indistinctly as the emergency dispatcher asked again, "What is your emergency?" from the phone now lying abandoned in the grass.

The child had no eyes.

Pete never saw the second and third children emerge from the crawlspace after him.

Part Two: Sophie's Life

11

The doorbell clanged loudly in its decaying yellow box in the hallway above the bathroom door. Mitch sat in the dark and ignored it, hoping that whoever had come would soon go and leave him alone. He had few enough friends who visited in good times, and in the last week they'd all kept their distance. It wasn't respect that kept them away, but fear. The LeRoux house was a peste-house. They knew without coming over to see for themselves that Mitch's despair was infectious. He was the spirit of gravity living only to pull others down and break their souls against the rocks and stones. No one had rung his bell since Sophie died and that suited him just fine. He didn't want to be responsible for anyone else's happiness or well-being—not anymore. He only wanted to sit and wait. For what, he wasn't certain.

Again, the hard, percussive clank and clang as the electric clapper struck. For anyone with a low startle threshold, the doorbell was a short road to an elevated heart-rate. Mitch sat quietly on the fraying sofa wishing whoever it was would give up and go away. He heard the doorknob rattle. For a second, he held his breath waiting for the hiss of the rubber door runner against the hardwood floor. Instead, the visitor resorted to knocking. And then pounding. And then shouting.

"God damn it, Mitch, open up. I know you're in there."

Liana.

She waited a beat and then pounded again. "The *police* came to see me!"

Mitch pushed up off the couch and inspected himself briefly in the reflection of the blank television screen. His face was sallow and sunken. He hadn't changed his clothes, shaved or showered in days. Although he wasn't deliberately starving himself, he had no memory of the last time he'd eaten. He figured he had an equal chance of starving to death as he did of feeling like getting up and finding something to eat, or even opening the curtains to let in light. This was suicide by inertia, just slowing down until he stopped. This was the "after." After Sophie. After happiness. After health.

After.

He got up and unlocked the door, stepping back before Liana could fling it open in a rage, shaming him for not calling after they'd slept together. Except she didn't shove it open. She cautiously turned the knob and pushed the door in a few inches, peeking around the edge. "Mitch?" she said.

He squinted, shading his eyes with a hand. She pushed the door open the rest of the way. Sunlight poured through the open portal, making her a shrouded figure surrounded in golden light, her kinky, tight hair a black halo framing a faceless angel. She shut the door, banishing the sun, and appeared as he remembered her. Warmly radiant. The shouting and harsh tone fell away, replaced by the same kind of effortless care she showed to Sophie the night of their date. It was what drew him to her: easy compassion, freely given.

"Jesus Christ, Mitch. What's happened to you? What's going on? The police wouldn't tell me anything except that they wanted to know who I was with last Saturday."

He thought of saying "Come in" or "Sit down" or any other number of perfunctory noises hosts make at their guests to signal that they are welcome. But, in the end, he chose to simply say, "I'm sorry." His voice cracked with disuse. He couldn't remember the last time he'd spoken either.

She slipped her arms under his and embraced him. The memory of their night together flooded back into his mind. Her firm breasts pushing against his chest, warm breath against his neck, her hands pressed to his back all called up in him the feeling of being wanted and loved. And then it drained away at the recollection of the following morning. A week had passed by in a moment—a week spent sitting, feeling nothing but longing and loneliness. Not thinking of the woman he'd spent the night with, or his job, or anything else. And he cried again for the millionth time since Braddock and Dixon left him to return to his empty home.

"Why did the police want to know about our date? What happened?" She pulled back and glanced around the apartment. Quiet and dark and empty. She cupped his chin in her hand and lifted his face to look him in the eye. "Where's Sophie?" she asked.

Mitch tried to look away, but her pleading gaze held him fast. No one looked at him the way she looked at him. Instead of judgment or disinterest, she saw him and reflected back warmth and caring. He tried to find a way to tell her. "She's..." *What? Gone? Passed away? Left us? No. She's dead. And I can't say it. Because saying it makes it too real. She's dead and no one comes back from the fucking dead.*

"Oh God!" Liana understood without being told. She pulled him in and held him tighter. He felt her tears dripping onto his shoulder. "How?" she asked. "When?"

He told her everything. It didn't take long; there wasn't much to tell. The police explained to him that an autopsy would be done, but it'd be weeks or months before the results would be made available. Braddock had handed him a card and told him to call the minute he saw his neighbors, if they returned. That was, if he wanted justice for his niece. *Justice.* He couldn't even conceive of what abstract ideas like "justice" or "closure" even meant. Deep in his grief, he'd only felt the pull of the void, asking him to dive deep and let it take him and his pain.

"I wish I could wake up. I wish I was opening my eyes and it was a week ago. Except I don't, you know? I kind of want it all be a dream. You. Sophie. This." His knees folded and he collapsed to the floor. Liana followed him down. They knelt together and she held him. "It has to all be a dream, because I can't live in a place where I win and lose at the exact same time."

Liana hung on to him while he shook and cried. Mitch hadn't ever wanted to be a parent—his own had convinced him that he had no taste for it—but when Violette had Sophie, he realized a kind of compromise in himself. He didn't want to be a father, but he wasn't about to let down a child who needed him. He stepped up whenever Violette followed their mother's example and found something better than parenting to occupy her attention. When she left, he found that what he wanted meant less than what was owed. *Someone* owed Sophie a chance, and he was the only one left to give her that. Now that he was free of his obligation to her, he felt crushed. And worse, he felt alone. He'd gotten so used to her excitement at seeing him, her enthusiasm over simple things he'd long ago become inured to. She could find joy in a plum in a way that mystified him. To Mitch, it was just another option in the grocery store—one that was messy and often had to be thrown out because he would forget he bought them and they went to waste. But in Sophie's hands, they were a delight. She would smile broadly and clap when he cut one up for her. She would devour them like there was no greater pleasure to be had and lick the dripping red juice off of her fingers without shame or self-consciousness. She taught him the things he needed to relearn about living after coming out of prison. She brought him back to life. Now, she was gone, and all his old wounds hurt afresh.

"Come on," Liana said, letting go and pushing herself up. She held out a hand and pulled him to his feet. "You can hop in the shower while I fix you something to eat. You look like you haven't had a thing in weeks." It had only been days, but Mitch didn't have a lot of weight to lose to begin with; he imagined his starved appearance was striking.

While he showered, Liana set about the task of cooking breakfast and helping straighten up the apartment. She opened the curtains and let the sun stream in, illuminating the dust motes floating in the air so thickly it looked like the apartment was under water. He dressed in clean clothes and sat at the kitchen table, watching her work while he ate. His hunger was an ember that roared into a lustful fire when properly stoked, and he devoured the eggs, bacon, and toast before any of it had a chance to cool.

When she finished putting the kitchen in order, she sat next to him and laid her hands on top of his. A touch of life returned to him at the feel of the warmth and softness of her skin. Finally, she said, "So, where is Sophie now?"

"I don't know. They still have her in the hospital, I guess."

Her neck straightened. "No one's called you?"

He shook his head. With Liana's alibi and Faye's disappearance, his chances of being arrested and charged in her death were diminishing, but it still seemed unlikely that anyone at the hospital was going to welcome him with open arms. He was not her father. Worse, she'd died in his care. Stuck in his own hole, he hadn't thought to ask how to claim her.

"Have you contacted a funeral home to come get her?"

Mitch stared at his empty plate. "I can't afford a funeral. I can't afford anything."

Liana scooted her chair around the kitchen table to sit closer. "Oh, hon." She pulled a smart-phone out of her purse and began typing into a search engine. After a few seconds she held it up to show a web page for a funeral home near Kingsport. "The man who owns this place took care of my cousin, Rawndell, after his accident. He'll understand. He helps people who don't have much."

"It's not that I don't have much. I have *nothing*."

"You have me," Liana said, dialing the number.

12

The consultation suite at the Tremblay Funeral Home was bright but sober. In the center of the room stood a varnished table with matching chairs that resembled a dining room table without place settings more than a sales desk across which to discuss coffins, cremation, and memorial services. Light filtered in through the long white sheers, but Mitch couldn't see outside. There would be no gazing out the windows at the people walking up the street. No daydreaming he was someone for whom an afternoon spent planning a child's funeral would be unthinkable. There was just this.

Mitch chose to sit on the chocolate-colored leather sofa at the far end of the room instead. Liana took a place beside him, holding his hand. Except to work, she hadn't left his side since the morning she'd come to his door. Her insistence on doing what needed to be done, whether or not it was doable, was starting to seep through his pores. He got up in the mornings, he showered, ate, and did all the things people who were alive did. He felt the stirrings of the kind of intention he'd known when Sophie was alive. Perhaps there was life after death after all. Given time.

An older man, simply but professionally dressed, entered through a door at the opposite end of the room. From his modest clothes to his undyed gray hair and neatly trimmed beard, he seemed immune to pretension. He walked toward the sofa and extended a hand directly to Mitch. "I'm Anthony Tremblay," he said. "But please, just call me Tony."

"Michel. But most people just say, 'Mitch.'"

"I'm happy to be able to help, Michel." Tony said his name perfectly. He grabbed both of Liana's hands and gave them a light squeeze before pulling a chair from the dining/conference table over in front of the sofa. Mitch wondered how hard it was to navigate all of the usual polite things that people added to welcomes and introductions like "It's nice to meet you" and "A pleasure to see you again." Tony seemed to be able to express those sentiments with a modest smile and a firm grip while maintaining the delicate reality of the situation: no one wants a mortician to say how wonderful it is to see you again. Because it isn't. Not on *their* turf, anyway.

Tony guided them directly, but sensitively, into a discussion of what he had on hand or would be able to order, showing Mitch pictures of caskets and urns in a binder catalog. He explained the details of each item, describing pillows and linings and exterior finish. He never mentioned prices. Though Liana had said he was giving a considerable discount, it was still money Mitch didn't have. Especially not since he hadn't shown up for work in over a week and a half. He hadn't even called in. Unless his boss took special pity on him and let him come back to work, abandoning his job wasn't going to go over well with his parole officer either.

Despite there being no prices listed in the binder, he tried to pick what seemed like the least expensive of every option available, saying, "I think I can afford this," or, "I might be able to make payments on that, if you'll let me."

Tony held up a hand. "Don't worry about the money. Liana and I have already discussed it and we're covering the entire expense. You just pick what you need for your niece. The two of us will take care of the rest."

Liana raised her eyebrows and shrugged like she had no idea that she and Tony had already colluded on how to settle accounts. Mitch gave half a smile and returned his attention to the funeral director. He thought about resisting and insisting that he be allowed to contribute something, even if it was just a token payment. It was clear, however, that his girlfriend—he dare not say that aloud for fear of being corrected—and her friend wouldn't accept anything he offered. Still, he picked what he would have chosen for Sophie had he been expected to foot the bill alone. A modest casket for a viewing and memorial followed by cremation and a simple urn. He imagined himself eventually trying to find someplace where he could spread her ashes. But she hadn't been enough places in her life for him to think of one that stood out, and he imagined they'd frown on it in a city playground. It didn't seem right to just walk over to the shore and throw her remains out into an ocean she'd never played in. He would have to work to come up with someplace special. Someplace that would have impressed her had she ever been. He wondered if he could sneak her into a local produce farm with a plum orchard.

"So what's next?" he said.

"I'll contact the hospital and see if they're ready to release Sophie to us."

"Why wouldn't they be?"

Tony sighed and straightened up in his chair as if the slight bit of extra distance between them might give his next statement time to soften along the way. "Although written results take time to come out, and there's a backlog for the actual examination... the child fatality review team should have ordered the procedure done right away. Either way, I'll find out where we stand and we'll get her here as soon as possible."

"Right. The autopsy." Mitch's shoulders dropped. "I guess we shouldn't have an open casket then."

Tony leaned in and rested a hand on his knee. "Don't worry, son. The Middlesex County pathologists are good at what they do. You won't be able to tell she's even been touched. Trust me."

Mitch wanted to trust him. Tony's easy manner and calm attitude surrounded him like a blanket, making everything he said sound okay, even when he talked about autopsies and medical examiners. "Can I come with you to pick her up?" Tony swallowed and hesitated for a second. Mitch guessed that no one had ever asked to ride along for a pick-up before.

"I don't think that's a good idea," he finally said. "They're good people over at the medical examiner's office, but it's not a nice place to visit. Let me bring Sophie back here and get her cleaned up for you. You can see her after I've had a chance to care for her."

Mitch shuddered at the thought of what "cleaned up" meant. It was a common phrase he used with his niece. *Time to get cleaned up for school. Let's get you cleaned up for dinner. Bed time—let's get cleaned up!* It was part of a routine, a way to prepare a young child for something that she needed to see coming in order to approach it without struggle. The rituals eased the transition from play to the necessary tasks of day-to-day living. It hurt so bad to use the phrase in such a final setting.

"Okay."

Tony squeezed his knee again and stood. Mitch and Liana rose along with him. Folding closed his binder and placing it under his arm, he took Mitch's hand again, shook it, and held on, placing his left hand over their grip. "Don't worry, Michel. You don't have to go through any of this alone." Liana leaned in and wrapped her arm around his waist.

For a minute, he believed them.

October

13

Mitch sat staring at Liana's laptop computer, searching the job listings on the Internet. He'd tried to return to work at the coffee shop, planning to ask if he could get an increase in hours as well as back on the management track, but, as he expected, his boss had already restaffed his position. The old man had been apologetic and offered to give him a call if something else opened up, but made sure to mention that he couldn't make any promises. He also didn't seem to feel like management was a likely track any more. If something eventually opened up, he said, barista was all they'd probably have. Mitch thanked him and said he'd check back. The boss looked like he wanted to say "Don't bother," but just smiled and shook Mitch's hand. On his way out, he caught glimpse of the old man pumping hand sanitizer in his palm, as if grief was catching.

Since then, he'd applied to every café across the city, but there were more people willing to pour coffee than there were shops able to accommodate them. Except for a couple of postings for an "assisted sales representative"—whatever that was—and something that looked like it might be a sidewalk food cart (*Love Asian food? Love working outdoors?*) it was all the same shit on the job boards as the last time he'd logged on. He stared at the computer screen. Unfilled, unskilled jobs in a college town were typically few, and in this economy they were even fewer. Liana told him she'd talk to Mike and try to help him get on at the grocery store. He'd filled out an application and she took it to her boss, but he was still waiting for her to say whether he'd gotten an interview. There seemed to be developing a limit to how much she could prop him back up. At first, she'd stayed a couple of nights at his house while trying to help put his life back in order. The apartment was as clean as it had ever been, and when she was there it felt almost like a home. But then she went to work and he had to try not to stare at Sophie's room, imagining what was and wasn't on the other side of the door he didn't have courage enough to open. Schrödinger's girl. One afternoon, he'd lost an hour just staring at a piece of yellow construction paper with the squiggly circles and crude smiley faces she'd made him tape to her door to indicate which room was hers. He'd helped her write her name below the face. *Those are* my *letters*, she'd told him. *My name letters.*

Before long, he started staying at Liana's place. It was both better and worse. He was able to focus, and mornings when he walked out of her bedroom, he didn't have to face the sign with Sophie's handwriting on it. But then came the guilt. He was starting to feel good for a little bit each day. And every day that feeling lasted a little longer. Sure, he was coping with his sorrow, but it was something else too. In the evenings, when he and Liana lay in bed snuggling, he felt free. Being held by the woman he loved and believed loved him, he realized that his life was his and no one else's. Freed from the responsibility thrust on him, without anyone to care for but himself, he had permission to *be* himself for the first time since his sister had split.

And the guilt of it was crushing him.

He closed the laptop and moved over to the sofa. Liana had a television, but it was an afterthought. No cable, a digital antenna that worked only half the time, and an age of filmy dust on the screen. She listened to music obsessively, and her immaculate record player held the position of most exalted thing in the living room. Under it, a collection of meticulously cared for vinyl and the plug-in for her dual processor lossless audio player. No iPod and lossy, compressed audio for her. He felt intimidated by her record collection. It was broad, but mostly made up of small label and indie bands he'd never heard of. Everything was inside a plastic slip cover and the first three albums he'd pulled out all had silver numbers drawn on the covers: 150/500, 15/100, 13/50. Limited editions that were irreplaceable if he accidentally scratched them. He carefully put everything back the way he'd found it and instead moved on to the bookshelves on the opposite wall.

They bowed under the weight of paperbacks large and small, but commonly available and well-read. Behind the books stacked in front were more arranged in rows. Nothing on that shelf said "worth more than you." She collected them the way he wished he could, habitually and without regard for subject or genre. He thought back to the last time he'd had time to read. It wasn't a memory he wanted to revisit. He scanned the shelves looking for one that intrigued him. They didn't appear to be in any kind of discernible order, but he noticed that slightly more of them were fantasy and science fiction than anything else. Even if he thought to look for a specific title, he wasn't sure how to find one in the chaos. Liana knew each and every one and he'd seen her get excited, jump up and magically produce titles she owned almost without looking. He randomly pulled one off the shelf and turned to the table of contents. *Short stories. Perfect!* He settled down on the sofa to begin reading in the silence. Liana had dog-eared one page in the book. He turned to it and began to read a story called "The Horrid Glory of its Wings," wondering what about *that* tale had inspired her to deface the book in a way she didn't any other.

An hour later, Liana interrupted his paralytic trance by bursting in the front door, manic and out of breath. Mitch shamefully wiped at the tears streaking his face and dropped the book on the couch, resolving to ask her what a story was about first before diving in next time. "You're home ear—"

"Quick! Get your boots on. We've got to go." She moved frantically, tossing his Docs at him as she ran for the bedroom, stripping off her uniform and throwing on jeans and a Chelsea Wolfe T-shirt.

He leaned over and peered at her through the open door. "What's going on, Li?"

"It's Tony," she called from the bedroom. "He won't say what the deal is, but he told me to listen to the thing that's all over the news. It's unreal!"

"What thing? What are you talking about?"

She came rushing out of the bedroom and grabbed his elbow, pulling him up off the sofa. He only had one of his shoes on and it was still untied. "We gotta go! Hurry up!"

Mitch fumbled his way into his other sneaker, Liana practically dragging him out the door as he hopped along trying to get his heel in. "I thought you were working until eight," he said.

"I am. I was. I told Mike I was taking a personal day. I don't really have those, but whatever." She didn't let go of his hand and continued to drag him down the stairway of her apartment building as he struggled not to trip on his laces and tumble down the stairs. Her car sat idling next to the curb outside. She ran around the front and jumped behind the wheel. Mitch slid into the passenger seat and she was off, tearing out of the lot and pulling into traffic before he could get his door completely shut and seatbelt latched.

Nerves worked up Mitch's stomach and into his throat, threatening to choke him. If it was a problem Tony had alerted her to, that meant it was a problem involving Sophie. He couldn't begin to imagine what that could be, but the images floating around in his head made him want to be sick. He had no stamina left for further indignities to be heaped upon his niece. It had been a month and he still hadn't been able to pick up her body. Tony explained that the backlog at the medical examiner's office didn't just effect results, but also procedures. Usually, they moved untimely deaths ahead of "unattended" deaths and children were given first priority, but in this instance, they were taking their time. The delay heaped an additional helping of powerlessness on top of that which Mitch already felt. He couldn't save his niece and he couldn't even give her a decent burial because no one would let him have what was left of her. He wanted to move on with his life and get on the other side of everything that was dragging him down. Grief, guilt, loneliness, and despair all sat on his chest like two tons of earth he'd shoveled over himself. Only Liana had extended a hand, offering a way up and out from underneath it all. And so when she said, *get in the car*, he did without question. When the safety tether goes taut, you follow where it pulls you. He knew that was no way to build a relationship. Eventually, he'd have to cut the line, stand up for himself, and bring something to their romance if he wanted it to last. Right now, though, he was letting the lifeline guide him.

Liana reached over and grabbed his hand. She gave it a hard squeeze and held on even though he would have preferred she keep both hands on the wheel, the way she drove. She banged a left turn ahead of oncoming traffic to get to the highway. Even though she was from outside Atlanta originally, Liana had taken to Massachusetts driving like she'd been raised with it. She was a wild driver, piloting a car like it was a rocket sled on rails and the only work to be done was feed it gasoline and lock the doors when they got out. Early on, she'd joked that her philosophy of the road was two-fold: "drive it like it's stolen" and "all you gotta do is miss"—meaning, miss the other cars on the road. It had taken him a week of riding with her practically every day to learn to let go of the door handles and relax. She was never stressed behind the wheel, no matter what she encountered. Today, however, she seemed more focused than usual. More in a hurry. Mitch had to brace himself against the door to keep from banging his head on the window.

"Let's see if they're still talking about it." Letting go of his hand, she clicked on the radio. He reached to change it from talk to some music, but she stayed his hand and said, "Just listen."

"I don't understand," he said.

"Listen," she insisted, turning up the volume. The car filled with the placid voice of an NPR host saying, "Religious figures around the country are calling it everything from God's mercy for bereaved parents, to the 'beginning of the end,' while scientists and physicians remain baffled. We want to hear what you think, listeners. Call us at 1-800..."

"What the hell, Li? I'm really not in the mood for The Old Time Bible Hour."

"Yeah, this is weird," she said, pulling the wheel hard to dart around another motorist. "It's *all* weird. Keep listening." He tried to focus on the radio instead of the danger posed by oncoming traffic.

"Our first caller is Steve from Dunwich, Massachusetts. You're on the air, Steve." Mitch sighed and tried to focus on the voices on the radio. Steve from Dunwich wasn't going to be encouraging or probably even coherent. Everyone up there was either some kind of religious nut or just a nut. It was a wonder that the call-screeners at WBUR didn't just have a block on any number originating from anywhere in the Miskatonic River Valley. He waited for the inevitable half-mad doom-saying to start.

"Thanks for taking my call, Robin; I'm a big fan of the show. I just wanted to say that I believe this is a sign of the Second Coming."

That's a bingo!

"Why do you say that?"

"Look at scripture. Isaiah 26:19 says, 'Your dead shall live; their bodies shall rise. You who dwell in the dust, awake and sing for joy! For the earth will give birth to the dead.' Mark 9:37 says, 'Whoever welcomes one of these little children in my name welcomes me.'"

"What does that mean to you?"

"This is Jesus sending 'the meek' to herald his return. God loves all the dead kids; if we reject them we reject Christ!"

"Thank you, Steve. That's an interesting perspective," the host said without a hint of exasperation or irony that Mitch could hear through the radio. "I'll give that to my guest, Reverend Chester Williamson of the Second Life Baptist Congregation in Lancaster, Pennsylvania. Reverend Williamson, do you think the events of the last couple of days have a *specific* religious implication?"

Mitch looked at Liana with concern as she pushed the car faster. They drifted across the highway, moving around slower moving cars and zipping dangerously close behind others hanging in the passing lane until they too moved out of the way. The dashboard began to rattle as she accelerated over eighty-five. She turned the radio volume up again to combat the growing road noise. The voice of the Right Reverend Williamson boomed out of the speakers like he was preaching to the seats in the back of a revival tent and not the ones in the front of a car threatening to rattle apart on the Mass Pike.

"The Bible is full of accounts of people rising from the grave. The one we know best of course is Lazarus, brought singly back by Jesus, but there are other references to the dead coming to life as well. Thessalonians tells us that at the Second Coming, the 'dead in Christ'—that is, the truly devout—shall be resurrected first. I'm not sure I agree with the caller's interpretation of Scripture, but Jesus did express an affinity for the innocence of a child-like faith."

The host broke in. "Dr. Emil Blomquist from Boston University School of Medicine, do you see things differently?"

"I don't know what to say, Robin. Medical science just doesn't have an answer yet for what we're seeing. That said, I do think it is important that we remain calm until we have had a chance to study in greater depth what must be, in essence, a new natural phenomenon."

"A new *natural* phenomenon?" Williamson interrupted. "Wouldn't this, if *anything*, fall into the category of the *super*natural, Doctor?"

"That I've never observed a natural process before, doesn't make it *super*natural. I'd liken it to when Pasteur confirmed the germ theory of infectious disease. The more we learn, the more we'll likely see a natural process at work here. It behooves us not to overreact and start alarming people unnecessarily by declaring that the sky is falling or that a religious day of reckoning is at hand."

"Overreact," the Reverend said, laughing. "I don't know what an *over*reaction to the dead rising from the grave would look like, but I suspect that a serious investigation of spiritual metaphysics is an appropriate reaction in *addition* to scientific inquiry."

"We're just about out of time, gentlemen. Any final tho..."

Mitch clicked off the radio, unconvinced they were listening to a live broadcast. It had to be some Halloween nonsense that accidentally got spooled up early by an intern at WBUR about to be fired. *They can't seriously be discussing the living dead on public radio.* "What are we doing, Li?"

"All I know is that Tony called me and told me we needed to come over right now and then I started hearing this weird stuff all over the place. People are freaking out." A sign announcing Exit 10 toward Worcester in one mile flashed by almost too fast to read. She cut off another driver, and sped up as they approached the exit. Mitch gripped the handle on the door harder.

"What stuff?"

Liana braked hard to avoid rolling the car around the rotary exit and pulled to an abrupt stop at the end of the ramp. She turned and looked him in the face. "I... I don't want to say. It's weird, Mitch. But it might be good weird, y'know?"

"I don't understand what could possibly be 'good weird.'"

"Do you trust me?" she asked. He nodded. "Okay. Then let's go meet Tony."

14

Liana checked the address on her phone again before shutting off the engine. She'd parked across the street from a blocky, three-story tan building with the seal of the Commonwealth just under the front parapet. The architecture displayed very little of the ornate flourishes that distinguished most other city or state-owned addresses. Unlike New England city halls and courthouses and even libraries, there was nothing adorning this edifice meant to make you stand in awe of its majesty. No columns or deco window arches to draw the eye up to a cornice ledge dramatically underlining the sun and blue sky above. Just tan brick and unassuming concrete steps leading to a pair of unadorned wooden doors below the circular seal and an address engraved in a plain font: 86 Garden St.

"Where are we?"

"This is where Tony told me to bring you." She leaned over and lightly kissed Mitch on the lips. "Whatever happens in there, I love you."

His throat seized up and he couldn't swallow. Between the radio and now this, he had no idea how to still his mind. It was racing from one unreal idea to another with such speed that he felt a sort of velocity disorientation. Every thought was moving so fast, he only had time to catch a blurry image of an idea before it was gone and his mind was on to the next one.

He took as deep a breath as he could and managed to hold a coherent thought long enough to say, "I love you too."

Liana was already out of the car and around on his side, pulling him into the street. She dialed Tony's number with one hand while she continued to guide Mitch with the other. As they climbed the steps, one of the heavy doors swung open and Tony emerged, ashen faced with twin ruddy spots on his cheeks. He looked like someone who'd witnessed something so horrible, the memory could only be overcome with alcohol. "Come in, quick," he said, shoving the door open for the couple to pass by. He cast a nervous glance up the street before ducking in after them.

On either side of the foyer in which they stood, stairways reached up to a landing where Mitch could see closed office doors. In the center of the lobby, dead ahead, wide marble steps led down. While the exterior of the building was unassuming, bordering on anonymous, the interior was rich with symbolic adornment. A pair of bronze sphinxes on either side of a center stairway froze Mitch where he stood. He shuddered as they stared at him with a flat dispassion, their hollow pupils fixing him in place. If asked, he intended to blame the shiver on the excessive air conditioning. Above him, on the front of the upper landing, was a gilt hourglass with outstretched golden wings. The words *Fugit Irreparabile Tempus* were engraved in the marble wall below it. Mitch asked Tony if he knew what it meant. "Time flees irretrievably," was the answer.

"Where are we?"

"The ME's office," Tony said. "Come on. This way." He was halfway down the steps before turning to see if Liana and Mitch were following. He paused and held out a hand to the couple. "Come on."

Passing through a pair of swinging doors at the bottom of the stairway marked STAFF ONLY, the building transformed a third time. This time to a sober and sterile-looking hospital environment. White walls and a gray floor with blue stripes on either side of the hallway led off to the left and the right. Doors with wire-reinforced windows were labeled with the names of people who spent their days behind them. Tony led them to a door marked MIRANDA DOWNUM, M.D. He knocked and opened the door, peeking in before swinging it wide.

Inside, a petite redhead with freckled skin and a black silk choker around her neck sat behind a desk much too big for the room. Behind her hung a painting of a dog-faced man in a golden headdress and skirt, holding a shepherd's crook and scales. She stood and came around the desk, reaching out to hug Tony. Pulling back, she said, "I thought you said you were bringing her family. Who's this?"

"This *is* her family." Tony held out a hand. "This is Michel LeRoux." He cleared his throat. "Her uncle. Her only known relative."

"No mother? Father?"

"It's just me, ma'am," Mitch said. Dr. Downum looked him up and down before sighing. He casually slid a hand over the tattoo on his forearm—a diamond inside a circle—but he was certain she'd seen it. When he'd gotten it, it was armor. Now it was a weakness—a signal to everyone else in the world what his vulnerabilities were. She was judging him based on his appearance while she looked like she hadn't graduated from medical school long enough ago to have filled her office so completely with clutter. Eventually, she reached her silent judgment and said, "This way," leading the trio out into the hallway and around a corner to two more swinging doors. These were marked with a simple numeral one. She pushed through without holding them open for the others following. Tony pulled a door open and allowed Liana and

Mitch to enter ahead of him. He shrugged as if to say, *Dr. Downum doesn't deal with people often. Not living ones, anyway.*

The trio stepped into a large, chilly room. Three steel tables bolted to the tile floor stood in a row along a far wall. Above each table was a recessed alcove with a sink below a hanging autopsy scale. On the opposite side of the room stood a door with a slender vertical window above the knob. Behind that, the room narrowed with one wall made up of square steel doors in rows from floor to fluorescent lit ceiling. And at the end of it crouched a man in blue scrubs with his back turned. He looked over his shoulder at Dr. Downum and smiled weakly. "You find them?" he asked, standing up.

"This is the uncle," she said without gesturing or looking back.

The man stood up and took a step to the side. Sophie's body sat propped up on a rolling office chair. Her blank eyes were open, staring off into the middle distance. Mitch felt a filter of rage descend over his consciousness. There was no word like widower for someone who lost a child, because it was just too terrible a thing to give a name to. He couldn't imagine the profound cruelty that would inspire such a show. He walked toward the girl to move her from the chair back onto a table where he could cover her. Preserve her dignity.

Sophie blinked. He stopped.

It's a trick. He tried to convince himself that he was seeing things. The result of a suggestion brought on by a terrible practical joke meant to drive him mad. He looked over at Liana and Tony—people he trusted—for assurance that they weren't in on it. It was a con and they were *all* being had. Liana was standing frozen, gape-mouthed and shocked. *At least* she *wasn't in on it.* Tony, on the other hand, had that fatherly look that he'd paraded around the funeral home. The face of a man whose job it was to feign empathy. *Well, fuck him and fuck Dr. Downum too. No one deserves to be treated like this.*

She's not a toy to be propped up and paraded around. If they think I'm going to take the bait and go running over like—

She blinked again and tilted her head.

"Sophie?" he said, the name catching in his dry throat like a hook.

She looked at her uncle and mewled softly, raising her arms in the gesture that had always preceded her saying, "Pick me up." He rushed for her, his hip slamming into the corner of an autopsy table, bouncing him off target and nearly into the wall as he ran. Correcting course, he plucked her out of the seat, hugging her tightly. Her little arms wrapped around his neck and they stood embracing each other. Holding on. He loved her so much.

She was ice cold.

15

While Tony and Dr. Downum argued over the issue of how to resolve documenting the release of the child, Mitch cradled Sophie, whispering to her, smoothing down her hair, trying to warm her with the heat of his body. She didn't look like his girl. Her hair was still curly, but it had lost all of its color, going a dull grey. Her skin was ashen and her eyes were washed out white with cataracts. Despite all the appearance of death, he couldn't deny that she nuzzled into his shoulder, searching for that comfortable nook where her head fit just right. She nudged and shifted and fidgeted until she found it. And the familiar comfort of holding her against him made everything but her irrelevant to Mitch. He didn't care how Tony and Dr. Downum worked out the paperwork, as long as they both acknowledged that he wasn't leaving without his niece. He quietly hummed a lullaby while trying to ignore the fact that he was sitting in an autopsy room, feet away from a refrigerated wall full of the as yet unrisen dead.

Shifting in the office chair, he adjusted himself beneath the girl, trying to make her more comfortable. She didn't seem to notice. She lay still on his chest, her fingers lightly playing with the beginnings of the beard on his chin. She felt lighter, maybe even smaller somehow than he remembered. She'd always been little. And while she grew, she remained small for her age, younger kids on the playground towering over her. Sitting in his lap since her resurrection, she felt lessened, as though some essential element of her was missing. Of course that was nonsense. She was embracing him. There was nothing missing.

Except her soul.

He pushed the unwelcome thought down. He wasn't sure what he believed in when it came to the universe and the afterlife, but he was certain that if there was a god and it was merciful, his niece had her soul just like everybody else. If there wasn't a god, then she wasn't missing anything. Just like everybody else. The only option left was that there *was* a god, but it was not a merciful being and it had kept the part of her that gave her spiritual substance while returning only a dead shell to him. Given what he knew about the world and its injustices, the last was as much a likelihood as the prior two options. Still, he preferred to willfully exclude it from his list of possibilities.

She's fine. She's sitting here and she's fine.

He closed his eyes for a moment and felt her fingers stroking his cheek, imagining that they were home on their sofa and that none of this had happened. Of course it had. She'd been taken from him—kept from him. They'd told him she was dead and had threatened him with jail. In that time, he'd lost his food assistance and was about to lose the rent voucher now that they would have to return home and needed it the most. He wondered how Liana would do with the two of them moving in to *her* apartment. It wasn't big enough for three. He *had* to find a way to keep their old place. That meant redoubling his efforts to find a job. And trying to get Sophie back into day care. There was so much to be done. He didn't have time to daydream.

Opening his eyes, he saw Liana standing against a far wall with her arms folded to keep away the coldness of the room, keeping her distance. Mitch wanted to call her near, bring her into the embrace, but she seemed to be coping less well with the reality of the situation than she had been with the concept. Her enthusiasm in the car had hit a brick wall in the morgue. It was one thing to listen to stories about the dead returning to life on the television or the radio. She had clearly been excited by the prospect of reuniting Mitch with the most important person in his life. But it was an entirely different experience to face the reality of what he held in his arms... and have it stare back at her. Sophie wasn't a corpse. She was awake and alert. She wasn't talking... was she breathing...? but here she was, holding on to him, and that was all he wanted in the world at that moment. He had his niece. He had a second chance.

She isn't a corpse, he told himself again.

Dr. Downum sat down at a small table and rested her head in a hand. "She's the object of a criminal investigation, Tony. I can't just release her."

"She's not an object," Tony replied. "She's a little girl. How many of these kids have you seen so far?" Dr. Downum looked over at Sophie and Mitch and sighed. She looked tired. She looked frightened.

"So far? Three."

"And where are the first two?"

Dr. Downum shook her head to indicate she did not want to say, not in front of Mitch anyway. Tony squatted down in front of her chair and grabbed her hands. From where Mitch sat, the mortician looked like a father trying to give a daughter comfort. He wondered if they'd known each other personally before they worked together, or if they'd formed that bond by tending to the dead in tandem. However it had developed, it was clear that the two of them would be coming to an agreement, not because they had to, but because they both knew the right thing to do.

"She's the only one a family member has come to collect," Dr. Downum said. "The other children... the... the chief ME took them after they... woke up. One of them came to *after* I started cutting, Tony!" The mortician pulled Dr. Downum close and held her.

Mitch didn't want to think about what had happened to the other kids any more than it looked like Dr. Downum wanted to. He tried to put the memory of the radio program with its doom and gloom callers out of his mind. People had said the most horrible things. One caller said the kids were an abomination. Another proclaimed that Hell was emptying onto the Earth, starting with the children. Overall, the consensus among the reasonable listeners of NPR was that they were witnessing the beginning of some kind of end. He didn't want to imagine what the callers to more reactionary talk radio were saying.

"Tony, they know I had *three* children here awaiting examination. I panicked when the first two came to, and called my boss. They took the boys away and refused to tell me anything about what they intended to do with them."

"You think it was possible they called the kids' parents to come get them?" he said.

Dr. Downum shook her head. "I don't know what happened to them, but I'm pretty sure it wasn't that. That's why I called you first this time. I have no idea what's going on, but I'm sure they'll be back once they remember I've got another one."

"It's okay," he said, pulling her away from his shoulder so he could look her in the face. "You did the right thing."

"But what do we do now?" Mitch asked. Tony and Dr. Downum looked at him, not surprised that he'd been listening, but seemingly concerned that he'd given voice to the question both of them were dancing around. He was appreciative of both of their help, but he just wanted to go home, and he wasn't leaving without Sophie.

Dr. Downum leaned back in her chair, wiped her eyes, and said, "If I write it up that the examination was performed and her body released to the funeral home, maybe that'll be the end of it." She paused for a moment as if searching for the least upsetting way to say what else was on her mind. "Of course, if anyone follows up and finds out she was never interred, they'll know I perjured myself and that'll be the end of my career, at the very least."

"Why do you have to write anything?" Mitch asked.

"What do you mean?"

He tried to lean forward. Sophie protested, groaning softly, and reached for the back of the chair to keep him in a position where she could rest her head on his shoulder. He said, "I mean, give us a couple of days to get settled and then say you... lost her."

Tony smiled and nodded as if they had never considered the most obvious solution. Dr. Downum hadn't gotten on board yet, however. She protested. "I can't say I *lost* a body. How do you lose someone who's..." The look on her face changed from consternation to skeptical understanding. "You mean, I say we left her unattended and..."

Mitch grinned broadly at the absurdity of it. But it seemed like an elegantly simple solution to him. He stood up from the chair and set Sophie on her feet on the floor next to him. He held out a hand like he did when they were walking to Khadija's house. She grabbed it and looked up at him with milky eyes and a wan, thin-lipped smile.

"She just got up and walked away," he said.

16

Mitch sat in the backseat of Liana's car with Sophie in his lap, facing him. She refused to let him buckle her in to a seat belt, so he'd climbed in with her, slouched down, and held on tightly, hoping a cop wouldn't see and pull them over on the ride home. Moreover, he hoped Liana's nervousness wouldn't get them in a wreck. She kept glancing up at them in the rearview mirror, taking her eyes off the road. He tried to make eye contact, but every time their eyes met, Liana quickly looked away. She braked sharply and accelerated just as abruptly, reacting to the other cars on the road more than driving deliberately.

They rode in silence until she took the highway exit closest to her apartment. She waited at the stop sign at the end of the ramp, seeming unsure which direction to turn. A car pulled up behind them and honked. Liana jammed her foot on the gas pedal and the car lurched into the road. A pickup truck in the oncoming lane honked as they peeled out in front of it. She hunched her shoulders and held her breath and she swerved away from the man treating it like a game of chicken. Mitch gripped Sophie tighter and squinted his eyes waiting for the impact. When it didn't come, he opened them again and looked at his little niece's face. Her expression hadn't changed. If she noticed that they'd been in danger, it hadn't registered. Eventually, she let out a long sigh and took another breath, her shoulders lowering slowly.

"I'm sorry," she said.

She's freaked out by this. If it was anybody but Sophie would I be losing it too? Of course, I would.

"It's okay. We can make it work," he said. From the back seat, he saw Liana's head shake ever so slightly. He could lie to himself about her silence on the return trip if he wanted, but he couldn't deny what her body told him. Just like before, winning one meant losing the other.

17

Liana's apartment was perfect for one. It was cozy for two. With three, all its limitations were laid bare. When they first arrived, she flitted around the place picking up bits and pieces of her life, repositioning them in an attempt to triage those things she judged most in need of childproofing. Before, Sophie would have been running around asking what this was, wanting to touch that, inquiring about details that caught her eye, however banal. Instead, though, Sophie seemed uninterested in any of Liana's possessions except one; she sat quietly on the sofa watching television. When the orange monster Murray announced "amplify" was the word on the street, she seemed to take an interest for a brief moment before returning to her placid impassivity. Mitch's breath hitched at the re-run. How they'd loved this episode when they first watched it together. Whenever something loud happened near them, a bus passing by the house, or something dropping onto the floor with a clatter, they both shouted, "AMPLIFY!" as loudly as they could and laughed and laughed as if it were the height of sophisticated comedy. They'd do it out at the grocery store, the playground, everywhere but the library, and get odd looks from strangers when they hit the same timing and tone like it was a rehearsed routine. No matter how many times they shouted the word, it never failed to make Sophie smile. It was their shield and a sword against sudden startling noises that frightened her. Today, she sat watching with a blank expression.

Mitch moved away from the television, and her eyes followed him. Despite the cataracts, she saw. She stayed put on the sofa while he chased after Liana, trying to get her to slow down and relax. He'd once dated a woman who burned off anger by cleaning her apartment. Every time they fought, she'd tear through the place like a cartoon cleanser mascot. They weren't well-suited for one another and Mitch hadn't learned to sublimate his anger yet; as a result, her apartment was always as clean as a surgery. Liana, by contrast, was comfortable with a little clutter and didn't tidy to cope. Not that he'd seen up to that point, anyway. In the short time they'd been together, she'd been in support mode. He was coping with his grief in his own way— by shutting down, doing his time quietly—and she was holding him up. Now, though, it was his turn to assure her things would turn out all right.

"It's been a… weird day," he said. "Let's just chill out a little and—"

"Don't tell me to chill out."

"I didn't say *you* need to chill. I said… *we* should take some time to chill and put things in perspective."

Liana's expression darkened and her full lips went thin. "Perspective? What kind of perspective do you think I need to contextualize what's sitting on my couch?"

He raised his hands, as if he could deflect her words. "Heyheyhey! *Who*, not *what*. That's Sophie over there. You remember meeting her? Remember our first date?"

Liana clenched her fists and seemed to be searching for a retort. She tilted her head and looked over Mitch's shoulder at the child. The girl was staring at the two of them, not the TV, and Liana's jaws clamped shut with an audible click. They weren't shouting, but neither were they whispering, and anyone could see the girl understood they were talking about her.

"You seemed so excited on the way to the… to Dr. Downum's office. Where did that go?"

She lowered her voice and said, "I was excited. I was excited for you. For us. But... you know, the way it sounded on the radio, it was... I don't know. They didn't say..."

"What is it? Just say it."

"I didn't know she'd be so... dead."

Mitch turned and looked at Sophie, not to confirm what Liana was saying—he knew—but to see if she had heard. He felt an urge to go over and scoop her up and tell her that Liana didn't mean what she said. But as much as he wanted to fight against the accusation, he knew what she said was true, even if he was unwilling to acknowledge it. She'd been dead, and now she wasn't. Sort of. There was no way to put it that didn't sound naïve. It was a miracle. She was getting better. Whatever measure he tried to take of it, it still sounded like a denial of the bare fact Liana laid out. Sophie didn't look like a healthy little girl. No matter how badly he wanted to ignore the fact, underneath her appearance was the truth.

"Her heart's beating," he said. "You can feel it." He reached for her hand, hoping that touching him would bring her closer. Liana shook her head and took a step back as if he'd reached out to drag her over to touch Sophie's chest. Maybe he'd meant to do just that. He wasn't sure what he intended to do from one second to the next.

"You need to give me some... time. I wasn't scared then, but I am a little now. Maybe more than a little. I need time." She took a breath and said, "I'm frightened, Mitch."

Mitch understood. She was being thrust into a situation she hadn't planned for—*couldn't* plan for. This was different than going out a couple of times with a guy who has a kid. Different than realizing their romantic life was going to revolve around babysitters and bedtimes. He'd been in her situation: single and living alone, only responsible for himself, and possessed of the choice to be involved in Sophie's life as *he* pleased. An uncle was supposed to be the one to come over and spoil her with presents that annoyed her parents and tell her it was all right when she and Violette clashed and later when she needed someone to talk to who wouldn't judge her. It wasn't his job to feed and clothe and shelter her, raise and educate her. It wasn't his job, and he wasn't the person for the task. Who would ever have picked a man like him to bring up a child? Then, Violette made the choice for them both, thrusting them together, and taking his autonomy with her on the road. But he'd adapted and come to terms with the situation. Mitch was all Sophie had. *And whose fault is that?* he thought. He felt the pang of shame at his responsibility for her father's absence burn and grow into anger at the people who'd placed them in these roles. In the one into which he'd placed himself. It poured life blood into the part of him that was reactive and desired to shut down whatever forced him to confront his own failings. And on it went, burning in his heart and his head. It wasn't Sophie's fault she needed him. But she did. And he came to love his responsibility because he loved her more than anything else.

And then she died.

Solitary freedom came back to him like the debt due on a Faustian bargain. The feeling of life without her was always there in his mind, in his heart. Accompanied by guilt brought on by fleeting moments of relief at only having to care for himself. At having Liana there to care for him. He'd begun to love those quiet moments — just the two of them, no children.

He breathed in and out, trying to be mindful of his emotions, like his counselor had shown him. Meditation he'd leaned on to survive three years at MCI Concord. He tried to find that calm center where rationality lived, and in the middle of the emotional tumult, Mitch began to feel a tiny point of calm. No matter how liberating that brief glance at independence had been, how unfair the suddenness of it was, he knew he needed Sophie as much as she needed him. He accepted his responsibility and saw the justice in being the one tasked with her care. Somehow, something had given her back to him. Whatever that something was, God or the Devil, a comet's tail, or a spill of 2-4-5 Trioxin, he didn't care. He had a second chance to get things right as far as she was concerned, and he wasn't going to squander it. Not like his own parents had squandered his and Violette's upbringing. Whether or not he'd asked for it, he had this chance to do it the way it was supposed to be done. And only this chance.

"I'm sorry. You're right. It's getting late, and I know I'm fuc—" He glanced at the child and corrected himself. "I'm frazzled, and need to rest. Sophie and I will sleep out here." He gave it a beat, and when Liana didn't smile, continued. "Tomorrow, I'll take her to scope out our old place. You've already done so much for me, and I can't ask you to—"

Liana leaned forward and awkwardly kissed him, shutting him up before he could finish. He didn't feel like she was stopping him before he could commit to leaving, but rather that she was thanking him for saying what she didn't have the heart to utter herself: he and Sophie had to go. He kissed her back and tried to memorize the various feels of her. Soft lips and arching back. Smooth skin and sinewy muscle. He tried committing them to memory, to last through his exile, like drinking water before heading into the desert. Of all the little physical things he took pleasure from, most of all he thought he'd miss her sweet breath, like spearmint.

He pulled away from her, though he didn't want to. She smiled with half her mouth the way he loved and half his grief came flooding back. He had no words. The idea of going back to the place where he woke up to find his worst nightmare lying in his niece's crib was more than he could face. But face it, he supposed he would have to. There weren't any other options. Although he still had some money in a savings account, he sure as hell couldn't afford a motel for a few nights, much less indefinitely.

He glanced at Sophie again. When the paramedics had come for her, she was in her pajamas. He didn't know what happened to those; he imagined someone in the hospital or perhaps the medical examiner's office had disposed of them. She was dressed in a cream-colored shift dress and a pair of tights that were too long and bagged at the knees. He suspected Tony had brought those clothes for her. It looked like a burial outfit, and he wanted her out of it as soon as he could manage. Even if they stayed at Liana's, he knew he'd have to go back to his sister's place at least once. That's where all of Sophie's things were. All of her clothes and books and crayons and dolls. Everything she owned was elsewhere, abandoned in his haste to run away from grief. Although there was no rational reason to hold on to those things before, he had to go see if he could at least get some of her own clothes and a few toys. If the landlord hadn't trashed everything. He couldn't go now, though. There was no way he could ask Liana to stay alone with Sophie while he ran to see what was left; she seemed perilously close to the tipping point. And he couldn't take Sophie with him. He couldn't carry her and everything he needed to bring back. Which, naturally, led him to realize that they couldn't stay with Liana, no matter how badly he wanted to. He'd give her space. Tomorrow. After he determined there was still a place for him and Sophie to go.

"Can I borrow a shirt?" he said. "Soph doesn't have any PJs, and I want to get her out of that weird mortuary outfit."

Liana's face clouded with a touch of the apprehension she'd worn only moments earlier before she relaxed again and sighed. "Of course." She walked into her bedroom and came back with a tour shirt for some band he'd never heard of. Unlike her others, it had no skulls or pentagrams or devils. Instead, it was a simple graphic sequence of the phases of the moon and an unreadable band name that looked like brambles.

"Perfect. Thanks."

Liana nodded but didn't say, "You're welcome." She stood watching while he tiptoed over to where Sophie sat watching him.

"Want to change into something better, sweetie? Tomorrow, we'll go get you some new clothes, okay?"

"'Kay," she said. Her voice was tiny and hollow like someone trying to speak at the end of a breath. She held up her hands the way she did when he told her it was pajama time, and he pulled the shift up over her head. She was pale. So pale. A chill shuddered through him, like she was made of wind and frost. In the window, Liana's air conditioner struggled against the late day heat. He pulled the black shirt down over her and asked her to step out of the tights. She did, and fell into his arms, wrapping hers around his neck. The babydoll style shirt fit her like a nightgown.

Liana sighed and Mitch looked over at her. She straightened her back the way she'd done when she was trying to motivate him to do something he didn't want to do—get out of bed, get showered, find a grief counseling group. This time, her standing tall wasn't something she was doing for his benefit. She squared her shoulders, took a deep breath and said, "Let's give it a couple of days, and... I'll try to get used to things. We'll figure it out together."

"You sure?"

She shook her head. "Don't ask me if I'm sure, because I'm not yet. But I'm willing to try."

He smiled and stood. Sophie kept a hold of his neck and wrapped her legs around his waist as he lifted her. Behind him, a puppet on the screen shouted, "Amplify!" and he felt a surge of contentment that made him shiver even harder.

"We can make it work," he whispered.

18

The child's tiny feet made no sound on the creaky hardwood floors as she tiptoed through the darkened apartment from the living room into the hallway that led to Mitch and Liana's bedroom. Her uncle had closed all the curtains before they went to sleep so the light from the street lamps in the parking lot outside wouldn't bleed into the apartment and disturb them. But she didn't need the light to see. Everything was easy for her to see, and the dark didn't frighten her any more.

Mitch had set her up to rest on the sofa, but she never stayed there. In the middle of the night when she could hear their breathing go deep and rhythmic, she would get up and wander into the bedroom and crawl in under the covers with him. She was always freezing cold. He would wrap his arms around her, lending her his warmth.

She didn't like this place. It was too small and none of her toys were here. Not even a set of crayons. Mitch promised they'd go get her stuff and bring it back, but she didn't want to go get anything. She just wanted to be there. She wanted to go home.

Pushing open the door, Sophie padded over to where her uncle and his girlfriend slept. It was a tall bed, too tall to climb into herself, so she had to wake him to get help up. He was more than willing to scoop her up and let her nestle in the crook of his arm, her head under his chin and cold feet pressed against the cozy warmth of his pajama-covered legs.

He'd scooted into the middle of the bed to make room for her instead of letting her sleep in between him and the girlfriend. Sophie wanted the middle, but she settled for the edge of the bed, if that's where Mitch wanted her to sleep.

But she didn't sleep. She closed her eyes and pretended, so if he got up to go to the bathroom, he wouldn't be worried or try to take her back to the sofa. Sophie would climb in bed with him and keep her eyes closed until she could hear his breathing go slow again. Sometimes he'd snore. When that happened, she'd open her eyes and look around the room. She'd try to get a glimpse of the girlfriend, but her uncle's body blocked her view. Except tonight.

Tonight she wasn't going to wake him to help her climb under the covers. Instead, she stood on the opposite side of the bed looking at the girlfriend. She was so nice when they first met. She seemed happy then when she sat down to play. Sophie had liked her. Now, she was different. Now, she was frightened. When she thought Sophie and her uncle weren't looking, she'd whisper things to people who weren't there. She talked to a Gran that Sophie couldn't see, asking her for help. For patience. And courage. Gran never answered and she was still afraid.

Sophie stood and stared at the girlfriend. She slept with her lips parted slightly, breathing slow like Mitch, but not snoring. Sophie wanted to be pretty like her. She wanted to have warm skin and bouncy tight hair and dark, pretty lips like the girlfriend put on before she went to work. But instead, her hair was limp and her lips were pale and she was cold. Everything was cold. Except Mitch and his girlfriend.

Reaching up, she held a finger near Liana's mouth trying to feel her breath. It was warm and moist on her tiny fingers. She wanted to lean in and try to inhale a little of that breath. Just have a taste of its sweetness and feel some of the heat of it in her mouth and her lungs. It sounded so good, and deep in her belly she could feel the ache of wanting it. She stepped forward and got up on her tip toes, but no matter how hard she stretched, she couldn't get her mouth close enough to breathe any in.

Sophie took a step back. She watched the girlfriend sleep some more, the woman's chest rising and falling with each soft breath.

After an hour, she slipped out of the bedroom and came back with the small step stool Liana used in the kitchen to reach things in high cabinets. It was heavy and hard to carry, but Sophie wanted to get close. She wanted just a little taste.

She wanted that warmth inside her.

Interlude: Scenes from a Revival

19

From the seats surrounding the amphitheater stage he heard a few murmured "amens" and "hallelujahs," but for the most part his parishioners were frightened and looking to him for guidance. The preacher stood in front of his congregation with his microphone at his hip, staring forward into the distance for effect, letting his last words sink in. It was taking less work than usual to rile up the crowd, but more than he liked to get them going in the direction he wanted. He took a moment to straighten his custom-tailored Savile Row suit and check his Omega watch, like he was pressed for time, before returning the microphone to his lips. A hush settled over the chapel theater as he raised his free hand above his head for them to be quiet and listen.

"Look to Revelation 11:13. The teaching of scripture is that 'thy wrath is come, and the time of the dead, that they should be judged, and that thou shouldest give reward unto them that fear thy name.'" He gave another pause for call and response before interpreting his selection. "Now, good people, is the time of the dead. You see it. They are rising from the grave as we speak. And they herald the wrath of the Lord!" A shudder of mumbled noise rose from the crowd. He felt a tinge of satisfaction in their discomfort. He would whip their growing unease into righteous revelatory ecstasy and stand bathed in it.

"The dead are rising and coming to be among us for the judgment of the Lord in these final days. But do they bring His love and grace? Nossir! No ma'am! I say, they do *not*. I tell you they are a mockery of His word, His son's work, and of the Holy Spirit. 'Behold a pale horse, and his name that sat on him was Death, and Hell followed!' These so-called 'children' are the minions of Death and the stink of Hell is on them. They are risen by the Prince of Lies to tempt us with their small bodies and innocent faces, but they are the souls of the damned given pleasing shape to tempt us to take them into our homes and divert our attention away from the Lord and his plan. I tell you, that God has warned us of this and promised to protect us from evil.

"Harken to Revelation 3:10. 'Because thou hast kept the word of my patience, I also will keep thee from the hour of temptation, which shall come upon all the world, to try them that dwell upon the earth.'" He raised a hand and pranced to stage right to give a little love to the cheap seats while the paraphrased scripture sank in. "We are being tempted by the children of the grave. Tempted by the least among us, those whom we loved and lost to the Lord in his wisdom. God has a plan! He took those children for His own reasons, according to His plan. And now the Devil returns them to Earth filled with demons and lies to tempt us with promises he cannot keep, and a desire to frustrate the works of the Lord, our God! But shall we allow ourselves to be tempted?"

"No," the crowd replied.

His cadence and volume was starting to work. They were following his train right out of the station and soon he'd be able to lead them out the front door, into the streets, and begin to exact God's plan. It would only take a little more goading for the sheep to rise up. "I said, shall we allow ourselves to be tempted?"

"NO!"

"That's right! Because we are strong in the power of the Lord. And he has promised to keep the faithful free from temptation in these final days. So what is to be done with these ghouls and the… the *deadophiles* who cling to them? What are we servants of the Lord to do?" He didn't wait for a response. There was nothing in it for him to let them ponder the question themselves. "We are called to stand and do His work."

The crowd simmered at the edge of a roiling boil, and then he applied the heat. "Deuteronomy says, 'There shall not be found among you a witch, or a *necromancer!*' One who can summon the dead. 'For all these things are an abomination unto the Lord.'"

"AMEN!"

"And what shall we do when the witches and necromancers call forth Hell to spew its filth up onto the Earth? When they raise the dead army of the Devil? Shall we stand back and allow corruption and sin to overtake us?"

"NO!"

"HELL no! Thou shalt not suffer a witch to live! Shall we instead send these demons back to their unholy master? And their deadophile slaves with them?" The cry that rose up pleased Pastor Roper. It filled him with a satisfaction that he could only find on the stage in this theater.

"God hates deadophiles!" the ebullient crowd cheered.

• • •

He looked at her. He strode to the edge of the stage and looked right at her. For a moment, she felt completely alone in the assembly as he gazed down from above and that smile of his opened wide, as if she was exactly who he'd been hoping to see. Of course, he didn't know her, but his intense blue eyes and perfect, gleaming smile said that he knew her heart—her soul. While she sat transfixed by his gaze, he lifted his microphone and said, "*You* are the hope that God's work will be done!" Her heart quickened and she felt out of breath. A fog descended around her consciousness and the noise of the hall dimmed until all she could hear was his voice echoing in her head.

And then he stepped to his left, pointed at another parishioner a couple of rows farther back, and repeated himself. "*You* are the hope..." And again.

The crowd roared back to life in her ears and she felt Junior's hand slapping her thigh as he shouted hosannas. In the couple of months that she'd been coming to the New Life Church, people boasted that they saw crowds of up to five thousand on Christmas and Easter. There had to be at least that many in the hall today; the place was packed and it wasn't even a holiday. People stood in the aisles and the doorways in violation of the fire code. Still, with the memory of Pastor Roper's eyes upon her, she felt fireproof.

The rest of the sermon was a blur as she watched Roper walk from one end of the stage to the other, wishing he'd stop and recognize her again. She crossed and uncrossed her legs, trying to hold her excitement at bay until she could have a private moment to release the tension in her belly, between her legs. She dropped her hand into her lap and let her thumb brush against the front of her jeans below her zipper. An electric charge shot up the small of her back. She thought about doing it again. Instead, she kept herself under control. Her ears slowly came back to life and she called out as Roper asked for "amens" and "hallelujahs," but nothing felt as rich as that moment he looked down and declared his faith in her. The sermon gave way to another song from Roper's wife at the piano, the choir backing her, and then a video on the massive central screen updating the congregation on their investment in the Jamaican orphanage and ministry. The faces of the children always made Violette sad. They made her miss Sophie.

The decision to leave her child behind had been hastily made and for all the wrong reasons, but it had led her here. To a reunion with Junior—her daughter's father—to the New Life Church, and Pastor Roper's ministry, and salvation. She was better for having left. And now that she was healed, it was time to go back and reclaim her daughter. Sophie would be better off with her than her uncle. It was the end of times, and her girl needed a mother. She needed a family and the Lord and Violette and Junior would ensure when the stars fell from Heaven, Sophie was not burned. She had to make certain her family was fireproof.

Part Three: Sophie's Afterlife

20

Mitch awoke alone in bed, well-rested for the first time in days. The first couple of nights in Liana's apartment were rough on everyone; it took a while to adjust to the new way things were. Sophie didn't want to be apart from her uncle for longer than it took to let him have a shower or fix a meal, and even then she'd sit on the floor just clear of what he was doing and wait. The rest of the time, she clung to him. Mitch had tried to revivify his routine as best he could. But no matter how much he wanted to pretend otherwise, he couldn't deny things were not as they'd been. Without a job, he couldn't afford to take Sophie back to day care, and he wasn't even sure Khadija would allow her in once she saw what had happened. Of course, he couldn't go on job interviews with her in tow, and he couldn't leave her home alone either. Being together in close quarters was already straining his relationship. Leaving Sophie with Liana while he went out would be the weight that broke it. He was descending in a downward spiral of "couldn'ts" that were standing in the way of fully getting their lives back on track.

Liana tried to hide it from Mitch, but he could see their constant closeness was clearly getting under her skin too. Their duo had become a trio. Although she put forward an effort, her fear of his niece wasn't fading. The reality of rescuing the child from the morgue weighed heavily on her. At first, she'd tried to engage Sophie like she had the night of their first date, but the girl didn't demand pyramids or drawings or any kind of cooperative play anymore. She sat. She observed. And she cleaved to Mitch. Liana was becoming increasingly aloof and defensive of her personal space. She had even banished herself to the far edge of the bed at night; they hadn't made love since returning from the morgue.

Liana sat him down after the second night and asked that he not let Sophie into bed with them. It was their space. *Her* space. She wasn't ready for a "family bed." So, he explained to Sophie as best he could that she needed to sleep in her own bed all night long. He'd expected an argument. Toddlers were little lawyers, and he paused, giving her the opportunity to point out the difference between her bed and a couch with a pillow and a few blankets on it. But she hadn't. She didn't say anything at all. When he was done explaining things, she just held her arms up and made the sound that meant she wanted to hold on to him. But last night, she hadn't risen from her temporary bed on the sofa. That was progress. Right?

He rubbed sleep from his eyes with the backs of his hands and lay there for a moment, listening. On a normal weekday morning, the sounds of Liana getting ready for work carried through the apartment. She was considerate, but was also used to living alone, and not having to worry about waking other people up. He loved it. It was like waking to the sound of life every day. Sophie used to be the same way. When she awoke, it was time for the whole house to rise. She'd call out to Mitch to come get her. She'd sing songs and talk to her stuffed animals and play. She *used* to do all those things. Since he'd brought her home, she hadn't said more than a word or two at a time, or eaten a thing. It made him wonder what she'd been through in the month she was gone. Whatever it had been like, she wasn't now who she had been before. She didn't play. She didn't laugh. She moved only enough to stay close to Mitch, mewling quietly when she wanted him to pick her up. He decided he didn't want to contemplate, if she had been someplace else, what that place was like, banishing his Catholic grandmother's ideas of Purgatory and Limbo from his thoughts.

Of course it'll take time for her to be her old self. She's been through... everybody needs time to recover after being sick. So does she.

That Sophie hadn't come into the room that night filled him with a sudden dread. Since she'd returned, he'd lived with a steady foreboding that took the form of wondering how long she'd stay. What if she hadn't come in to sleep because she was... fully dead again. He sat upright, stomach clenched, and took a deep breath trying to convince himself to calm down. Everything was fine. Sophie was fine. *It's just a quiet moment. Maybe Liana is being extra quiet because Sophie is still asleep on the couch for a change and she doesn't want to wake her.*

He slipped out of bed and pulled on the previous day's jeans and T-shirt. In the living room, he found Sophie sitting cross-legged on the sofa staring at the television. It was tuned to the news. He walked over and gave his niece a hug before changing the channel to PBS. When she saw her favorite characters on the program, she turned and smiled before returning her attention to the cartoon. A smile! Her cheeks had a hint of rose color in them, and her milky eyes seemed clearer. His heart beat faster.

It's happening. She's getting better.

He found Liana in the kitchen sitting at the table warming her hands around a cup of coffee. She was still wearing her pajamas and didn't have that strong-scented body wash fragrance she always wore after her morning shower. He poured himself a cup. "Did you see Sophie?" he asked.

Excited by a step in the direction of "normal kid appearance." It wasn't until he sat down at the table with Liana that he noticed, despite the midsummer morning warmth that would soon turn to humid afternoon heat, she was shivering. And her new gray hair.

It wasn't collected at her temples or in a patch adding a dramatic flair to her curly black and fuchsia hair; white strands spread here and there throughout. *Salt and pepper.* The small wrinkles at the edges of her eyes seemed deepener, and the bags underneath emphasized how tired she looked. *She's just tired.* Sophie's midnight wanderings kept both of them up. But the combination of wrinkles and gray made her look years older.

"I didn't know you dyed your hair," he said. "I mean, other than the red parts."

She looked up from her cup. "I *don't*." A shiver ran through her body and she took a sip of her coffee, hunching up trying to hold its warmth closer.

"Huh. When did you start going—"

"You have to find somewhere else to stay," Liana said. She wasn't a curt woman. She had a Southerner's penchant for friendly small talk and filling the spaces in between moments with cheerful reflection. They'd spent long nights sitting on the sofa discussing his past, her past, their future. She knew everything about him and his family, and she had told him all about her own. They'd shared stories about what had led them to where they were physically and emotionally while they sat, hands intertwined, and made plans for the future together. Time reached out from those moments like a bright highway he couldn't wait to travel. But now, her tone suggested that she didn't want to talk about her hair or her eyes and had nothing else to say on the subject of his departure. She was asking him to leave. *No. Not asking. She's telling me to go.* Mitch felt like he should put up a fight.

Something in him said that he could have his lover *and* the girl. He wanted to say he understood how she felt and that they could make it work. Things would get better. But the face of the woman sitting in front of him put that all to rest.

"I'm going to go stay with a friend," she said. "So, you don't have to get out today. End of the week though—before I get back. Okay?"

"When can I see you again?"

Liana looked over his shoulder at the girl sitting on her couch, watching television. "I don't know. Maybe never, I think." She dropped her head down so he couldn't see her face. Her shoulders jerked and hitched and he heard her sob. Mitch put his hand on her shoulder and she batted it away. She said, "I have to go now."

"I—I don't understand, Li." Except, he understood entirely. Liana was frightened by Sophie. She wasn't a normal little girl. Despite Liana's considerable efforts to conquer her fears over the last few days, she was still struggling. "Please don't make me choose," he said.

"I'm not offering you a choice. Look at me." She widened her eyes. The crow's feet that used to only appear when she smiled now remained no matter what expression she wore. The gray in her hair was more than just noticeable.

"I'm sorry. I don't—"

"Take a good look. She did this to me," she said as she stood up. "I need you to be gone by the time I get back. I'm sorry, Mitch." She wiped tears from her cheeks, grabbed her keys from the counter, and walked out the door.

Mitch picked himself up and turned toward his niece. She sat watching the characters singing and dancing on the television, and looked like a normal little girl. Liana had aged, and Sophie looked healthier. That was his fault. Everything was his fault.

21

It took less time for Mitch to gather together their meager things than he'd anticipated. He'd been packed and ready to go in under ninety minutes. Although he'd prided himself on having a simplified existence, he felt like he was walking out of Liana's apartment with fewer things than he'd carried out of MCI Concord. That *his* life fit into a single, large duffel bag didn't bother him. He wanted the opposite for Sophie, though. He wanted her to have everything he didn't. A house full of things that brought her pleasure and gave her roots. A real home.

Though Sophie looked better than she had when they'd picked her up from Dr. Downum's office—he tried not to think of it as the morgue, though it was—she still drew stares from other riders on the bus as they made their way to their old apartment. The back of the bus, already mostly empty, owing to the overheating compressor above the rear seat adding to the late summer heat, emptied out completely when they sat down. It suited him just fine. The distance home from Liana's was over six miles. Though she never seemed to tire, he couldn't imagine asking Sophie to walk that far, and he couldn't carry her the whole way along with the bag holding their things. So they took the bus, and he sat trying to ignore the side-eyed stares from other riders.

She nuzzled under his arm, and stared at the floor while Mitch tried to pay attention to the route. After a long ride feeling like they were on display, he pushed the button signaling they wanted off at the next stop. When the bus pulled to the curb, he picked up the bag and Sophie and clumsily made his way to the rear exit. When the doors didn't open, he called out, "Back door," hoping the driver would let him disembark without having to walk the gauntlet of other passengers to the front. Nothing happened, and he repeated himself a little louder. He began to fear the driver was going to pull away without letting them off when the rear doors finally swung. On the sidewalk outside, he thought he heard a passenger aboard say something, but it was drowned out by the hydraulic hiss of the kneeling bus and the dinging indicating they were pulling away from the sidewalk. He wasn't the kind of person who got directly confronted often. Not outside of a bar. And he didn't go to bars any more. But from the safety of the bus, with him on the sidewalk, someone felt emboldened. *Fine. Whatever makes them feel righteous.* He took a breath and then another until he no longer wanted to get back on the bus and make that person repeat themselves to him, clearly and within reach.

He tried to set Sophie down, but she clung to him, so he carried her and the bag the rest of the way home. It was only two blocks. She weighed next to nothing and a slow stroll wasn't exactly cardio. Still, by the time he approached their place, he was sweating out the last of the moisture left in his body. Drinking a glass of water was going to feel like diving into the ocean in April. From halfway up the block, he saw it, though. An orange paper rectangle stuck to the door, across the jamb. He climbed the steps, knowing what it declared before he was close enough to read it.

WARNING: THIS IS A NOTICE TO VACATE THE FOLLOWING ADDRESS

He stared at the door. The eviction notice sticker stared brightly back at him, plastered on the window. Written in black Sharpie beneath the warning was his address and a date by which he was expected to remove all his personal belongings before a county sheriff came to take them away instead. Under that, it read: "Removal of this seal is a crime." Looking at the shining new deadbolt lock for which he didn't have a key, he wondered how he was expected to get his things out of the apartment at all. He assumed they expected him to call the number on the notice and arrange a time. That also assumed he had someplace to take those things. Somewhere else to live. He peeked in through a side window and saw the furniture and their other possessions where he'd left them.

After he moved in with Liana, it had only taken a single trip for him to gather all the things he required, and feeling no need for the constant reminder of all that he'd lost, he hadn't been back. He'd locked the door and walked away, knowing this was a probable outcome, but not caring. Now, all those things he saw as unnecessary entanglements with his sister and her selfishness were necessities once again. He chided himself for not planning ahead before remembering there was no way to anticipate something that had never happened before. Not to him, not to anyone. Not ever.

It didn't seem like it had been long enough since abandoning the apartment for the landlord to have gone to court and gotten an order of eviction. He was uncertain how such an order even worked, but he was pretty sure someone had to notify him they were going to be changing the locks and give him a chance to get his stuff out ahead of time. Then again, the landlord only seemed to poke his head up if the section eight rent checks were late.

He jiggled the door again. The fresh deadbolt held securely. They were locked out, and out of luck.

Letting Sophie down onto the front porch, he took a seat next to her on the front steps and tried to keep himself together. Panic was creeping up his spine. He had no idea what he'd do if he couldn't keep it pushed down and it reached his brain, overwhelming his ability to think clearly. He tried to imagine where they could find shelter for the night. He was sure there were places homeless families could just show up and find a spot to sleep, but again, like evictions, he had no experience with them, and didn't even know how to get started. Braddock's words at the hospital echoed in his memory, "Appointed by the court, right?" The power of attorney his sister had left him was locked in the house with the rest of their stuff. He imagined a whole new set of problems arising if he—a single man—showed up at a shelter with a child in arms he couldn't prove was his to care for. Especially one in her state. He was running low on hope that the future would turn out all right. *The future!* He didn't want to think a week or even a day ahead, as it seemed each hour brought a new horror, a new reason to close his eyes and wish that none of this was happening.

His niece looked up at him, her eyes questioning why they weren't going inside. Although her skin had a more vibrant color and fewer of those unpleasant purple veins were threading through it, her eyes were still... dead. Clearer than the day before, but not alive. She tried to climb into his lap and he pushed her gently back onto the stoop beside him. "Just give me a minute, Soph. I need to think, okay?" She stared, wrinkling her forehead quizzically. "I can't open the door," he explained, "and we've got nowhere else to go, hon. I need to think."

She pulled on his arm. "Open it," she whispered.

Mitch stood and followed her to the door. She pointed at the keyhole and he pulled his keys out of his pocket and slipped the old house key in, jiggling it so she could see it wouldn't move. He shook his head. "See? They changed it." Mewling again, she pointed and stood up on her tiptoes. "You want to try?" he asked. He stepped aside to let her turn the key and learn for herself that it wouldn't do what she knew it was made to do.

Sophie reached out with a slender finger and caressed the shiny brass cylinder of the new deadbolt instead. From under the tip of her tiny finger, thin tendrils snaked out across the cylinder. They turned the metal from a shiny brass hue to brown and then black. The rot spread under the cylinder collar and ate through the wood of the door. She withdrew her finger as the dark rot began to crawl back up her nail. The corrupted lock fell to pieces, clattering dully at Mitch's feet. He stepped back from the wreckage, not wanting to let it touch him. He looked at the remains of the deadbolt and imagined the gray ruin creeping up her arm. The thought made him feel ill. Like so many other unbidden images he'd imagined of late, it was burned into the backs of his eyes, always there, haunting.

He grabbed her finger and held it up in front of his face. The purple-black veins were back and her skin was fishy pale again. The slight clarity in her eyes he'd noticed that morning had gone as well. She looked almost as bad as when he'd first picked her up from the morgue. Whatever meager healing she'd enjoyed, it was undone. She'd given it up to get them inside. Hefting her tiny body up in his arms, he gave her a big hug and held on. She squeezed back. Her hold on him was weak and limp. Destroying that lock had taken a piece of her life away. It felt like part of him died along with it. Despite that, he no longer had to think about where they were going to stay for the night. He turned the doorknob, careful not to touch any of the rot, and pushed the door open. The musty smell of a house that hadn't been opened for weeks in the summer heat greeted them. He stepped over the threshold and breathed in the familiar scents of home that still lingered underneath.

Laying Sophie down on the sofa, he returned to the door and stripped off the eviction sticker as best as he could. The orange top layer came away easily, but left behind a sticky white square of gum and paper. He thought about picking at the rest with his fingernails, but realized he didn't care. They were in, and the orange part was off. For tonight at least, they had someplace that was theirs. He'd face tomorrow's problems when they arrived.

He grabbed the duffel bag off the porch and shut the door on the world, thankful that there was a slide chain to at least add a measure of security. At his feet rested a pile of neglected mail shoved through the slot by the mailman. He bent down and inspected it. Most of it was junk: credit card applications for his sister and enticements to switch his non-existent cable company. Halfway down, he found an envelope from the Commonwealth of Massachusetts, Department of Housing and Community Development. He tore it open and read the notice of suspension of his participation in the Housing Choice Voucher Program—or rather, his sister, Violette's participation. Another lack of foresight in the unimaginable future. The state had quit paying their part of the rent. His inertia had set wheels in motion—ones he couldn't stop turning, even if he lay down underneath them.

He took the mail into the kitchen and dropped it all in the trash. There was no point appealing the decision of whatever bureaucrat at the HCVP had signed the letter. Doing so would only bring unwanted attention, and right now, he was focused on realigning his powers of social invisibility. And doing a bad job of it. There was a knock at the door. He looked at Sophie wondering if he should scoop her and their bag up and make for the back. Instead, he told her to stay quiet and out of sight, and walked to peek through the faceted window.

Two familiar men stood on the deck: the detectives from the hospital. He hadn't seen them since they'd released him from custody. *What are they doing here? Did someone see us break in and call the cops? There's no way they could have gotten here that fast.* "What do you want?" he asked through the cracked door.

"Mr. LeRoux, I'm sure you remember us."

"Who could forget?" He knew they had just been doing their jobs, but he also knew what doing their jobs meant to a guy like him. Sometimes it meant three years of your life.

"We've been waiting a while for you to show up. We'd like to talk to you?"

"I already told you everything at the station."

"Please," Braddock said.

Mitch pushed shut the door, his hand hovering in mid-reach for the security chain as he thought about refusing to let them in. If they kicked it in, he would have nothing left to keep them safe. A chain was better than nothing. It was a tiny something, and right now, every little thing mattered. He undid the chain and opened the door.

Still dressed alike in dark suits despite the heat, Mitch had a hard time remembering which one was Braddock and which was Dixon. He thought he recollected Dixon being shorter, but he couldn't remember.

The taller one glanced at the remnants of the deadbolt lying on the porch while the shorter one said, "You haven't been home in a while. You neglected to let us know you were taking a trip." The shorter one was Dixon; he was "bad cop." Mitch got the feeling it wasn't a shtick either; Dixon might always be on the simmering edge of a fit of rage.

"I never left town," he said, trying to keep the tremor from his voice.

"Well, that's not true, is it?" Dixon said. He tilted his head as if Mitch were a child lying about taking a cookie from the counter.

"What do you mean? I've been staying with my girlfriend."

"Yeah, Ms. Halliday. She seems like a firecracker." Braddock winked at him, smirking. Mitch didn't return the smile. The fear spreading through his body kept him from feeling anything other than a building fight or flight response. Neither one of those biological imperatives was going to be worth a squirt of piss on fire against these two. Even if he didn't have Sophie to care for, he couldn't outrun or outgun a pair of cops on the job.

"May we come in, Mitch?" Braddock said. "Maybe we could all sit down and have a chat."

Mitch unconsciously stepped to the side to let the men in before thinking better of it and moving back into the doorway to block their entrance. This wasn't prison and they didn't have the right to shake down his house any time they wanted. "Not right now, guys. I'm not feeling good and I just want to... take care of some stuff."

"Yeah, I imagine you've got a lot on your plate," Dixon said, peering over Mitch's shoulder.

"Have I done something wrong, detectives?"

"You been to Worcester lately?"

"Why do you ask?"

"Don't fuck us around," Dixon interrupted. "You think we don't know? Dead girl's body goes missing, *you* go missing, the dead come back to life and here you are, home again. Where is she?"

Mitch tried not to turn around to check on whether Sophie was doing as he'd asked. If they were asking where she was, she hadn't poked her head up. He tried to stay calm.

Braddock put a hand on Dixon's arm. Bad Cop glanced at his partner and the two shared a silent communication. Dixon sighed heavily through his nose. "We know you've got your niece in there," Braddock said. "Since she disappeared from the morgue, we've been watching the place, waiting for you to come home. We saw the two of you sitting on the steps. Look, as far as we're concerned, the investigation into her death—before she came back—it isn't closed. It's just become... complicated is all. I don't care what the DA says, someone's going to be held accountable for that kid in there being a living corpse instead of a living girl. Do you follow me?"

Mitch felt their stares peeling away his skin and chipping at bone looking for the truth. The way Braddock referred to his niece, it was clear that *both* men were bad cop, no matter how nice one of them acted. It took every ounce of his will not to slam the door and try to run for it. Still, they weren't arresting him yet, so he resolved to stand his ground at least for a minute longer. If he slammed the door in their faces, they'd just kick it open and take her.

"Didn't you find Faye?" Mitch asked. "She's the one you need to talk to."

Braddock nodded his head. "We did. Tracked her down at her boyfriend's place in Revere. She says she's been staying there since she hurt her back... uh, what was it?"

"'Helping a friend move,'" Dixon said, hooking air quotes with his fingers.

"Yeah, helping an unidentified friend move from one undisclosed location to another. She claims she was laid up with a Percocet and a cocktail on the davenport up there the night you say she and her kid, Meghan, were babysitting. The daughter and boyfriend both confirm her alibi."

Hope slipped out of Mitch's body like the last whisper of warmth before winter. He wanted to scream, *she's fucking lying! Don't believe her lies!* Instead, he quietly asked, "You can't believe her? She and Meghan were *here* that night."

Both detectives nodded. "She's full of shit and the boyfriend's no stranger to the court, as we say. He's got a hillbilly heroin problem. Against their triple bullshit, however, all we've got is your story and your girlfriend corroborating that someone matching her description was babysitting and left on foot before you two... turned in for the night. We got bigger problems than he said/she said, though."

"I don't get it," Mitch said.

"Did you know the girl—Meghan—isn't even her kid?"

Mitch wondered what kind of game the detectives were running on him. He stood waiting for the hand to play itself out, wondering if he'd even see the trick card slide out of Dixon's sleeve. "No."

"You know what a 'private re-homing' is?" he asked. Mitch shook his head. "It's when someone signs their kid over to someone else because they don't want them anymore."

"Like Violette did with Sophie," Braddock added. Mitch took an involuntary breath in, but didn't respond.

Dixon continued. "We figure Faye's where your sister got the idea for the power of attorney she left with you. See, it turns out your neighbor has been collecting kids for years. She adopts them off of a site where people go when they realize that little Vladimir or Q'ian have too many problems for them to handle and they just want to be clear of a kid they can't control, but can't send back to Russia or China. Here comes Faye and her boyfriend and they'll take the kid off your hands for nothing. Just a piece of paper saying that they're the new guardians of the child. Then they get the public benefits and tax breaks..."

"And whatever else the boyfriend wants off the kids," Braddock added.

"Then they're off to ditch them with some other shitheels looking for a 'non-legalized adoption' online."

"I've only ever seen Meghan over there. She doesn't have any other kids," Mitch said.

"Not there. She's a middle-man. She takes 'em and trades 'em. We're not sure to who, but however it works we're certain the original adoptive 'parents'"—Dixon said it with such contempt that Mitch was certain he was going to spit on the porch after saying the word—"ain't coming forward to find out what happened to the kid they dumped."

"Why don't you arrest her then?" Mitch asked.

"There's no law against it in the Commonwealth yet. It's not an adoption as far as anyone is concerned, so there's no law being broken."

"What has this got to do with me... and Sophie?"

The cops looked at each other and sighed. Braddock rubbed at his head looking as if he expected more from Mitch. "You ever hear of *corpus delicti*?" he asked.

It was Mitch's turn to shake his head.

"It means 'the body of a crime.' Some people think it means that you have to have an actual body in order to prove there was a murder, but that's not *exactly* right. What it really means is that in order to convict somebody of something, a crime must first be *proven* to have occurred. Now if you, say, killed someone and chopped up the body before stuffing the pieces into a septic tank or whatever..." Mitch's blood chilled and he felt faint. The cop continued like he hadn't just seen all of the color drain out of his face. "You could still be arrested, tried, and convicted as long as we could prove that someone who used to be alive is now dead, and you're the one who did it. You follow me so far?" Mitch nodded. Braddock continued. "But if I can't prove that you killed a guy, for example, because he's walking around doing stuff, well then, there's no *corpus delicti*, is there?"

Dixon took over the explanation. "A little birdy in the coroner's office told us that the victim in our homicide case just... What did she say, John?"

"Got up and walked away."

"Right! Got up and walked away. That means, no wrongful death, no case, and no arrests. But, there's still somebody *responsible* for what happened to your niece. Right? And without her, we have nothing to hold them accountable. So, you see our problem with her just up and taking a stroll home. She's our only evidence in the case."

"She's all we've got to try to stop Faye Cantrell's revolving door of kids."

Mitch shivered at the way the men spoke about Sophie. "She's not evidence; she's my niece."

"That's what you think," Dixon said. "She's a corpse, Mitch. Walking around, yes. We've seen other kids like this in the last couple of weeks and it's not pretty what happens to them as time drags on. Believe me when I say you don't want to be around when it starts to go bad."

"And you don't care what she did to Sophie. You only want her so you can stop this other thing."

"We care, god damn it," Braddock said. "We care about both. What she did to Sophie was unconscionable. But you need to understand, Mitch, that while it may have been accidental, it wasn't unintentional. She's a piece of shit. We want to stop her before she kills someone else's kid. We want her to be held responsible for what happened to *your* child."

"I'm only Sophie's uncle."

"Funny. Way I look at it," Braddock said, "for the last thirteen months you've been her father whether you wanted to be or not. Now it's time for you to do the right thing by her."

"What am I supposed to do?"

Braddock shrugged, looking genuinely apologetic as he said, "Help us. Let us take her. I promise she'll be treated as humanely as possible." The addition of "as possible" turned Mitch's stomach. It meant that there was a point at which they anticipated fully humane treatment was not practicable. They said there were others. Maybe it wasn't anticipation. Maybe it was experience.

"And if I say no?"

"Give it a day or two, Mr. LeRoux. Take your time. And when you realize that this is bigger than you can handle, you call us. We really do want to help you." Dixon held out his business card. Mitch took it, though he already had one. He figured they assumed he'd just thrown it away. The detectives turned to leave, but Dixon stopped and looked over his shoulder.

"One more thing," he said. "You know what Oscar Wilde said about children?" Mitch shook his head. "He said they begin by loving their parents. But when they get older, they judge them. That... little girl in there is going to hold *you* accountable, Mitch. If you're lucky, she'll forgive you. I don't want to think about what will happen if she doesn't have it in her heart to do that. I don't want to think about it because I've seen what happened to other people living with their dead kids. But, then again, maybe you deserve it."

The detectives turned and walked away.

22

From their car across the street, Dixon watched Mitch peek out from behind the curtains and wanted to go back to the door and let him know that if he intended it to appear like no one was squatting in the apartment, he'd have to stay away from the windows. At the same time, it would make his job simpler if Mitch was easy to spot when they came back. It'd been difficult keeping an eye on him at the girlfriend's place. Her apartment was on the third floor and he apparently hadn't felt the need to look outside to confirm no one was watching.

While no one in homicide actually knew how the dead kids coming back to life was going to affect their cases, what was certain was that the DA was a political coward who put media attention and elections ahead of her prosecutors' judgment and experience. Dixon's girlfriend was an ADA who'd graduated to the child protection unit—her dream job—and was now looking to go into private practice. She had enough in less than a year in the special division, and Julie could put up with a hell of a lot. She was still dating him, after all. The common consensus among Julie and her colleagues was, with the amount of media attention focused on these kids, any homicide prosecution centered on a murder victim who was walking around was officially closed. The parents weren't organized or numerous enough to present a threat at the polls, and, dead or alive, kids don't vote. But TV stations eat, breathe, and shit sensation, and FOX 25 would love to get a picture of DA Maria O'Brien standing next to a horror movie monster only a few weeks before the polls opened.

Braddock hung up his phone, balled up his fists and listened to the sound of his abused knuckles popping. He said, "The word from on high is we're back in rotation tomorrow. What do you want to do?"

Dixon said, "Let's head up to Revere. Faye Cantrell should know the girl she shook to death is home." He smirked at his partner. "In case she wants to drop by with a fruit basket and apologize."

"You're a bad man." Braddock put the car in gear and pulled away from the curb. Dixon held up a hand to wave at Mitch staring out from the curtains.

23

After two days of isolation in the house, Mitch started to feel cagey and restless. He didn't like confinement, even if he was the one confining himself. His original plan to wait and surface once the world had sorted out the problem wasn't looking like a short-term endeavor. And he was hungry. Though Sophie wasn't noticeably affected by the lack of food in the house—she seemed to be doing fine subsisting on what little they had—Mitch still needed sustenance. His stomach growled constantly and cramped periodically now that he'd exhausted the dry and canned goods left behind in the pantry. He'd had the last can of soup the night before and was down to a final packet of Ramen. The cupboard was bare and he needed to come up with a solution.

Looking through his wallet, he found his sister's SNAP EBT card—Supplemental Nutrition Assistance Program—"food stamps." No working Internet in the house meant they had to venture out to check the balance on the account —a proposition that he found only slightly less daunting than starving. So far, most of the other services they'd been subscribed to had taken their time to cut him off. Cable was gone, but they still had electricity and natural gas. The utilities were going to run out eventually and even if they lasted a while longer, the sheriff was coming in a week to evict them. Even if he had enough cash in the bank for a first, last, and deposit on a new place, he couldn't pass a credit check without a job. He needed an income stream to keep them going. *This is how people become homeless.*

He'd called Khadija to see if he could bring Sophie back for a day or two a week. He thought he could scrape enough together for a week or two, hopefully enough time to find work and save up a little more. She'd been compassionate and kind, like always, but told him she couldn't accommodate a child "in her condition." He told her he understood, and didn't press the issue. She was a decent person, and he could hear how difficult it was for her to say no. Even so, without day care, he couldn't return to work. And no matter what Sophie's "condition," he couldn't conceive of leaving her alone in the house for an entire work day—especially one that started as early as it did for a barista in a coffee shop. He was falling down a steep spiral. The only thing that could hold back the seemingly inevitable tide was money. And he didn't have any other way to get money without work. *This is how people end up in prison.* One *of the ways, anyway.*

After giving Sophie a bath to try to dispel the odor that was beginning to haunt her, he dressed her in clean clothes and tried to make her as presentable—alive looking—as possible. He tried darkening her skin a little with some of Violette's makeup, but was worse at that than even his diminished expectations had prepared him to be. The result was worse than simply asking her to let her hair hang in her face a little. He washed her a second time, tried again, and when he thought he'd finally done a passable job, they left.

The half-mile walk to the branch library was more like a mile by the time he'd led them down side streets and through alleys after strangers started shouting, "Ghoul!" and, "Deadophile!" at them from passing cars. He figured it was her gray hair that gave them away at a distance and regretted not bringing along a hat for her to wear.

They pushed through the library doors and paused by the checkout desk. He wanted to take her over to the children's section to find a book or two she'd enjoy, as they had every Monday before she died. They could pretend to be normal and sit on the carpet under the hanging purple gauze with the cardboard stars and pick out some of her favorites from the picture book bins. They'd read and she'd look up and together they'd pretend they lived in a place where light pollution didn't blank out the stars from night sky. He was pretty certain that wasn't a good idea, however. Several of the parents and nannies who were lingering after the ten o'clock sing-along were hastily shoving their things into diaper bags and grabbing their kids, dragging them out through the rear exit. The children cried at their sudden departure, calling out for the promised book or DVD that they hadn't yet checked out. Hisses to be quiet and assurances they'd come back some other time answered their protests. Instead of heading for the children's room, he led Sophie to the computer station.

They sat down at an open terminal and he signed in. They were limited to twenty-minute sessions on the public computers. That was more than enough time to check the EBT account and go. Sophie sat on his lap, staring at the screen. In the past, she'd have been trying to "help" him by reaching for the keyboard or mouse and clicking at things randomly. Instead, she sat quietly and watched him work.

He accessed the SNAP cardholder login and clicked on his account. Two hundred and forty dollars remained on the card. He checked the date. A fresh deposit. He resolved to zeroing out the balance as quickly as he could before they shut the account down. It meant taking Sophie to the grocery store maybe two or three times, buying as much as he could carry home on each trip with her in tow since they were without a car again.

Whatever it takes.

He logged out of the food assistance account and, despite his better judgment, surfed over to CNN.com. A picture that had been shown over and over again on the television and had even made it to the cover of TIME stared back at him. A gray-haired boy of maybe seven or eight, face twisted in anguish as a man struggled to wrench him from his mother's grip. The headline read, THE BATTLE OVER THE CHILDREN OF THE GRAVE. He skimmed the first article, although it told him nothing about why things were happening. There was plenty of speculation split down the lines he'd already heard on the radio and the nightly news at Liana's. Talking heads searching for meaning without any facts to supply it other than that some kids who'd been dead had now come back. Not all of the children in the world who died came back. Just a few. But a few were enough to set off a shit-storm of panic, public hand-wringing, and moral grandstanding. While scientific experts were "baffled," religious leaders were making hay of it. Either way, for the churches it was a win. More people than ever were suddenly interested in attending service. The comments at the end of the article were even less encouraging. Most of them encouraged stockpiling ammo and shooting the kids in the head—armchair attorneys advising it wasn't murder to kill something already dead.

Behind him, a quavering voice said, "Mitch? I, uh, think it's time to go." He looked away from the monitor and saw Kathy, their favorite librarian. She'd doted on Sophie ever since he started bringing her to the library, promising her she could check out anything she wanted, and overruling Mitch when he didn't want to get something he thought was too commercial or reinforcing of gender stereotypes. "Her books, her choice," she'd say. "My Sophie gets to read what she wants." Except today, Kathy wasn't asking for a hug or taking the girl off to show her the latest books in the "New Arrivals" bin. Today, she looked like she was staring at a ghost.

Behind her, hovered a man he recognized from prior visits to the Wednesday sing-along. Curtis something. They'd bonded in the past as the only two men who regularly attended the free toddler events at the library. Curtis stared at Mitch with a barely contained hostility. Mitch swallowed hard as his vision narrowed and his heart raced.

"I still have time on the computer, Kathy. It's only been five min—"

"Shut the fuck up," Curtis said. "You heard the lady. Take that... ghoul... and get out."

Kathy shot the guy a look telling him to be quiet and returned her attention to Mitch. "Please. It'll be better if you just go." Mitch felt frustration and despair stab at him. She had been more than a friend: she was an ally, always making him feel welcome, usually waving his late fees, and even once helping with the online application for heating oil assistance after he'd moved into Violette's house. Coming to the library always meant a few minutes of relief a couple of times a week as Sophie sat quietly and "read" a picture book to herself or played with the librarian. Today, Kathy looked terrified, and had even brought backup. If Mitch had any allies left, their numbers were dwindling.

He held up his hands and said, "We don't want any trou—"

The man pointed a thick finger at Mitch and Sophie. "I said—" The child reached for his hand and sent him backpedaling away, arms pinwheeling, a look of terror on his face. However frightened this guy was of Sophie, he'd regain his bravado as soon as he found something to even the odds like one of the heavy sticks used to prop open the windows in the spring and autumn. It was indeed time to go.

Mitch shouldered his empty messenger bag and stood up, hefting Sophie onto his hip. She stared at the man who kept backing up until he banged into the checkout counter yelping in pain and fear. The guy searched left and right for somewhere else to retreat, all of his macho bluster robbed by a little girl.

Mitch looked at Kathy, silently pleading with her for understanding. She shook her head and pointed toward the door. As they passed, Curtis slid along the edge of the checkout desk, saying something about Mitch knowing what was good for him. Sophie reached out with a finger and sent a thin line of rot snaking across the countertop toward him. The man jumped away, scrambling to swing a chair around in front of him. With his equalizer and shield, a fresh line of invective spewed from his mouth. Mitch didn't listen. Instead, he walked out into the daylight, headed home to hide.

24

Sophie tagged along beside him for only the first block before starting in with her pleas to be carried again. She stepped out in front of him arms raised, almost causing the both of them to tumble onto the pavement. Despite the heat and his nerves, he picked her up so they could move faster. Mitch was as pleased to cuddle with the girl as she seemed to be clinging to him. Her arms and legs wrapped tightly around his body. If he let go of her, he felt confident she'd stay right where she was, clinging, nuzzled against his chest where her infrequent breaths cooled him. He started out taking the same back alleys and side streets to get home, but couldn't shake the feeling they were being followed. The man in the library was a coward—he could tell. Incarceration had given him an almost failsafe threat detector. Face to face, that guy was as dangerous as a Tibetan monk at prayer time. What he also knew, though, was that guys like that were the type to hide behind a wall with a section of pipe, or around the block in his car, waiting for the anonymous hit and run that'd lead the evening news. Mitch returned to the main road and detoured toward Mount Grove Cemetery, a sprawling necropolis in the middle of the city where no one would be able to ambush him, or run them over and get away. He also needed the walk to clear his head. It didn't help that when Mitch felt stress, confined spaces amplified the feeling and distilled his worst fears into physical manifestations like shortness of breath and headaches. He figured if the other MBTA riders weren't upset enough by the dead girl in his arms, his shaking and heavy breathing would put them over the top. "If we can just stay out of sight until I figure out what it was that made you better that first time, Sophie, we'll be fine." He said it more to reassure *himself* that things would eventually get better, because they had to. He wouldn't allow himself to contemplate the opposite outcome, even though the purple black veins in her arms and legs were getting worse and she smelled faintly of something he refused to acknowledge.

He loved to come and sit in the quiet of the landscaped garden and meditate under the open sky—no walls, no bars. There was peace and solitude and an unspoken agreement among all visitors not to disturb each other. People in the city outside the necropolis minded their business too, but it wasn't peaceful. They talked loudly into cell phones and shouted out their car windows at other drivers. They catcalled women passing by, begged for change, bitched about people who wouldn't clear the subway car door fast enough, and lingered in doorways as if no one else needed in or out since they had found themselves in a place worthy of a pause. In the necropolis, people did none of these things. They whispered, and walked quietly. They set up cameras on tripods and waited patiently to get pictures of the hawks and owls making their nests in the larches and oaks. They strolled in the narrow lanes and sat at the edges of the ponds looking out over the water. Some even came to talk to the dead. And all of them gave plenty of room to each other.

Sometimes, he'd climb the winding staircase up the sixty-foot Adams Tower in the center of the cemetery and sit atop the landing behind the parapet wall staring into the vast expanse toward Kingsport Bay. There were no joggers, bicyclists, or pets allowed in the park; it was the only green space in the city where someone could truly amble without having to dodge people exercising or indulging their animals. It was as peaceful a place as he'd ever known on Earth and if he could have spent every moment of the day there, he would. Though he hadn't been back since Sophie died.

They passed under the Egyptian revival gatehouse entrance. Thick columns rose up beneath the gap in the monolithic stone arch, at the top of which was engraved, "THE DEAD SHALL BE RAISED."

This isn't what they meant.

He toyed with the idea of walking in and finding a place to sit down, perhaps by the Ward Dell, where he could sit and watch Sophie chase frogs in the algae-covered pond. She likely wouldn't chase anything though, instead choosing to cling and cuddle. He didn't mind as long as they could rest for a while and he could convince himself that no one was after them, lurking, looking to do either of them harm.

They continued along the main road until finding the narrow garden path that led off toward the dell. At a hundred and seventy acres, most visitors needed a map to find their way around to the various landmarks. Not Mitch; he'd committed every square foot of the cemetery to memory. He knew where Richard Upton Pickman and Randolph Carter were buried. He knew right where he was going. On the way, he passed a woman kneeling near a grave and tried to give her a wider berth, respecting that she wasn't there to bird watch or meditate. She looked up from the grave in front of her and stared as he wandered away. He glanced back a time or two to see if she was still watching. She sat there, mouth open, eyes fixed on him, and the anxiety he'd begun to shed under the gates came flooding back.

"You!" she called out. "Excuse me!" He hurried his step a little to get over the next rise and out of sight. He and Sophie weren't an attraction; he didn't want to be on display. He just wanted to have a quiet minute beside the pond listening to the frogs instead of the constant hum of traffic rumbling through the city like a cosmic drone. The narrow concrete path back to the Ward Dell was a cul-de-sac bordered on three sides by steep hillsides, and he didn't want to be cornered there. Mitch changed direction and started up a walkway away from his destination. "Stop, please!" he heard her call out. Sophie lifted her head from his shoulder and looked at the woman. Mitch continued apace. "Why do *you* get her back?" he heard her shout. He slowed and stopped. Turning to look, he saw the woman standing in the grass at the end of a family plot, the headstone in front of her, bright and unstained by the elements. It wasn't hard to find the markers for children. Their headstones were topped with lambs or sleeping cherubs and were as tiny as their little bodies had been. They littered the old cemetery, reminders of a time when raising children to adulthood was not the proposition it was today. Still, he'd learned surviving childhood was never guaranteed. Death was no stranger to any family. But being familiar wasn't the same as being welcome.

He glanced down at another small marker to his left adorned with a cherub reclining on the front. *Trevor. Son of Calvin and Annabel. May 10, 1934 — November 2, 1935.* The grass surrounding it was green and a little long. No toys or flowers had been left nearby. Trevor's parents were likely in the ground near him. His siblings, if he had any, resting also, or soon to join him. How many generations would grief last for someone who never got to develop into a person of unique character and accomplishment? He figured a single one, if that. Trevor died, and the world moved on without him, leaving only this piece of stone to mark his brief existence. Nothing else lasting in the world was altered by either his birth or death.

He walked slowly back toward the woman. All she wanted was to talk, he hoped. She looked at him with red, wet eyes. "What did you say?" he asked.

"Why do *you* get her back?"

"I don't know," he said, holding Sophie a little tighter. "Did you... lose a..." He trailed off, not knowing how to ask the question. The woman wiped her tears away and looked down at the stone in front of her. Mitch read the inscription.

CHERIE MARIE WRIGHT
MAY 15, 2015 - JULY 29, 2017
BELOVED DAUGHTER

He shuddered to think at what a child, months in the earth, would look like if she were to return. He held Sophie tighter and quietly thanked whatever merciful force had brought her back for not doing the same to this woman. "I'm so sorry," he said, not knowing how else to express the creeping sense of guilt that seemed a tincture of every moment now.

She stood and reached out with an unsteady hand, he took another step out of range of her caress, not wanting her to touch Sophie, not wanting Sophie to touch her. The woman's face fell and her eyes welled up with tears. "Will you help me?" she asked.

"Help you, how?"

"Help me get her out."

Mitch looked at the headstone and saw that she had been clawing at the ground in front of it, long tears in the grass where her fingers had pulled at the earth. What he first thought was the smell of the necropolis was actually the woman. She stank of dirt and grass and sweat. Her fingers were brown and mud caked under her ragged nails.

"No one will help me. They say she's not coming back, but I know she's down there. I heard her scratching the day they covered her up, but no one will listen to me. You understand, though. You know. And you can help me. You look strong. I'll buy a shovel—two of them—and we'll come back and get her."

He felt breathless. The thought of a living child trapped down there made his stomach cramp and his vision narrowed. He felt the stirrings of the kind of instinctive reaction that came when he saw someone walk across the exercise yard or the cafeteria *that way*. A con would get that look of vicious resignation and he'd walk like a thing, not a man. And then the world would go wild and blood would fly and the screws would come to lock everyone down and someone would go to the infirmary, or worse, to their family. "I can't," he whispered. He took a breath and repeated himself, a little louder. "I just can't."

"What's so special about *her*?"

"What? I—"

"My Cherie was special too!"

All his desire to sit under the sky on a still day fled. He had no idea how to help this woman. He didn't know how to help Sophie or himself, and he couldn't be responsible for this woman and her daughter too. "I'm sorry," he said.

She lurched forward and slapped him. He staggered back, tripping over another low stone. "No, you're not. You're not sorry. You have her and *my* daughter is down there. Why do *you* get her back? Tell me, god damn it!"

He backed away, feeling in shock. His cheek where she'd slapped him was stinging and hot to the touch. His fingertips came away dirty from where she'd left part of her child's grave on his face. "I don't know what to say." The woman took another step after him with her hand raised. *No one* put their hands on him. No one touched him unless he wanted to be touched. Not anymore. This woman, though, didn't care who he was or what he'd been through. Maybe she'd earned the right to be upset with him and resentful of his fortune, so he allowed her a free shot. But now her account was square. He gave her a hard stare and her expression changed.

"Give her to me!"

"What!"

"You can't take care of her like a *mother* can. Give her to me and I'll love her. A girl needs a mother."

She was beyond reason, and he was only making things worse trying to talk to her. It was past time to go. He turned and felt the flat slap of her hand on his back between his shoulder blades. It stung and the urge to shove her away made him hesitate. He forced himself to take another step toward home.

"I'm so sorry," the woman said. She sobbed and let out a low keening sound. "Please don't go! Don't leave me here."

He didn't know her story, how her daughter died or why she was here alone. He didn't know how long it'd taken her to break and become so desperate she was going to dig a corpse out of the grave with her bare hands. All he knew was that he needed to be back in the house with the curtains drawn. He and Sophie just had to hunker down and wait this out. *Once people get their heads wrapped around it...* His train of thought was broken by Sophie lurching over his shoulder. She hadn't moved so suddenly or forcefully since she'd returned. She practically launched over his shoulder... at her. He heard the woman gasp and the sound of her falling to her knees again. He spun around to see her holding a gray-skinned hand, wrinkled and veiny. New liver spots grew in front of his eyes as the ashen color crept up her flesh. She tried to scream but only a thin strangled sob came out of her mouth. Reaching out, he tried to apologize. She clambered away from him—from Sophie—scrabbling backwards across the grave, clutching her withering arm and wailing into the light of the uncaring clear sky above.

He looked at Sophie. Her skin was a little less sallow. Her eyes, brighter. His panicked mind reeled with rationalization. *I'm looking at her in the sun is why she looks better. This is how she looks! She didn't just take something from that woman.*

He knew that wasn't true. He knew it. And he knew more than that, but wasn't ready to give words to the idea yet. "What did you do?" he asked. She didn't reply. Instead, she nestled her head back into his neck and held on as before, her breath a little warmer than it had been a moment ago.

He hurried out of the cemetery toward home. The necropolis, his refuge no longer.

No one was welcome anymore in the city of the dead.

25

Mitch jammed a chair under the doorknob. The combination of it and the slide chain weren't going to keep anyone truly motivated out of their apartment, but at least it kept the door from blowing open in the growing breeze. Mitch's nerves were shot and the noise it made when it banged at the end of the length of chain was like a hammer fall every time. He was feeling jangly and getting worse. It was one thing to suffer dark stares and judgments whispered under breath on the bus, it was another entirely to be rejected by a friend and threatened by strangers. Mitch had sprinted home from the cemetery clutching Sophie to his chest without concern for drawing the attention of anyone in the neighborhood. He wanted behind a closed door. Drawing the wrong attention, or even *any* attention for a prolonged moment, could lead to decisions and actions that had to be opposed, countered, and couldn't be undone. He could take care of himself, but he didn't want that kind of life for Sophie. The life you want and the life you have rarely intersect at the time you need them to, and in his experience, the gulf between them was full of painful longing no matter how narrow.

He peeked through the curtains at the street outside. It was as empty as it ever got, which was to say that traffic moved on, and the people on the sidewalk kept their eyes trained on cell phones or the ground. Still, he couldn't help feeling that someone had followed him home. That there was an ill-intended mass of angry people converging on them. He let the curtain fall back into place and sat heavily on the floor. Sophie looked at him with a kind of understanding he didn't want her to possess. Not yet. Her tiny doll's face was drawn and her eyes always seemed to carry a kind of aged weariness. Her resting expression used to be one of open wonder. Now, it belied the kind of emotion he'd expect to only see from a war widow—from someone who'd survived the worst existence could throw at them. Like the woman in the necropolis.

The room grew dimmer as a billowy white cloud moved in front of the sun outside. It suited Mitch. Darker felt more hidden. It felt safer. He drew Sophie nearer and asked, "Why did you do that to that woman back there?"

She looked at him with slightly bluer eyes, and whispered, "She hit you, Yunka."

"You can't do that to people, sweetheart. Even if they hit, okay?"

The girl's brow furrowed. "She was being mean."

"No. She was…" He didn't know how to explain it. Not to a child; not at all. The woman's derangement was too close to Mitch's own recent experience. How do you tell a child what it's like to go insane from grief? "She was sad, Honey. She used to have a little girl like you and she died. Like you. It made her sad," he repeated. "And sometimes, that makes people do things they wouldn't otherwise do. Like yell and hit."

"But she was *mean* to you." Her little brow furrowed as she tried to process what he was telling her.

"It's okay. I can take it. Just promise me you'll never do that again, all right?" She shook her head. "Please, Soph. Promise me."

She frowned and looked at the floor, suddenly very much a child again. "I promise."

I can take it. I think I can, anyway.

Sophie crawled into his lap and he held her close, caressing her hair. It was dry, and a little matted. He tried to gently tease out the tangles with his fingers, trying not to pull or tug at her hair. When he did, she didn't complain like she had when... before. She patiently let him disentangle the knot and continue preening her.

His stomach growled, and while he was aware there was money on the EBT card, he was resolved to the idea he'd have to go without food for another day, at least. He couldn't face going outside again, and the grocery store was infinitely more daunting than the library. During daylight hours it was almost certainly going to result in a confrontation like he'd already fled twice today. Someone would get it in their head that Sophie's mere presence would contaminate everything, and that guardian of integrity would step up to offer a line of defense between the living and the dead. Maybe they'd never even make it inside. If he was going to go, he either had to go alone or when the chances of running into anyone else were at their lowest. The Star Market on Langan Ave. was open twenty-four hours. It was *never* empty, but in the past he'd been there after midnight, and it was quiet then. He could try to sneak Sophie in at maybe two or three in the morning when the employees were tired out and there were fewest customers. After the bars were closed, but before the dawn rush. Not tonight, though. They'd try tomorrow, or maybe the next day, if his hunger could hold out. His stomach rumbled again. Sophie said, "Shh," and pushed a finger into it playfully. It'd *have* to be tomorrow. He'd have to find a way. She looked better now than she did this morning. Maybe he'd have more luck with the makeup if he tried again.

"Hon?" he said. She looked up at him from his lap with a furrowed brow. "When you were... gone. Do you remember anything about it?" She nodded. He felt a lump grow in his throat. The kind of fearful anticipation that comes in the silent moment right before disaster. That space between seeing the ball of fire, and hearing the explosion. "What was it like?"

She shrugged.

"You don't remember?"

She shook her head. "I 'member. It was nofing." Despite her precocious emotional maturity—what his mother used to refer to as being an "old soul"—she still couldn't pronounce TH, saying it like an F like some London child. The sound pierced him. She'd barely spoken since their reunion, and her voice was as welcome and familiar as a favorite song once forgotten. Then, the content of her answer dawned on him. Nothing. It reminded him of being wheeled into surgery for an emergency appendectomy when he was fifteen. The anesthesia nurse asked him to count backwards from a hundred, and he remembered getting to maybe eighty-nine before the next thing he knew he was waking up in post-op with a completely different nurse checking on him and a profound sense of weakness. The space in between eighty-nine and opening his eyes was a perfect void. No dreams, no consciousness, no memory of anything other than the moment before and that there was a blank space in between where, if the universe existed, he wasn't a conscious part of it. The thought of that moment of oblivion had both comforted and terrified him for years afterward.

"You remember... nothing? Like, *being* nothing?"

"Uh huh. Kinda."

"Were you scared?"

She shook her head and laughed once, the first such sound she'd made since dying. "Nofing can't be scared, silly. Nofing's nofing."

He felt his chest tighten and his eyes blurred with tears. "Are you happy to be back?" She nuzzled closer and made a contented sound he'd never heard her utter before. It was and wasn't the answer he'd hoped for. If she wasn't content to be in the body she inhabited, he hoped maybe she was happy enough with him. He could live with that for now. But her non-answer weighed on him. His heart ached and he cried, powerful hitching sobs no one had ever seen him cry, until her little hand caressed his cheek and he heard her shushing and whispering, "'T's okay," and he finally realized that the intersection of the life he had and the life he wanted was right here. Now. He was something and so was she. All he wanted was to be the two of them together, because, together, they were something worth being.

The chair by the door screeched as it slid forward on the hardwood floor. The door closed, and the seat slid and fell with a terrible crash that made Mitch's heart thunder. He scooted Sophie off his lap and scrambled to stand, but his legs were weak and unwilling. Clutching the girl, he pushed onto his knees and prepared to scoop her up and run for the back door. There was no easy exit from the postage stamp back yard, except to return to the front walk between their house and Faye's—the back was only an escape from fire. A James Whale scene of pitchforks and torches appeared in his mind, and he thought fire was a clear possibility. "Sophie," he whispered. "Go wait for me in your room." She whined, and he told her more forcefully, "Go. Now!"

The door hit the end of its chain and banged again. A woman's voice called out: "Michel! Are you in there?"

26

Liana lay curled on the living room sofa, clutching a fleece blanket close like the chill of a winter storm was blowing in through the gaps in the window frames. In the kitchen, Mike wiped the sweat off his brow and twisted the string around the sodden teabag and spoon, forcing out the last drops of Earl Grey into the cup below. He'd turned off the air conditioning, and the temperature in his condo, while tolerable, was starting to rise as the afternoon sun shone through the west-facing windows. He set the mug on a coaster on the coffee table and asked if she needed anything else. She shook her head, pulling the blanket higher up over her shoulders. He crouched in front of her and put a hand to her forehead. She flinched at his touch and he jerked his hand away as if she'd burned it.

"What?" he said.

"Your hands are cold."

Eyes darting toward the steaming mug he'd just been holding, he flexed his fingers and frowned. They were anything but. "Li, I'm giving you the rest of the week off."

She pushed herself up on the sofa, and pulled the blanket tighter. "I can't afford to take a week of sick time."

He held up a pinched thumb and forefinger and said, "Zippit! You just relax and try to feel better. Don't worry about sick time; I've got you covered. Your job today is to try to feel better. We'll talk more about it later when I get back." The way he looked at her, Liana didn't need a mirror to know she didn't look like herself. She'd spent the better part of the day staring at her new gray hairs and the small wrinkles around her eyes. She looked maybe ten years older than she had last week. Though that meant she looked closer to her actual age instead of forever young, the change coming so suddenly, and coupled with a profound inner chill, made her feel afraid and lonely. Mike stood. She almost reached out to stop him, but she knew "having her covered" meant that he had to go to work, if for no other reason to stamp her timecard in and out again at the end of the day.

"I promise, I'll only be a day or two," she said. "Mitch needs time to get settled."

Mike smiled and tilted his head, giving her the kind of sympathetic look you give a person with a hangover. *You're hurting,* it said, *but you just have to ride what you did to yourself out.* "Stay as long as *you* need," he said, pointing at her. She thanked him and watched as he gathered his things together and left for work. She closed her eyes and tried not to dream of being alone on Arctic landscapes.

• • •

After a short, fruitless attempt at a nap, she sat up again and tried to find something to occupy her restless mind. She turned on Mike's big screen LCD TV more to get rid of the reflection in the blank screen than out of any interest in watching something. If she had her druthers, she'd read and listen to her records, but she wasn't home and didn't have her druthers. Mike wasn't much of a reader and his music collection wasn't anything she'd wish on an enemy. So, television it was. She surfed away from the game show on the local channel and searched for something that wouldn't make her head hurt. Easier said than done. The news stations were still in a twenty-four-hour resurrection of the dead cycle, saying nothing at all and adding even less understanding to what was happening, but damned certain to cover every single minute with punditry and conjecture. Even a minute of it made the fear and panic come surging back. She clicked over to a nature show that somehow made astrophysics seem as shallow as celebrity gossip, but with pretty animations. She tuned out Michio Kaku talking about black holes like they were walking the red carpet at the Oscars and tucked her legs up under her, hoping to warm her feet a little under the blanket. Looking around to see if Mike had another fleece tossed over a chair somewhere, her gaze rested on his stove. Atop it sat the kettle he'd warmed her tea in, and under that glowed a light blue flame from the gas range, still lit and on low. Downing the last of the tepid tea from her cup, she got up to make another.

Her knees ached from being folded underneath her. She could feel the cold floor through her socks and slippers as she shuffled into the kitchen. The teapot radiated heat and she held her hands around it, feeling the light warmth rising from the brushed aluminum. She dropped a fresh bag in her cup, pouring steaming hot water over it before returning the pot to the stove. The smell of tea reminded her of her Gran. When she left Atlanta to come stay with her cousin Rawndell in Dorchester, the old woman had said, "I hear those winters up there in New England can get real cold. Take warmth." She'd pressed into her hand a small lacquered pin depicting an open Bible below a single flame like a candle: the fire of the Holy Spirit. Back then, Liana had laughed at the idea of being able to take warmth with her. "It's not something you can pack, Gran." Now that no matter what she did she couldn't find any relief from the cold infecting her, she dwelled upon her Gran's gift. Liana wasn't religious anymore, but she could use some of that Holy Ghost heat now. She tried to imagine herself back down South, sweating in a room with a slow-moving fan, waving a butterfly-shaped piece of cardstock stapled to a wooden handle under her face while listening to the preacher. In those moments, she'd ignored the sermons and daydreamed of living somewhere cool. Not knowing what real coldness was like. Not until now.

You don't know what you have in life until... it's taken from you. That's it. Sophie took something from me and she left some cold, dead hole in its place. And now I'm frozen like Dante's Devil in his lake without even a single sinner to chew on to stay warm.

She turned the oven dial to BROIL and knelt in front of it, waiting. After a few minutes, she opened the door, and a wave of heat washed over her like sinking into a warm tub. Of course, she'd already tried that. The comfort of scalding hot water only lasted a few seconds before it became unbearably cold. The water heater had been unable to keep up with her demand.

She held her hands out like it was a roaring hearth at Christmas; the air in front of the open appliance wavered with distortion, but she barely felt it. A chill still resided in her body like she'd been the one rescued off the slab. Leaning forward into the box, ignoring the smell of her singeing hair as it brushed the top, she took a deep breath, hoping it would help to have warm air inside as well as out. It still felt like the chill was beating back the heat, pushing it away. She touched the tip of a finger to the rack. A pleasant sensation of thawing spread up to her second knuckle.

Then the unbidden thought came, *I could climb in.*

Gripping the rack with both hands, she pulled it out and tossed it aside. The hot metal tore away from her searing palms, filling her nostrils with the stench of burning flesh. It clattered in the corner smoking and stinking of her skin and scorching the floorboards. She didn't care. It had felt good to touch it.

She reached out and put her hands on the hot surface inside. The smell and smoke rising from her blistering flesh threatened to choke her, but it just felt like the hot water closing around her—like climbing back into the womb. The cold was retreating, so she leaned in further.

Take warmth, she thought.

27

Violette stood in the open doorway looking like an entirely different person than when she'd skipped out on her daughter. Mitch almost didn't recognize her. She wasn't the jam band groupie dressed in a halter top and a knit Rasta tam who'd left for "a couple of weeks" more than a year ago. She'd cut off her dreadlocks and wore a long cotton skirt with a loose, button up blouse that covered the tattoos on her shoulders. "Can I come in?" Mitch held the door, resentment tickling at the back of his skull. He wanted to question what right she had to just show up after more than a year away with no word, no calls asking how Sophie was doing, not even a postcard to let them know she was all right. *No. You cannot,* he wanted to say. He let go of the door and stepped back from the threshold.

"I suppose so. It's… your house."

"What's this?" She swiped a finger down the paper and glue residue from the eviction sticker. He ignored the question, knowing there'd be plenty of time to discuss how badly he'd stumbled trying to preserve the life she'd abandoned.

"You just dropping in or are you back for good?"

"I'm back. You should, um, know I brought somebody with me."

Mitch sighed. "Did they kick whatshisname out of the band?"

Violette shook her head and said, "I'm not with him anymore." Before Mitch could snark about whether it was too hard on his other girlfriends to have a band wife along, she turned and waved her hand at the car parked across the street. Out of it climbed Junior Wilson. Sophie's father. The man Mitch had put in the hospital, who'd put him in prison in return.

"Oh no. You can't—"

"We've reconciled, Michel. Junior and I got married six months ago." She held up her hand to show him a plain gold band around her third finger. "We've been working hard to make up for our past sins and live a life in grace. We have a new place to live and we're part of a community and... we're here to pick up our daughter."

Mitch's vision darkened and Violette's last words seemed spoken through a long tunnel. They were faint, but they echoed in his head as he tried to make sense of the man climbing the front steps. He'd also changed his appearance. Instead of the Southie hoodrat baggy shorts and oversized Celtics jersey that had been his constant uniform, Junior wore a pair of tan slacks and a white golf shirt. The only hint of his tough guy past was a pair of unblemished tan Timberland work boots. His face was how Mitch remembered it, though. His nose was crushed and one eyelid drooped from nerve damage where Mitch had broken his supraorbital margin—that's what the medical expert had called it at trial. His jaw had healed nicely though. Junior smiled asymmetrically; his dental implants looked like the real thing. His eyelid dropped a little more until it almost looked like he was winking.

I did that.

"Can we come in, Mitch? There's a lot we'd like to talk about," he said.

The terms of his parole fired in Mitch's head like cannon blasts. *You shall not come within one thousand feet of your victim, James Michael Wilson Jr., for any reason whatsoever. You shall not associate with persons who have a criminal record without the permission of your Supervision Officer. You shall make a diligent effort to satisfy the restitution order of the Court that has been imposed. Failure to abide by these conditions shall result in a resumption of your sentence for the duration of your remaining sentence, plus any additional time deemed appropriate by a court of the Commonwealth of Massachusetts.* Junior's presence was a very present testament to the many reasons why Mitch would likely end up back in prison before the order of eviction stuck to the door could be executed.

Mitch felt like chances were equal that if he tried to speak, he might vomit as likely as utter a word. He cleared his dry throat and said, "I'm not allowed to be anywhere near you." His voice was a croak and he thought maybe only half the words were audible.

Junior held up his hands in a what-can-you-do kind of gesture and said, "*I* came to *you*. No one can hold that against you, can they?"

"You'd be surprised."

Despite not wanting to let either of them in, Mitch gestured into the house. If Braddock and Dixon spotted Junior on the front porch that could be the end of everything, right then and there. Maybe Junior was right. That he had brought himself to Mitch's doorstep seemed like something a reasonable judge wouldn't hold against him. But then, a reasonable judge had ignored Mitch's plea for leniency when he asserted that he'd been misled into believing that Junior was beating Violette. Mitch's old "friend" Sully knew exactly how to pull the trigger on his violent temper. A few glasses of whiskey, but not so many he couldn't stand and swing a fist, and then a story convincing enough to a drunk man to get him to get up off the barstool and walk out with a bullshit story ringing in his ears and dark intentions growing in his head.

That wasn't to say Junior had been wholly innocent; he was into Sully deep for an Oxy habit he didn't want to pay for. Mitch wasn't an enforcer; he was, however, a talented amateur boxer with a bright future, a trusting naïveté, and a short fuse when it came to family. Why wouldn't he believe Sully when he said Junior had been tuning up Violette? Junior was a pill snorter who'd let his habit get ahead of his ability to pay. That didn't mean he deserved to get beaten so badly he couldn't smile without almost closing an eye, or speak clearly. But that's what he'd gotten from Mitch. And the judge hadn't cared that he'd done it for his sister. "Did you ever think there might be a way to help Violette without destroying another man's life?" No. Mitch *hadn't* ever thought of that. People like him didn't possess a receiver attuned to those possibilities. Until prison, he was exactly what you would expect from a man raised by wolves. He'd been that man right up until prison broke him, and Sophie domesticated him.

Mitch closed the door and put the chain back on. He led his sister and her husband toward the sofa and asked if they'd like some coffee. He didn't have any left, but the offer sounded like the sort of thing civilized people did, and he was civilized now. Junior shook his head and politely declined. Violette looked around the house at the debris of life with a child. The clutter wasn't as bad as it had been when Sophie was better and Mitch was working, yet it was there: toys randomly abandoned in the course of seeking other toys; pajamas discarded in the middle of the room because it was easier to dress her in front of the TV than in her room; a snack bowl filled with uneaten Cheerios going soft from humidity and stale with time.

"Where is she?" Violette asked.

Mitch nodded toward the rear of the house. "In her room." Violette stood up and started back. Mitch put a hand up. She stopped. "Vee, there's something we should talk about first," he said.

"I want to see my child."

"I'm not kidding. I think you need to know what's happened since you've been gone. Things are... different." Junior stepped in between them. Mitch faced the man he'd put in the hospital. Time had been good to Junior. Not only did he look like he'd kicked the junk habit, he appeared to have been working out. He had muscles he didn't possess before, and a new confidence that was pushing against Mitch's desire to remain civilized. He told himself, *it's not his fault. He didn't do anything.* Still, he wondered what the next few seconds would bring, waiting to hear the ring of the bell from his corner.

"I want you to know we forgive you," Junior said. Mitch blinked repeatedly, trying to decide for what transgression he *deserved* to be absolved. "I actually *owe* you for what you did. You put me in the hospital, and they gave me that good stuff that I really loved. Morphine is fiiiine, man. And when I got out, I cleaned up enough to help put you away, and *then* I went chasing after it hard. I chased all the way down to rock bottom. And when I got there, he lifted me up."

"He?" Mitch asked.

"The Lord God! He reached down and picked me up and helped me get clean. He helped rebuild my body *and* my spirit, and I am a changed man standing here in front of you. It took a while for me to find the path, but once my feet were on solid ground, I walked straight toward the Lord and his grace."

"And then Junior found me and showed me to the light," Violette said. "We've been born again, Mitch, and we want to take our daughter home, to be a family."

Mitch nodded, but he took a step back, keeping his hands up to hold back his sister and her husband. "That's all... great. I'm happy that you've both got... your lives together, but, I think you should stop for a minute and listen to me about Sophie."

"I want to see *my* daughter."

"Let her go, Mitch," Junior said. His voice took on a familiar darkness.

Violette pushed past him and walked out of the room. Mitch turned to follow her, but felt Junior's hand tighten on his bicep.

"I'm saved, and I forgive you," he said, "but don't think I'll let you keep me from my family. Thank you for looking after Sophie, but we'll take care of our own from here on. This is God's plan for us." What remained unspoken in Junior's declaration seemed every bit as clear as the words he'd uttered: *This is God's plan for us. And it doesn't involve you.* Mitch squared up, trying not to put his feet in position to throw an overhand right, but finding himself with his left foot forward anyway. Looking at Mitch's balled up fists, Junior added, "You can go home now."

"I... have nowhere else to go."

"Well, you can't stay here. It's a violation of your parole." Junior's grin widened. He looked like he might have winked. Mitch wanted to hurt him for it.

The scream from the back of the house interrupted their standoff. Junior's eyes darted over Mitch's shoulder, and Mitch's hand ached with the memory of breaking itself against Junior's skull. For a second, he craved the same kind of pain. But he was civilized. And Violette had just discovered what he'd done to their daughter.

Junior shoved past Mitch and ran toward the girl's room. He followed.

Violette was backed up against the far wall, hands clamped over her gaping mouth while Sophie sat on the floor staring at her. She looked at Junior and then Mitch, and sprang to her feet. Junior jumped away as she darted past him leaping up into Mitch's arms. He caught her, holding her close.

"She's a... she's a..." Violette stammered.

"I tried to tell you. We've been through a lot. And—"

"She's a ghoul!" Junior said.

A red veil fell over Mitch's vision and he wanted more than ever to jump forward into trouble. He ached to tell him to shut his fucking mouth or the beating Mitch gave him before would feel like kisses from his sister. But the girl held on tighter, and he held himself back. "Everyone here has changed from who they used to be, but we're all the same people. This is Sophie. She's still your daughter, Vee."

Violette wept and Junior's face darkened with blood. "What did you do?" he shouted.

28

Liana's eyes snapped open, wide and fearful and she screamed a shrill, long wail of panic. She kicked against the arm of the loveseat as the feeling of it against her feet still held the memory of the confining oven. She tried to free her arms from the blanket twisted around her body, but it held her. Mike leaned in, and pulled at the fabric, trying to help her get loose. She flinched away from his touch, fearful of being burned. He yanked the trapped end of the blanket out from under her hip, and her hands came free, whipping in an attempt to smother the flames she still felt in her hair and on her skin. He fell back, while she batted at her head with sweaty, wet hands. He told her it was just a dream, and that she was all right, but she was still half-trapped in the nightmare, dying in fire, cooking herself alive.

The room slowly came into focus, and her friend's face emerged from the smoke that engulfed her semi-conscious mind. An image of comfort in extremis. He wore the same worried expression he'd had all those years ago when he found her beaten and barely conscious on the side of the road. She pushed up on the sofa, trying to get her breathing under control and her heart to slow its frenetic beating. He leaned forward and tried to pull the blanket back up over her shoulders, but she gently pushed it off. She was finally warm.

Perspiration soaked through her clothes and slicked Mike's leather sofa with a sheen of moisture. She felt as embarrassed as a child who'd wet the bed, and tried to stand so she could assess how to clean it up. He shushed her and told her to give herself a minute. She began to cry and apologize. "I'm sorry. I'm so sorry, Mikey."

"Hush, you. You're okay. This isn't anywhere you ever have to be sorry." As many times as he saved her from threats both real and imagined, Liana knew she would never be even with him.

"I am sorry," she whispered, unable to shed her twin feelings of shame and panic. And one other: a fear she hadn't felt since she was a little girl—the fear of utter helplessness at the hands of adults making decisions about her in which she neither had a say nor even a tiny bit of control. Inexplicably, a memory of sitting on the front step as the man in their house yelled at her mother for buying Liana another toy when they couldn't afford to put gas in the car. The sound of the slap, a body hitting the floor, and the breaking of the new precious thing. And then her mother's crying. More shouting and louder crying as the man she'd invited into their home established his place in it by force and intimidation. She remembered the sound of the front door slamming open and the feeling of the hand on the back of her dress that dragged her inside. And then the hand that fell across her backside because she'd had the temerity to ask for a pretty thing at a moment her mother was feeling generous.

How she hated that man, and imagined doing terrible things to him in his sleep. Instead, years later she slipped away in the night to go live with her Gran in another town. Time and distance cooled her worst inclinations toward him, and her absence seemed to fade her mother's memories of him screaming at Liana and hitting her for nearly any insult, no matter how slight. And in his last days when he sat skinny and wasted from the cancer that ate him, she stood, clad in black and made bold by the music that thrummed in her heart, and she told him he was nothing. He lurched at her from his chair, and she was nine again, terrified and perfectly weak. That week, she left for New England, and never thought of him again.

And now, she felt that fear, but wasn't certain why. She felt it from a gulf of distance that did not reach from Atlanta. No. He was long dead and couldn't hurt her any longer. But the threatening in her heart was as close as the man next to her. Except, not the man actually next to her. Mike was her sanctuary and protector. No, the threat was not in this place. It was in Mitch's apartment. She knew it wasn't Mitch, and… not Sophie. There was something else threatening *them*.

"I can feel her," she said.

"Feel what? Who?"

"Sophie. I can feel her. She's afraid."

Mike sat back on his heels. "I don't understand."

She stood up, and staggered a step, hovering dangerously over the glass top coffee table before finding her balance. She and Sophie were a part of each other now. She wanted to be a mother someday, but was terrified that despite her Gran's loving example, she'd fuck it up like her parents had done. Like being absent and angry was genetic. She knew it wasn't. That the choice to be a good parent could be made. That she could follow her Gran's example instead of her mother's. The feelings were beyond her ability to control, but her actions weren't. Her body was hers alone, and while it had been hijacked by this child, she had a choice. She could walk away, and her life would be hers alone again, or she could go after the girl and answer her call for help. Her choice.

The girl was calling out, and she was maybe the one person who could hear.

"I have to go. She needs me."

"What about what she did to you?" Mike brushed a finger along his temples, indicating her gray streaks and crow's feet.

Gran's nickname for Liana had been "Magpie." Whenever she saw something shiny, no matter what, treasure or trash, she picked it up and put it in her pocket. She loved anything that sparkled and had to possess it, even if it later ended up forgotten in her "Little Box of Ephemera," and was lost among all the other discarded jewels of the street. She had it, and she was comforted by the fact that whatever it was that had been cast off or lost was hers now and no one could take it. The little pieces of the world she collected gave her control over a part of her life she'd been denied. And understanding came into clear focus. "Sophie took something from me. A little piece of my fire. I don't think she wanted to hurt me, though. I think she wanted a connection. A piece to keep so she could always have me with her so she could be warm."

She snatched her leather jacket off the coat tree next to the door. Instead of sliding into it, she draped it over her arm and dug her car keys out of a pocket. Mike stood and held out a hand for her to give them to him. She shook her head. "No. Sophie needs me," she said. "I have to go."

"I understand that, but I don't think you should drive. Give me the keys. I'll take you."

"You don't have to do this."

He planted a hand on his hip and said, "Do you think you can stop me from coming with?" She knew she couldn't. Not without a Taser and a lot of duct tape. Liana dropped the keys in his outstretched hand and hugged Mike as firmly as she could. It wasn't hard, but she felt her strength returning. She felt the fire inside her burning, getting warmer.

29

Mitch sat on a dining room chair with Sophie in his lap while Junior and Violette stood in front of the sofa. A long silence had descended over the room after Mitch finished summarizing the events of the last month. He left out facts he thought Violette and Junior didn't need to know, like staying at Liana's and the encounters at the library and cemetery, but the salient facts were out in the open. Sophie died while the neighbors were watching her, and Mitch had gotten her back once the children began to return to life. Violette wept quietly while Junior listened with a stone-faced glare, staring at Sophie with an expression Mitch couldn't quite figure out. He'd never had a face anyone would call genial, but the damage Mitch had inflicted on him left him looking permanently ill-natured. *Or maybe it's just me. This is what I do to people.* Finally, Junior opened his mouth and said, "We can take her to Pastor Roper. He'll take care of this."

"*Pastor* Roper? I don't know if you've been watching the news, but religious types don't seem to like kids like Sophie."

"Ghouls."

Mitch stood, clutching the girl. He said, "Say that word again and we're going to have a problem." His threat felt empty, coming from a man clutching a child, but still, he felt committed to holding firm to the promise. He was fucking tired of hearing Junior call her that, and he was coming to the end of his patience with live and let live.

"Pastor Roper will know what to do," Junior repeated. He held out his hands. "Give her to me." Sophie clung tighter to Mitch, even though he made no motion to hand her over. "Now!"

"No. I don't know who this Pastor Roper is, but if he's like the rest of them, he's got no intention of 'helping' a single kid like Sophie. You're not taking her to a snake charmer to be 'healed.' I'll find a solution to her problem without faith healers and conmen."

"You think doctors have an answer? Scientists? They ain't gonna solve this problem. They don't know a thing because this ain't a worldly affliction you can study in a lab or a hospital. It says in Proverbs, 'The human spirit can endure a sick body, but who can bear a crushed spirit?' This is a *spiritual* condition, and it needs a spiritual solution."

"She. Not 'it.' And I don't believe in the same things you do. What makes you think this preacher can do something that no one else has been able to figure out yet?"

"You need to have faith in the Lord, Mitch. What more proof do you need of the divine than the dead coming back to life?"

Mitch wanted to argue, but he held back.

"Please, give her to him," Violette said.

Not to me or us. To him. Mitch felt his frustration deepen. Whatever change had occurred in his sister to get her to stop following the band and think of her child was not as strongly personal as he'd hoped. He couldn't see the puppet opening between her shoulder blades, but he felt like it was Junior's hand moving her mouth while he spoke for her.

"No. She doesn't want to go with you."

"Children never want to do what's good for them," Junior said. "You think she'd like to have chocolate pudding instead of steak for dinner?"

Mitch furrowed his brow. "She doesn't eat steak. She's four."

"You know what I mean. Hand her the fuck over!" Junior stepped forward, reaching again for Sophie. Mitch backed up and stopped when his back pressed against the wall.

"Touch her, and you'll regret it," he said. She loosened her grip on him and turned to look at the man approaching. She held out a hand for Junior, and he stopped. He frowned and seemed to share Violette's reticence in touching, or being touched by Sophie as soon as he got a look at her eyes, and the blue/black veins in her skin. Whatever his spiritual convictions, his natural aversion to touching something dead remained. For that, Mitch thought, he should be thankful. An image of what happened to the woman's arm in the cemetery slipped into his mind, and he smiled. Not at what she'd done to that woman, but at what he wanted her to do to Junior. If Sophie was a little brighter at a moment's touch, how much improved would her condition be if she got to give Junior a big long hug? He banished the dark thought. It wasn't fair to ask her to do that, no matter what his feelings for Junior were. And he'd made her promise not to. They'd find a way to make her better without having to sacrifice her innocence, or anyone else. There was another way to solve her problem that didn't involve ruining another life. He was sure of it. There had to be. It would just take time to figure out what that was.

When Junior pulled the pistol out of the back of his pants, he knew time had just drawn short. Mitch turned, putting his body in between Sophie and the gun. "Put it away, Junior. This isn't how you want this to go."

"What are you doing?" Violette said.

"This is what has to be done." Junior told Violette to pull the car into the driveway and open the trunk. "Keep the engine running," he said without looking away from Mitch and Sophie.

"What are you doing?"

"Just fucking do it!" Violette ran off like she had been snapped by a riding crop. Mitch wanted so badly to work terrible violence on the man standing in his house. But now, he had to get past the gun. He'd missed his chance to face Junior as an equal. He had to keep the girl safe, and he couldn't do that if he was shot and bleeding. He couldn't save her if *he* was dead. Not a single adult had come back from the dead. Not yet.

"This isn't going to end the way you want it to," Mitch said. "I promise."

Junior shrugged and nodded his head toward the door. "We'll see who keeps their promises. Remember what I said to you in court that day?"

Mitch recalled the judge reading the verdict of the jury declaring him guilty. He didn't wait for a reaction, but immediately went into thanking the jury for their service and telling them that they had answered the call to serve and preserve a civil society of laws. And while he droned on, Mitch heard the voice of his victim from behind him in the audience gallery. Junior had said, "I'll see you in Hell. I promise."

Mitch was pretty sure they were all already there.

Violette reappeared in the door and told Junior the car was ready. He smiled and waved the pistol in her direction. "Let's go."

Outside, the sun was setting in a beautiful haze of orange and yellow above houses that had stood along this road for over a hundred years. Mitch wondered if anyone was looking out their window at them. At the man holding the gun on a man and a child, ordering them to climb into the trunk of a running car. If they were, not one of them made even a gesture to acknowledge Mitch and Sophie. No one peeked out their window with a phone in hand letting him know they'd called the police and he'd be safe. They'd be found and all would be right in the world.

The police.

He looked up the block for Braddock and Dixon's car. They would help him, wouldn't they? But they were nowhere to be seen. He and Sophie were alone. Like always.

"Get in. It's nice and roomy." Junior pointed to the trunk. It was a newer car, and the space was big enough for the two of them. All the tools and the spare were under a pull-up cover and rough felt covered all the surfaces; the very last place Mitch wanted to be confined was there. He'd have preferred a grave—at least then he wouldn't have to live in fear of what was about to happen to them. No. Not the grave. Not while Sophie needed him. *Stay alive. For her. Do whatever it takes to stay alive for her.*

"Now!"

Mitch climbed in and his breath abandoned him when Junior slammed the trunk.

30

Everything seemed off in the way that absolutely nothing appeared to be amiss. A bus stopped to drop off and pick up riders, a woman walked a small dog along the sidewalk, and houses stood silently waiting for their occupants to return from work and school and fill them with life. At the center of it, halfway up the block, a door stood open. No one came out. There was no car in the driveway with an open back hatch half-filled with groceries, waiting for the next trip. Just an ordinary house and an open door that said *all you count on in the world to be right, is wrong. And this is the threshold of chaos. Nothing through here is what you want it to be.*

Mike pulled up in front of the house and Liana jumped out, running to the door. She disappeared inside, reemerging a moment later, looking up and down the street as if they'd just missed Mitch and Sophie. But they'd seen no one leave. There was no way of telling how long they'd been gone, other than Liana's gut feeling that they had been here only a moment ago. They had been in trouble. And that trouble had moved on.

"Are you sure what you're feeling is right? It's not the dream or—"

"I know I'm right. I feel her, but she's somewhere... dark now." Liana stood on the porch with her eyes closed for a moment. She pushed out with her mind, trying to feel what she'd had after waking up on Mike's love seat. The call across space to that place in her where the little girl she once was still lived. She searched for the feeling, starting to get angry with herself when she couldn't find it. Her shoulders dropped and she opened her eyes. "I don't know. I can't..."

It was there, in the dark spaces in between her memories. The girl was moving farther away in darkness, and like her so long ago, was headed north.

"I know where she is. I think."

"And?"

"And we need to get going. She's moving."

Part Four: Sophie's Judgement

31

Perspective was capable of remaking the world. Standing outside an open car trunk with a suitcase in hand, it seemed large. Accommodating, one would say; more room than was needed. Staring into it with an eye toward climbing in oneself, it shrunk. The same space became frighteningly smaller and darker. And inside with the lid closed, it became smaller still, and even more terrifying in motion. The confined space was hot and the air was thin, tainted with exhaled breath and car exhaust. Lying on his side, each bump in the road and every acceleration and deceleration shifted the proportions of the space, jabbing Mitch in the back, forcing his head against the wall. It felt like they were on the highway.

He tried to inhale and was frustrated in the attempt. He coughed and gasped and coughed again as more of the invisible gas that filled the space invaded his body, denying him the simple satisfaction of a deep breath. In front of him, Sophie shifted. She whimpered in sympathy at his discomfort. He felt her sound through her back in his stomach more than he heard it over the engine and road noise. Through the seat and the bulkhead wall behind him, he could hear the faint sounds of a man's voice. At first, he thought Junior was yelling at Violette, but it kept on, without pause. They were listening to something. Talk radio, he figured, as if they hadn't just kidnapped people at gunpoint. He heard the muddy voice shout, "Amen!"

He held Sophie tighter and tried to soothe her, but was really comforting himself. *She* showed no outward signs of fear, just the same kind of concern for him that had been worthy of comment from so many who'd met her in the time before. "She is so empathetic," they'd say. "I've never met a four-year-old who wanted to know how I felt." Sophie had been a caring child. She still was, and that was how he knew she wasn't just a living dead girl—a ghoul. Even if she didn't play the way she used to, or eat, or even breathe much, she was still Sophie. She was still the child who crawled into his lap when she sensed he was feeling overwhelmed and afraid. Even now, she pushed back against his chest and belly, not to seek comfort, but to give it. No one had to tell him. He knew this one thing, more than any other.

"Hon," he said. His throat was raw, and his breath shallow. She moved, hearing him above the noise that drowned out everything else. "Hon, can you... can you do that thing you did... with the lock?"

Her head turned and tilted back. He felt her trying to look at him. Maybe she could see him in the dark. He had no idea what her pale eyes were capable of. He couldn't see her. Nothing was visible in the blackness of the trunk. Not even a line telling him where the seam between trunk and lid was.

"I don't want you to open it." The thought of the trunk popping open at eighty miles an hour on the highway terrified him almost as much as the idea of it staying closed and suffocating them. "Can you... make a hole in the side, so we can breathe?" Her shoulder shifted against him and he felt her reaching forward. A few seconds later, above the stench of exhaust, he smelled an unpleasantly musty odor like something left in the rain to decay, followed by a metallic iron smell that reminded him of blood, but he knew to be rust. A pinprick of light shone into the trunk, brightening the length of Sophie's arm. It grew as she pushed against it, flaking away what she'd ruined of the trunk lid. The noise grew painfully louder, but more importantly fresh air rushed into the space, whipping around them. It wasn't fresh like the air on the paths through the necropolis, or even the city park smell of Boston Common, but it was breathable, and he pulled as much of it into his lungs as he could.

"Thank you," he said.

"We'come." Her voice was scratchy and thin, and he barely heard her. He knew she didn't breathe much, not like he did. But she did breathe. She wasn't dead. She was alive. And if it could steal her breath and her voice, something like an enclosed trunk and car exhaust could hurt her body too. He pushed down the spark of anger he felt. Sure, he was barely holding on, sublimating his terror of confinement and trying to stay calm, so when the lid finally did open, he would have his wits. He was going to hurt Junior. He wanted to have her rot through the opposite wall into the cab of the car so he could crawl through and strangle the man from the back seat. Instead, he waited. Eventually, they'd stop, and he'd have his chance. He wouldn't let anything happen to Sophie. Not on his life.

As if she knew what he was thinking, she pushed back against him and sighed. He counted the time before he felt her take another breath. Five minutes.

32

The car slowed and Mitch listened, trying to get a sense of where Junior had driven them, but there weren't any echoes of activity he could hear that would help identify a place—not like the sound of gas pumps or a fast food drive-through speaker. He hoped this was their destination and not a casual stop, mostly because he was certain he couldn't handle another hour or more locked in the cramped darkness without losing his already tenuous grip on reason. He was ready to go mad. His right arm and leg were numb from lying on his side. His hip hurt and his head was pounding. Even with his wits, he wouldn't be able to spring out of the trunk to fight for his and Sophie's lives. Wherever Junior had taken them, he hoped cooler heads awaited his freedom from the box. At least until he could get his feet beneath him.

The car turned and he heard a primitive road under the tires—dirt or gravel. Eventually they slowed and stopped. The radio shut off, and he heard a power window roll down and the sound of footsteps. There were a few exchanged words before a harsh voice outside the car told them to pull up to the main lot, promising he'd radio ahead. Junior said something in reply and the window hummed back up. The car lurched forward; Mitch hit his head against a bulge in the trunk and saw stars flash behind his eyes. His head ached with renewed throbbing. He couldn't tell if his vision was blurry or if there was just nothing to see in the fading light through the rotted-out hole in the back of the car.

After another couple of turns, the car rolled to a stop and the engine shut off. Junior barked something at Violette that he punctuated by slamming the door. Footsteps crunched around the side of the car, followed by Junior's angry howl: "The fuck did you do to the back of my car?"

The lid lifted and Mitch was barely able to blink the sun out of his eyes before the fist landed on his cheekbone. It drove down two more times before he heard in the haze behind his fading consciousness, "That's not how we do things, Brother Wilson." The owner of the voice told someone else to get Mitch cleaned up and take him somewhere. He missed what the man called it.

"Take the girl to the safe room."

Blind, Mitch tried to keep hold of Sophie, but she was pulled out of his hands before he could find his grip. Then, hands were on him, pulling him upright. Junior said something about it being "the only way to get them here," and then Mitch's head knocked against the side of the car as rough hands hauled him out and his vision blurred again.

He tried to stand, the ache in his hip spreading down his leg as stabbing pins and needles replaced the fading numbness. His balance was unsteady and his knee wanted to buckle. He heard someone say, "Hold him up." The hands on his arms tightened painfully, as the men who'd pulled him out of the trunk tried to stand him up straighter.

A shape stepped in front of the late day sun. Mitch looked up into the blankness of the backlit giant until his eyes found details to resolve into view. The man was tall and athletic. He wasn't misshapen with steroid muscle, but looked like a gym rat nonetheless. The kind of guy who wants to look like he might bust out of his tailored suits as likely as hang them up at night. Thick dark brown curls lifted up from his forehead above a hatchet face. His lips peeled back in a rictus grin revealing as much of his gums as teeth. When his cheeks raised in the smile, his chin seemed even more pointed, and his head became as triangular as a caricature of the Devil. "I'm Pastor Gideon Roper," the big man said. "I apologize for the manner in which you've been brought here. Brother Wilson is enthusiastic, and, well, I understand you two have history."

Mitch laughed once, triggering a coughing spell that hurt his throat and pulled a muscle in his side. The men on either side of him held him up, but Mitch could feel them leaning away, as if he was contagious. Pastor Roper's eyebrows raised, but he didn't offer Mitch a handkerchief or a drink of water. He waited, smiling, for the paroxysm to subside and said, "Nothing funny about forgiveness, Michel—can I call you Michel?" He didn't wait for an answer. "Will you pray with me?"

His throat was raw from breathing exhaust, and he tried to hold in another bout of coughing, barely succeeding. His ribs ached with the effort of speaking. "I'd rather not, if it's all the same to you."

Roper clicked his tongue as he shook his head. "I understand you spent time in prison. One would hope you'd've used that time inside to look for the light of the Lord."

Mitch blinked his eyes clear and looked at the men holding his arms. They wore black shirts with a shiny gold cross that became a sword blade at the long end. Above and below the cross it read "GOD'S WARRIORS" in big red letters. They had long guns slung over their shoulders—not the MCI issue AR-15 rifles he was used to seeing in the tower, but something else he didn't recognize. The weapons looked like the ones guys who led fantasy lives about the apocalypse preferred: black on black and with enough folding parts to be as much transforming toy as firearm. The men scowled at him, but they were soft-eyed. He knew them better than they knew themselves. They were the kind of guys who'd brag about having Special Forces experience and then end up in the prison infirmary over a tray of Tater Tots or a piece of cake. Fakers with superhero dreams but no smarts or heart. Problem was, guns gave guys like that a measure of the power they worshiped and didn't have otherwise. And a man with a little power wants to use it; he just needs something to aim at. It didn't take any kind of special insight to know Mitch was the only target around. "I did my time the way I did it," he said.

Roper looked at him disapprovingly. "Well, we'll have to have that discussion another time, I imagine. I'm sure you'd like to have a moment to relax and recover from your less than comfortable travel accommodations." He nodded to the men holding Mitch and said, "Take him to the Parents' Ministry." He turned to go.

"Where's Sophie?"

Roper stopped and turned. "She's with the other children in her condition. Safe." He walked away, leaving Mitch in the hands of the men holding him up.

"Welcome to the New Life Church," Junior said.

"I'm not impressed."

"You have to have faith in the Lord, Michel."

"All I see around us are people, and what I've seen of them leaves me cold."

"I understand jail must've been hard on you." Junior smirked. "The sex-u-al abuse," he said with a drawl suggesting he didn't find the thought repulsive, at least not in the context of it being inflicted on Mitch.

"Nobody touched me inside. I'm not a punk."

"Yes, you are." Junior threw a straight right into Mitch's face. The shot hit high on the bridge of his nose, halfway up on his forehead. His head rocked back and he saw stars again.

As a boxer, he'd been hit a lot harder and a lot better, but not bare knuckled while a couple of goons held him still. He tried to brace himself for another shot, ready to drop his head and let Junior drive a fragile fist into the top of his hard skull, but none came.

Mitch tilted his head to get a better look at Junior. His vision was still a little blurry. "I thought you said you forgave me."

"That doesn't mean you don't still owe." Junior grabbed Violette's arm and dragged her off in the direction Roper had gone. Mitch saw him shaking his hand out, flexing his fingers as they walked, and he hoped Junior had at least sprained his hand if he didn't break it.

"If anything happens to Sophie, what I did to you back then will feel like kisses from my sister!" he called after them. The "guards" spun him around and started to march him away. He shook his head trying to clear away the cobwebs. Sucker punch or not, the fight had been taken out of him and although his leg was feeling better, he was as weak as he had ever been. No matter how badly he wanted to shake the men dragging him away from the car, trying now wouldn't get him anywhere. He looked around, attempting to make sense of his surroundings. The place seemed somewhere between a mall and a small university: a campus of buildings arranged around a central, modern mega-church style chapel. A garden courtyard with patterned brick walkways cut through the spaces in between buildings. He was led toward one on the periphery of the complex. None of the structures were marked with names or numbers like a university. They all looked alike, but his guides knew where they were taking him.

They might call it a church, but it felt like just another prison to Mitch.

33

The robot woman on the line directed Liana to leave a message. She disconnected, thinking that if Mitch hadn't responded to the three messages she'd left already, a fourth wasn't going to change anything. Especially if his battery was dead and he couldn't access his voicemail. She hoped that was what it was—his phone battery was drained, and he hadn't noticed yet that he had no service because he was driving and couldn't look at his cheap-o prepaid flip phone. But then, Mitch didn't own a car. He wouldn't be driving anywhere. She thought back to driving him and Sophie home from the morgue, him in the back seat with her in his lap, the pair of them clutching each other. The memory made her worry more. He had agreed to ride like that because they had no choice about leaving at that exact minute with the child. She knew he'd balk at going anywhere else with Sophie without a car seat. But yet, they were moving. Or had been.

When she first felt the stab of fear, it was coming from Mitch's place in Kingsport. Then, it moved. It headed north and she felt it growing more distant—but no less insistent—until they got on I-93 and drove toward the New Hampshire border. Then, for a while, it seemed like they were moving at the same pace together. Now, it felt as if the pull had come to a fixed point, and they were drawing nearer. Wherever Sophie and Mitch were going, they had arrived. If that's what it really was, and she wasn't just going mad.

She checked the volume on her smartphone again, making sure it was at its loudest setting, and slipped it back in her jacket pocket. Though she knew he wasn't calling back, she kept a hand on it to feel for the vibration, just in case she missed the sound of her ringtone over the car noise. She looked out the window at the road, watching the scenery pass by in a blur. Everything felt like that. Since he'd asked her out, Liana's feelings for Mitch had developed as quickly as the landscape moved, and everything else that followed upon kept the frenetic pace set by their first date. She was swept along in its wake like a lost feather chasing a passing semi-truck.

"Anything?" Mike asked. He'd asked the same question at the one mile notice of every approaching exit. She had only been able to say yes or no within a quarter-mile of any turn they needed to take. That meant they had to drive in the right lane so he wouldn't have to cut across traffic at the last second, and that was slowing them down. It was better than blowing past the exit they needed, though. Liana's sense was more like steering by stars in an overcast sky than it was like following a GPS. She'd failed to direct them off I-93 at the right exit and then spent almost an hour fidgeting and fighting with her seat while they moved away from her feeling at twice the speed they'd previously been pursuing it. Mike took an exit at Manchester and she directed him west, getting them back on track. Travel on the two lane state highway moved slower, especially when it took them through towns like the one they were passing through now. But they hadn't "lost the signal" since getting on Route 101. Now, however, there were no warnings or exits. Only side roads and intersections. It was harder to predict where to go without having to backtrack.

"I don't know. They've stopped moving and it doesn't feel the same."

"Stopped moving?"

"Yeah. The... pull... is... We're getting closer, but I'm less certain about... Now! This one!"

Mike said, "Dublin Road?"

"Yes! Here!"

Yanking the wheel and standing on the brake, he skidded around the corner in front of the Dublin Fire Department, to the annoyance and insistent honking of the pickup truck following too closely behind them.

The new road was increasingly rural and the points of exit were even harder to see approaching in the tall trees and growing late afternoon shadows. Mike leaned forward in his seat straining to see. He slowed, taking the blind corners more carefully.

Liana clutched at her throat and gasped.

"What is it? What's wrong?"

"I can't breathe. Oh god! I need to get out of this car. Now!" She banged a fist on the door and shouted, "Pull over! Pull over!" Mike angled onto the narrow shoulder. The sound of plants and a rock scraping underneath echoed inside the car. Liana threw open the door and lurched out into the trees before he stopped completely. She slipped on loose pine needles and mud and slid down the embankment into the forest. She tumbled ten feet or more down an embankment before catching hold of a tree to stop her descent. She held on as if it were a piece of floating debris in a vast ocean, rattled from the sudden drop, and the breathlessness overwhelmed her. She gasped and pulled for air. Her lungs filled with it, but the suffocating sensation remained. A few seconds later, she heard a loud horn blaring behind her and a shout from the window of some throaty monster vehicle passing by on the road above. She looked up to see an ashen-faced Mike, scrambling down the hill after her. He skidded on his heels, using the trees for stability until he reached her.

"Are you okay? What the fuck was that, Li?"

She took another deep breath, trying not to hyperventilate, but unable to rid herself of the irrational feeling she was underwater. "I panicked. I'm sorry." She took another huge gulping breath and let the cool forest air fill her. Everything smelled like pine and earth. She tried to focus on the scents and the feeling of breathing instead of the other sensation that had sent her into a panic. "I felt like I was drowning."

"You're not drowning."

"I know that." She put a hand on Mike's arm and let him help her up. Together, they climbed back up to the car, idling with her door hanging open as if they'd pulled over to take a quick picture of a scenic overlook. Mike circled around the rear of the car, and stopped to look for traffic before heading for the driver's door. No one was coming. He paused when he saw Liana still standing beside her door, not getting in. "What is it?" he asked.

"I'm not drowning."

"No. That's what I told you."

"I thought I was, but I know what it is." She looked over the roof of the car and said, "Mike, I think they buried her."

"What?"

"I think they buried Sophie alive."

34

One of the weekend holy warriors dragging Mitch along grumbled about doing all the work. The man on his other side told the guy to be quiet and hold him up while he unlocked the door. He shaded the keypad with a hand, entered the code, and threw wide the door before grabbing hold again of Mitch's arm to drag him inside. Mitch resisted the hands pulling at him, wanting to see—needing to know—where they'd taken Sophie. The goon's fingers dug deeper into his bicep and he was roughly ushered into a narrow stairwell. At the bottom of the stairs waited another armed man sitting in a folding chair outside a closed door. Like Mitch's guides, he wore all black "tactical" clothing and a God's Warrior T-shirt. The door behind them slammed shut with a bang echoing in the hallway that made Mitch want to be sick. He hesitated and one of the goons bounced him off the wall. He stumbled and feared that his guide would let go and let him tumble down the hard steps, but the man's grip didn't loosen and he was righted and steadied before being escorted down. On the landing below, the men spun him about and another wave of nausea hit him, blurring his vision and disorienting him to his surroundings. The guard on the plastic chair said, "Another one for the fire?" and they all laughed. He heard the sound of keys jingling and then a click before the hands were back on him and he was flung backward, this time with a hard shove in the chest that did send him sprawling.

"Church starts at dusk," said the one who'd shoved Mitch. He lay on the floor listening to the sounds of laughter and another door slamming that echoed through the room. Mitch was wracked with several cramping dry heaves. He'd never felt thankful before to have an achingly empty belly. With all of the indignities of the day, not lying in a pool of his own vomit seemed like a small mercy. He rolled over and pulled his knees under him letting the dirty linoleum cool the side of his face. Sleep hovered at the edge of his consciousness, tempting him. The auto exhaust from the long car ride wasn't in his lungs anymore, but he guessed it was still working in his bloodstream and brain. He got up onto his hands and knees and pushed himself up onto his heels. Opening his eyes, the fluorescent lights above made his head ache. He squinted at the door. There was no window in it. It didn't matter that he couldn't see through. He knew there was an armed man keeping watch on the other side. So many guns. He didn't know if anyone on the compound was actually willing to shoot—he figured they'd all be willing to *draw* at least—but the pistol on the guy's hip convinced him to come up with a plan before trying to walk out of the room. He didn't feel the need to learn by experience. *Do your time smart, not hard,* had been his mantra, but Mitch had no intention of doing this time at all. And he sure as Hell wasn't waiting around for "church," whatever that entailed.

It took a minute to fully comprehend where he was. The room looked like a cafeteria, maybe. There was what looked like a shuttered serving window at one end and a small stage with an upright piano at the other, and in between, a lot of open space. A dining room, maybe. If it was, the tables were gone and only a few plastic folding chairs remained. Scattered around the room, a handful of other people looked at him with a mixture of apprehension and a little pity. They reminded him of the anger management group therapy sessions he used to attend. A couple of them seemed surly and impatient, on edge, and ready to explode. The rest appeared tamed by the experience, if not broken. The group was mixed evenly, men and women, and the atmosphere held that essential blend of *I don't want to be here* and *whatever it takes to get out* that always seemed to fill the inmate classroom.

One couple sat on a pair of old sofa cushions shoved up against the wall. Two more people sat a short distance away from them, also resting on pillows on the floor instead of one of the chairs. One man sat with his legs stretched out ahead of him, ankles crossed. His wife, Mitch guessed, lay on her side with her head in his lap. She wasn't sleeping; her haunted eyes stared into the distance. A man in an ill-fitting suit with his tie loosened looked over from where he leaned against a square post, gnawing on his thumbnail like he was trying to get to the chewy center of his digit. On the small stage at the far end of the room, a single woman picked at a worn spot in her jeans, worrying it open wider. In the far corner, another lone woman sat in a folding chair. She stood up and approached him. No one else moved.

He tried to get up from his knees, but his vision swam a little and he stayed put. Although his head was clearing, it still wasn't completely clear. Another wave of nausea swept over him before receding again like the last remnants of a hangover. He was sweating and felt his heart beating hard even though he hadn't done anything exerting. If he'd been in a bed, he imagined it would be spinning.

The woman took him tenderly by the arm and helped him to his feet. She led him toward a plastic folding chair and eased him down again. Unlike the goons who'd brought him there, she let him do most of the work, offering just enough support to steady him. She crouched in front of him and asked if he was okay. She raised a hand, letting it hover in front of his face as if she wanted to wipe something off his forehead, but was afraid of hurting him. He wiped his fingers at the spot her eyes seemed focused on and they came away stained with dark, half-clotted blood. Junior must have been wearing a ring and cut his face when he sucker punched him. Mitch wondered what kind of horror movie victim he resembled and looked around for a reflective surface. Aside from the woman's wide eyes, there were none. He took a deep breath, trying to find that center of calm he sought in hard times. It eluded him.

"What is this place?" he asked. His voice was rough and his throat hurt. He tried clearing it, but that only made the pain spark, and did nothing to improve the quality of his voice.

The man on the sofa cushions snorted and answered. "This is the 'Parents' Ministry.'"

"Yeah, I got that much from the..." He almost called them "screws," but changed his mind. He'd put a lot of effort into shedding that skin; he didn't want to crawl right back into it, no matter how familiar and comfortable. Moreover, he didn't want these people to think of him as a con, ex or otherwise. Not if he needed their help. "I got that from the guards. What's that mean? Parents' Ministry? What are we doing here?"

The man leaning against the pole huffed, pulled his thumb out of his mouth long enough to say, "It's a waiting room," and returned to work on the nail. The woman on the stage snorted at his statement and the guy shot her a nasty look.

"What are you waiting for?"

"To atone for our sins."

"We're all here because we have kids who died," said the man on the floor. He stroked his wife's hair as she continued to stare silently from his lap. "You do too, or else you wouldn't be here."

"She's not..." *My child?* "She's not dead," he said. The woman who'd helped him into the chair sighed. She pulled a chair up next to him and sat, holding his hand. He didn't know her; she had no reason to want to console him. But she did, and he didn't push her away. The small touch helped him keep calm. She didn't say a word of comfort. She seemed to just need to make contact with another person. The couples had each other, and the man on the post and the woman on the stage didn't seem interested in cuddling.

"You sure about that?" said the thumb-chewer.

Mitch didn't answer. Getting Sophie back was more important to him than arguing with a guy over semantics. He'd have plenty of time for a therapeutic awakening when Sophie was back with him and they were out of this asylum. This room was just another symptom of the larger problem plaguing him: he might be outside the walls, but he was still doing time with his head down. Always a step behind when it came to their well-being, and letting other people lead him around. Being a pacifist and hiding in the shadows wasn't making life easier. In fact, it had the opposite effect up to this point. He felt like he needed to do what he'd done when he first went inside: make a clear declaration he was no one's punk and hurt someone. If he didn't stand up and do something decisive to ensure his survival and hers, someone else was going to solve their problems the way *they* thought best. If it wasn't already too late to prevent that.

He looked at the woman sitting next to him and said, "What's your name?"

She blinked rapidly, and she replied in a small voice, "I'm Amye, with an E at the end. My son's name is Brendan. Who are you?"

He looked in Amye's face and saw a spark of expectant hope that he would be the one to help her out—out of the room, out of the compound, out of trouble. He'd seen that look before. Until now, he was nobody's savior except his own. If she was willing to help him, however, he decided they could help each other. Instead of doing things the way he always had, he took the lesson he'd learned from Liana. He shouldn't be so quick to turn away an ally. "I'm Mitch. They have my niece, Sophie."

She pointed toward the couple on the sofa cushions and said, "That's Steve and Izzy. Their daughter is Michelle. Over there are Nick and Alexa; they have a boy named Jack. Sitting on the stage is Kristin. Her daughter's name is Cassie." Kristin looked up from her jeans at the mention of her name. She had a black eye and a swollen bottom lip. It looked like he wasn't the only one who'd had to be convinced to come to the Parents' Ministry.

"Don't you want to know my name?" the man against the post asked.

Mitch turned to face him. "It depends."

"On what?"

"Whether or not you want to help us get out of here."

The man huffed a laugh through his nose. Mitch clasped his free hand over Amye's for a moment and squeezed. He let go, stood, and took a step toward the man, holding out a hand to shake. The man didn't take it.

"Don't bother," Kristin said from her perch on the stage. "The rest of us are here because we don't want to go along with this shit. Byron there is locked up because he's too fuckin' eager to get started. Aren't you, you son of a bitch? Why don't you tell him what you did?"

The man took a step toward her. "You shut your mouth, whore, or I'll—"

Mitch gave the man a hard stare. Byron stopped and considered Mitch for a moment, making the decision whether this was a ring he wanted to step into. He had no choice, though. Whether or not he wanted to participate, the fight had already chosen him. Mitch wasn't offering monkey dance posturing and hollow promises of conditional violence to come—he promised a present brawl with pain and consequences. Violence was here. The man backed away, trying to look nonchalant instead of cowed. "That true, Byron? Do I need to worry about you?" The man didn't reply. He kept his eyes focused over Mitch's shoulder instead of returning his gaze. He wanted to escalate the fight with the girl, not Mitch. That made him a punk. And that meant *he* was the one Mitch had to keep the closest eye on if he didn't want to be blindsided.

He turned toward Kristin, careful to keep Byron in his peripheral vision. "That guy, Roper, called it the 'New Life Church,' but this isn't like any church I've seen. What is this place?"

"It's a religious retreat," Byron said. "Pastor Roper hosts spiritual getaways here where we study and pray and learn to be our best selves."

"All that's missing is the Kool Aid," Kristin said.

Nick pushed up, trying to straighten his spine without ejecting his wife from his lap. She protested and he caressed her hair. "Kristin's right," he said. "It's not a church; it's a compound, and this is a doomsday cult. It might be wrapped around the semiotics of a kinder religion, but it's no different than the Branch Davidians or the Church of Starry Wisdom." Mitch didn't understand everything Nick said, but he heard "cult" clear as day.

While Mitch and Kristin showed signs of coercion, no one else did. He didn't imagine all of them had been abducted at gunpoint. "So how'd you all end up here if you're not true believers?"

Nick fought back tears, his eyes glistening. He looked like he'd reached the limit of his ability to stay strong for the woman lying on his lap, and might break any minute. Still, he held it together and said with a clear voice, "Our neighbor is one of them. Her daughter... came back too. We were taking care of Jack and her... and then Abby convinced us to bring them both here. She said that Pastor Roper had... 'a special insight' into the kids and wanted to help. As soon as we saw what was going on, we knew that 'insight' was more bullshit. We tried to leave with the kids, but they stopped us and locked us up in here."

"My ex-husband brought me here," Kristin said. "He *forced* me to come here."

"I came with my husband," Amye said. "He said it would save our marriage. I mean, we started coming here before, you know, *they* came back. I thought this place was good for us. He was depressed and drinking a lot after Brendan died, and I was all alone. We started listening to Pastor Roper's sermons and coming here and he stopped drinking and spent more time at home. I had people who'd listen to me. But then Brendan came back and they changed. Everything's changed."

"That's true," Steve said. "We had friends who said he could help, but when Pastor Roper started preaching about stuff like demons and exorcisms and whatnot, we got scared."

The air felt like it was getting thicker. It was starting to remind Mitch more and more of the counseling circle. He was out of the trunk, his head was clearing, but he still wasn't free. Eventually the conversation would circle around to him so that he could confess his wrong doing and why he was there. But he wasn't going to confess. No amount of mea culpas and making moral inventories was going to get them out of that room. He had nothing to atone for, and neither did anyone else who was doing the best they could for their children.

"That's all... I appreciate you sharing. But I'm getting the fuck out of here. Anyone who wants to come with me should get ready to go."

"The kitchen's locked up. We tried it. And the windows don't open either," Kristin said. "What makes you think you can find a way out when the rest of us haven't come up with anything in a day and a half?"

Mitch pointed toward the way he came in. "There's the door right there. I'm walking through it."

"Leaving isn't as easy as arriving. It's locked, with an armed guard on the other side," Nick said.

"I'm aware." Mitch walked over to a tapestry hanging on the wall and tore it down. At the top, a rigid wooden dowel squared the fabric on which had been printed an image of a blond, faceless Crusader on horseback. At the bottom of the flag it read, *Behold a white horse; and he that sat upon him was called Faithful and True, and in righteousness he doth JUDGE and make WAR.* Next to it hung another, depicting a more troubling image with the scripture, *And he was clothed with a vesture dipped in blood: and his name is called The Word of God.* It unsettled Mitch to think of the focus all around the room paid to judgment and violent death instead of redemption and life. He doubted he'd find a tapestry here telling anyone to turn the other cheek or love thy enemy. They all depicted warlike angels and saviors. All of them with faces as smooth and featureless as mannequins. He shoved the dowel through the end of the tapestry, dropping the cloth on the floor. Without the flag attached, it felt light in his hand, but it was still almost three feet of inch thick pine dowel. As a truncheon, it wasn't cracking any skulls, but he reckoned it wouldn't feel good across the bridge of someone's nose. Thus, it was better than nothing. There were maybe a half-dozen tapestry flags including the one he'd just defiled. Enough for everyone who wanted one. He swung the improvised baton and said, "He's armed, and now so am I. Just because he's got a pistol and a ninja costume, doesn't make him god damn Franco Nero."

"Who?" Amye said.

"Never mind." A glint off of something at the far end of the room caught his eye. He walked over to get a closer look. He handed Kristin his stick and climbed up onto the small stage.

"What are you doing?" she asked as she watched him drag the piano out of the way so he could reach the crucifix hanging above it. It was sturdy looking wood, maple maybe, or oak, with a heavy, metal Christ on the front. He stuck his fingers into the slender gap behind it and tried to pry. It was screwed into the drywall and barely moved. But it moved. Digging his fingers into the slight space between it and the wall hurt his fingers, but he kept on until it started to give. When he had a decent enough gap, he took off his belt and slipped it behind the upright beam of the cross. He slid the strap down until it was closest to the bottom where he had the least resistance and the most leverage. He threaded the end through the buckle and cinched it. Looping the other end around his fist, he braced a foot against the wall and pulled. After a couple of tries, the drywall gave way with a soft cracking sound. The thing whipped at him. He ducked and swung the heavy ornament around and back toward the wall where it collided and left a big triangular dent before clattering to the stage floor. Mitch picked the thing up. It was shorter than the dowel, but much heavier, with points and sharp edges. He reckoned it could leave a dent in a man's skull shaped just like the one it punctured in the wall. Or worse. He smiled. That was just fine with him. He was done being sucker punched.

Stepping out from behind the upright piano he'd shoved out of the way to get to his new weapon, he paused and gave it another small push. He turned and asked Kristin, "Do you think you can push this thing off the stage when I give you a thumbs up?" Her brow furrowed, and then she seemed to gather his plan. She stood, and stepped over to the instrument to take a practice pull at it. It rolled on its wheels smoothly, but was heavy. She'd be better off with help, Mitch realized. "Steve, can you give us a hand?"

Steve came over to the stage. "What's your idea?"

"I want to get someone's attention." Mitch said. "When I give you the thumbs up, I was hoping you and Kristin could send that thing over the edge. Think you can make it happen?"

"Damn right we can!" Kristin said.

Mitch lightly pounded a fist on Steve's shoulder and gave Kristin a nod. "When it goes down, you two get down. Preferably behind something that can stop bullets."

"Where are you going to be?" Kristin asked.

"In harm's way." Mitch stepped off the stage and walked into the middle of the room. He glanced at the door, quietly thankful there was no window in it. In order to check up on them, the guard would have to come in. He took a couple of deep breaths to work himself up enough to address the rest of the people in the room. While violence came easy to him, leadership did not. But, if he was going to start shit, he felt like the others should at least know about it so they could choose to either get in on the action or out of the line of fire. "In a few minutes," he began, "I'm going to get that door open. And then I'm leaving through it. The rest of you are welcome to follow me. In fact, I'd like a couple of people backing me up. Your choice."

"They have guns. You're going to get everyone killed." Byron said.

"I'm starting to think that's already on the agenda. Old time religion style: join or die. Why else would we be locked away in here?"

Alexa lifted her head off of Nick's thighs and said, "I'll help. We both will." Nick looked apprehensive, but nodded in agreement.

Izzy stood and put her hand in. "Me too."

Mitch went around the room, yanked down the rest of the tapestries and liberated the dowels inside. He handed one to each of them and took one back to Steve. Kristin held hers up proudly, as if she couldn't wait to break it on someone's head. Alexa swung hers awkwardly like a flag. Mitch walked over and showed her how to angle it. She was small, there wasn't much muscle in her, but he knew heart when he saw it. "Swing it at his mouth. If you miss and hit his nose or throat instead, it's still all a win. But the mouth is your best bet. Get him thinking about his teeth. You follow?" She nodded, eyes wide with apprehension at the idea of bashing a person in the face. But she didn't let go of the stick or step away. *She's in*, Mitch thought. Heart counted every bit as much in a fight as strength. Maybe more.

Mitch took the last dowel to Amye and held it out. She shook her head. Unlike Alexa, violence, no matter how reluctant, didn't appear to be in her. Mitch put a hand on her arm and squeezed lightly. "It's all right. Stay back and keep up, okay?" She nodded quickly, afraid, but still standing.

Against his better judgment, Mitch offered the last stick to Byron. "You want in?"

"I'm *not* getting shot for you," he said, ignoring the fact that Mitch wasn't asking anyone to take a risk for him alone. Everyone was welcome to walk out of the Parents' Ministry if they wanted.

"Fine. Stay in the corner. If you get in my fuckin' way, I'll burn you down."

He set down his dowel and cross by Izzy, asking her to keep an eye on them, and dragged a chair over to the door. Climbing up, he inspected the hydraulic return arm at the top. "Anyone got a dime?" Nick dug in his pockets and handed him one. After a few minutes of work at the arm, he dropped a small bolt in his pocket and handed the dime back to Nick. "Thanks."

Climbing down, he picked up the crucifix, feeling its heft and balance. It felt good and deadly. This was as premeditated as the DA had claimed Junior's beating was. If only that lawyer knew what it felt like to stand in *this* place. That elected asshole calling that assault cold and calculated was like a priest giving a sermon on having a healthy sex life.

Mitch kicked the last stick into the far corner of the cafeteria and took his place behind the door. He took a deep breath and found his center of calmness. The place where he would go right before the bell rang—right before diving into someone's cell to take back what they stole out of his.

The place where violence lived in him was quiet.

35

Asphalt gave way first to gravel and then a rutted dirt road that pulled at the wheels as if trying to dissuade Mike and Liana from continuing forward. Mike slowed as they approached the next turnoff. Painted in large white letters on a bold, blue sign above a pair of hands clasped in prayer it read:

NEW LIFE CHURCH
A RELIGIOUS RETREAT AND COMMUNITY

Below that, in smaller text, contradicting the typical church sign message of "All are welcome," was the warning

PRIVATE PROPERTY
NO TRESPASSING

"Are you sure this is it?" Mike asked.

Liana squirmed in her seat, drawing in a deep breath with a hand on her chest, and nodded. "She's that way." Pointing past the sign, she said, "I can feel her."

"So what now? It doesn't look like they like visitors."

"It's just a sign. Keep going."

Mike let out the clutch and drove on. As they rounded the next curve in the road, they came upon an electric lifting gate beside a small security building that looked like it should've been at the end of a Hollywood star's mansion driveway, and not a church in the middle of rural New England. Mike stepped hard on the brakes as a pair of black-clad men wearing rifles stepped out of the gatehouse. He turned to Liana with a fearful look and quietly implored her to let him turn back.

"She's in there."

He gritted his teeth and pulled forward slowly until one of the guards raised a hand for him to stop. Liana stared out the window at the two men approaching the car. They carried their guns in a ready position the way soldiers in the movies did, up high with an elbow out, barrel pointed toward the ground. One bent over and leaned into Mike's window to ask where they thought they were going. Mike's mouth gaped open for an insufferably long second while he seemed to search for the lie that would open wide the gates.

"Um, hi," he said, forcing a smile. The man did not smile back. "We're not sure where we are. A friend of ours invited us up for a couples' getaway, but we're pretty lost." He held up his cell phone and the gunman took a step back raising his rifle slightly. Mike tried not to flinch. "I can't get a signal, and I have no idea what else to do. Do you have a phone we could borrow?"

"You two are a *couple*?"

"Don't we look like it?" Mike said. He tried to mask his fear with a nervous laugh. Liana gasped, taking another deliberate deep breath she didn't actually need.

"What's wrong with her?"

Mike said, "Asthma. She's got bad asthma and we forgot her inhaler. I'm running low on gas and like I said, my reception way out here is non-existent. Could you just let us in to use the phone? We won't be long, I promise."

The guard's eyes narrowed. "We got no phone in the guard house. Just these." He nodded his chin toward a black and yellow two-way radio clipped to one of the MOLLE straps on his vest. "You two head back that way," he said pointing away from their car. "Follow the road about twenty miles and you'll end up in Keene. They got cell towers *and* gas there. We got neither." He stepped back from the car, hands still on the rifle. Although he kept his finger outside the trigger guard, Liana felt certain he was itching to slip it in. She'd seen that look before. If she couldn't exactly read his mind, it wasn't hard to discern his thoughts. They were hot and unpleasant. On top of that, the feeling of breathlessness and confinement was growing steadily worse. She wanted to spring out of the car and run into the open to get a deep breath, but, the way they looked, she was pretty certain these two were already itching for a reason to switch their safeties off. She stayed put. The gate guards backed away and the one who'd told them to turn around jerked his chin at them, encouraging the couple to take his suggestion and head to Keene.

Mike looked at her, gesturing with his hands on the wheel to say "What now?" She nodded behind them. He put the car in reverse and started to back up the road, breathing a deep sigh of relief. When they moved away, however, her breathing seemed more labored and desperate. "Thanks anyway, fellas," he called out the window. He regretted it immediately.

She saw the gateman whispering at each other as Mike backed the car down the road, and the one who'd given them directions spoke into his radio. Liana couldn't hear what he said, but he wasn't taking his eyes off the car. It felt like being in some classic spy film, getting stopped at the border checkpoint between the U.S.S.R. and Poland while the lonely outpost soldiers checked to see if their papers were legitimate. But she wasn't a Bond girl; she was a supermarket checker who sometimes liked to get in the pit at concerts. She wasn't afraid of a fair fight, but her elite combat training was limited to listening to people bitch about the price of quinoa and not tripping over her own boots in the circle pit. And she sure as hell was afraid of men with guns. She felt for the reassurance of the never-used baseball bat she kept in the backseat foot well. A purchase inspired by her ax handle beating. Right next to it was a catcher's mitt, in case anyone ever had reason to ask why she had a bat in the car. As if anyone would ever think she was sporty.

"What now?" Mike asked. He stopped at the end of the drive, waiting for Liana to tell him which way to go before backing out onto the highway.

She pointed the opposite direction the man with the gun had directed them. "That way. Go maybe a half-mile and find a place to pull over. We have to walk the rest of the way."

"Walk? Where?"

She widened her eyes, looking at the sign ahead of them for the *New Life Church*.

"Did you *see* the guys with the guns?"

She sighed. "Uh huh. I did." She turned in her seat to face him. "You don't have to come with me. You can wait with the car; I'll go by myself. That way, when I come out with Sophie and Mitch, you and Octavia can be ready to get us out of here, tout suite."

"You named your car 'Octavia'?"

Huffing a wheezing laugh, she patted the dashboard affectionately. She loved her car, and whenever she had extra money, she made sure to take it to a mechanic friend to be tuned up and serviced. Still, it was old, and she hadn't had extra cash in a while. Octavia was past due for his attention, and while it was reliable for city driving, she had no idea how hard or for how long they could push the engine before something broke. That she could rely on Mike was an immutable certainty; relying on Octavia was another matter.

"Let's go," she said. Mike pulled out onto the highway and did as she suggested. He drove until he found a space on the shoulder big enough to park the car completely off the road. He made a U-turn and nestled Octavia into a patch of wild grass next to the tree line.

"How are you going to keep from getting lost in there?"

Liana stared out the window into the woods. She was as outdoorsy as she was sporty. That a pair of Dr. Martens might be suitable for hiking was only accidental fitness for the occasion. At home, she oriented herself to tall buildings and main roads, and her friends joked that she could get lost in Public Garden. But, looking into the thick trees and underbrush, she knew the way. "I guess the same thing that got us this far will get me through there."

"And once you're through?"

She shook her head. "I have no fuckin' idea." She opened the door and pulled the black "Brooklyn Crusher" bat from behind her seat. It didn't resemble anything anyone would actually take to a game, but it suited her aesthetic better than a Louisville Slugger, and was more deniably a weapon than the telescoping police baton she used to carry. She left the glove on the floor and dropped the seat back into place. Mike shut off the engine and climbed out of the car behind her. "You sure you don't want to wait here," she said. "You've already done way more than—"

He held up a hand to stop her. "You're not the boss of me," he said. The tremor in his voice belied the joke, but he didn't back down. Mike was stand up all the way.

Liana stepped away from the car to take a couple of practice swings, almost throwing the bat away on the first one. She tightened her grip and tried again. However devastating the polypropylene bat was advertised to be, it felt ridiculous to contemplate bringing such a thing to what was most likely going to be a gun fight if it was any kind of fight at all. Then again, having a club, knife, or even just a big rock seemed better than showing up empty-handed — which Mike still was. She leaned back in the car and opened her purse, feeling around until her hand closed on a "tactical" pen. Constructed from non-reflective hardened aircraft aluminum, it included a sharpened, scalloped edge euphemistically described on the original packaging as a "DNA catcher." That feature was designed to dig out a chunk of flesh and make a person bleed as you jammed it into their throat or face. The pen was a ridiculous thing she bought as a joke. "Weaponize your life!" she told friends when using it to sign a bar tab. But then, so far, she'd never been denied entry to a club with *it* in her purse. As often as she ran into guys at shows who asked the question "What are *you* doing here?" with more than a little racial animus in their voices, she felt better with it in her purse. Though she'd never actually used it — she was better at avoiding shit than finishing it — it was better than nothing. She held it out for him to take; he looked at the pen like she was trying to hand him a snake.

"What the hell is that?"

"It's mightier than the sword, as they say." She showed him the scalloped edge. "You can jam this end into a dude's eye or temple or something. The writing side will hurt real bad too." He took it and timidly practiced thrusting it into someone's face. "Yeah. Just like that." She winked and started off into the woods.

Everything she stepped on in the overgrown forest floor seemed to crackle or crunch no matter how much care she took to be quiet. Behind her, she heard Mike stumble and curse under his breath. The two of them were very possibly the worst trackers in the history of the woods. More than once, she imagined the sound of a hidden twig snapping was that of the rifle shot that was going to end her or Mike before they even caught sight of the New Life Church. But the shot never came, and the farther they hiked through the woods, the more strongly she felt the pull, almost like Sophie knew she was near and was drawing her on harder. Breathing still wasn't getting any easier.

They slowed as they crested a steep incline. It gave way on the other side to a clearing and, beyond that, a complex of buildings arranged in a diamond. As they scuttered down the hillock, the glass and steel dome of the central building rose up like a blue halo around a statue looming over them. It was a caped, crowned, and faceless figure holding a massive sword aloft that looked more like a wraith from a fantasy novel than the gentle savior she remembered her Gran praying to. Though eyeless, it seemed to glare at them with hot malevolence as if about to come to life and strike them down. She remembered some of the parishioners in her Gran's church talking about the avenging savior who'd someday return to cleanse the Earth of the wicked. *Is that us? Are* we *the wicked?* Her blood ran cold.

Despite the desire to turn back and flee up the hill, she stood her ground, feeling for the pull in her heart to tell her where to go. As badly as she wanted to follow her instincts, she followed Sophie's call.

36

Kristin and Steve wheeled the piano up to the apron edge of the small stage and waited for Mitch to give them a thumbs up. He positioned himself by the door, and raised his eyebrows to ask if they were ready. They nodded, and he raised his hand, thumb extended. Rearing back, they gave the instrument a violent shove toward the edge. It banged loudly as the front wheels cleared the apron and the piano pedals jammed into the lip of the stage. Then it toppled forward, seeming to hang in the air for a quantum eternity before crashing to the floor below. The sound was a musical explosion. An echoing wooden crash accompanied by a couple hundred strings all vibrating with sour notes at once. The piano lid swung open and clapped closed and small fragments of the thing went scattering across the floor with their own random percussion. The disharmony filled the tile-floored room, bouncing off the shutters at the opposite end, surrounding them in a medley of tatters, broken strings ringing, snapping wood and faux ivory clattering on the floor. It all echoed in the room like the Devil's concerto.

Through the door, Mitch heard the faint reply: "What the hell?" The sound of a key scraping in the lock followed it almost immediately, as he'd hoped. The guard pushed the door expecting resistance from the hydraulic arm above. With the crucial pin removed, there was none, and the door swung open violently. He practically fell into the room, propelled by his expectations and excitement. He entered as Mitch had expected he would, leading with a drawn gun. "What on God's green

Earth is going—" he shouted, losing his train of thought as he stumbled a step farther inside than he intended. Mitch swung the crucifix at his weapon hand. The feeling of the man's forearm snapping resonated up the cross, providing an instant sense memory of other bones that had broken under his hands. The sound of the gunshot in the room refocused Mitch and he swung with the back of the cross, driving it flat into the man's face like a tennis racket. Overweight, over forty, and caught full in the face with a piece of oak, the guard crumpled to the floor. His pistol clattered across the room. Mitch watched it slide right up to Byron's feet, as if he'd pulled it toward him telekinetically. The man bent over and picked it up. Mitch waited to see what he would do with it. He was too far away from Byron to close the distance fast enough to take it. He had to hope Byron wouldn't turn it on them.

He had no such luck.

"Am I in your way now, asshole?"

The sound of Amye's stick snapping against the back of his skull echoed in the room like a lightning crack. He staggered forward a step before swinging around with the gun. Amye shrieked and collapsed in a ball as he tried to draw a bead on her. Mitch skipped across the room like he was coming out of his corner after the bell and delivered a hook into Byron's neck just below his ear. The man fell, stiff legged and slack faced. His head made a sound on the floor like someone dropped a coconut. Mitch grabbed the pistol out of his hand and tossed it away behind him. He folded Byron's arms and rolled him over onto his side so he wouldn't choke on his tongue or vomit. He put his hands on Amye's shoulders. "Are you okay?" She looked at him with wide frightened eyes and nodded mutely. "Thank you," he said, helping her up off the floor.

He turned and said, "Is everyone okay?" The others nodded and mumbled their state of good health. Looking around, he searched for the gun he'd tossed aside, finding it untouched on the floor near Nick and Alexa's feet. He walked over and picked it up. He didn't know guns. Their makes and models were as foreign to him as high performance cars. Hell, any car! All he knew was that one went fast and the other shot bullets. The feeling of it was comforting, though. Its weight was potent. He imagined it kicking in his hand, sensing the power of sending something faster than the eye could follow into someone else to tear and break flesh and bone. His ears were still ringing from the guard firing it into the floor. Though he couldn't see smoke, the smell of spent gunpowder in the room lingered, lightly tincturing the air with sulfur. There was nothing this thing couldn't ruin. He held it out to Steve, who cocked his head as if to say, "Who, me?" Mitch nodded. Steve took the gun, thumbed on the safety, and held it at an angle away from his own body and everyone else, pointed at the floor. Mitch instantly felt good about the decision to give it to him. He didn't want that kind of power.

The two of them dragged the guard the rest of the way into the room next to Byron and Mitch searched him for another gun, finding a small pistol in an ankle holster. The guard was snoring loudly, but Mitch didn't feel bad for crushing his nose. The old fart had been ready to shoot him; he was lucky to get out of it only needing a CPAP mask.

"Time to go," he said. The parents filed past him toward the door. As Izzy walked by, he handed her the throwaway piece. He figured if Steve knew what he was doing, maybe she did too. She didn't disappoint. "Where did you guys learn to handle guns like that?"

"I'm a New Hampshire woman," she said, without elaborating.

"Live free or die," Steve echoed.

"I'm all for the first part! The rest I'd rather put off as long as possible."

"Where did *you* learn to move like that?" Izzy asked.

"I used to box."

"That part with the cross didn't look like any pay-per-view I ever ordered," Steven said.

Mitch glanced at the others. Amye had a starry-eyed look of admiration he was certain would die as soon as he told them the truth. He couldn't help thinking of reading Yeats in his cell. This was the moment where the center either held, or the ceremony of innocence was drowned. If he told them, would it change anything? He hoped not; these people were all he had at the moment. "I might've learned a thing or two in prison."

Amye gasped and took an involuntary step away. The others stood their ground.

"What did you do?" Steve asked. His question wasn't loaded with threat, but Mitch had seen people's attitudes toward him pivot drastically when he'd been honest about his past. The new spark of fear in Amye's eyes gave him pause.

"I... hurt someone I thought was threatening my family. I almost killed him, but I got lucky and he lived." *Lucky.* The word felt wrong on his tongue, as if the sound itself objected to its utterance in that context. Mitch wondered whether everyone would have been better off if he *had* killed Junior. He'd have gotten a longer sentence, and maybe Violette wouldn't have had someone to dump Sophie on when she wanted to go on the road. She would've had to stay home and raise her daughter instead. But, that's where the alternate timeline broke down in his imagination. Eventually, he realized, she would've wanted to go have fun with her friends. He imagined her leaving Sophie with Meghan, coming home late to find Faye in her living room, demanding money with bourbon-stinking breath and swaying on her feet. He saw Sophie lying in her crib, dying in the next room just as it had actually happened. That he couldn't even imagine a better world than the one he lived in nearly broke him. He took a long shuddering breath. Everything he'd resented about Violette leaving—the sudden unwanted responsibility, the stress, the loss of his independence—he missed all of it when Sophie died. That she'd been taken from him again was unbearable. He'd do anything to get her back, and that frightened him even more. He couldn't do *anything*. He had to do the right things, or he'd fuck up both their lives all over again.

Alexa put a hand on his arm. "Are you okay?"

"I guess so," he told her. Suggesting he was in any kind of way all right wasn't honest, though. He felt as far from okay as he felt from Sophie. "I did my time, and I've worked real hard to learn how to manage my... violent impulses. Sometimes, it all feels like it was for nothing, though." He trailed off, fearing he'd lost them. All the allies he'd earned would see him for who he was and abandon him, as they should if they had any sense.

"I'm glad you still have work to do," she said, squeezing his arm. "Don't give up now. We need you. Your girl needs you."

The others drew near and reached out for him, grabbing ahold of his hands, his shoulders, pressing their palms against his back, over his heart. They touched him and told him to stay strong. Izzy said, "Keep your gloves up. Keep fighting."

He looked in the faces of the people around him, and, for a moment, felt a glimmer of hope. They were afraid, but not of him. Still, they couldn't draw around a campfire and sing "Kumbaya" just yet. "It's getting late. We've got to get moving," he said. He gestured toward the door hoping no one noticed how badly his extended hand shook. They let go of him and started to file out of the room. Mitch stood waiting with his hand on the key the guard had left hanging in the door, waiting to twist it as soon as they were all clear. Byron groaned and coughed and sat up, rubbing his neck like he was coping with a bad hangover. Mitch found himself hoping it felt at least that bad. He pushed down his resentment; Byron wasn't his problem any longer. There was no reason to hold that grudge. Not after the deadbolt was thrown. He started to pull the door shut.

"Wait!" Byron shouted. "You can't leave me here."

Mitch sighed and hesitated a moment. "You had your chance. If we find your boy... we'll try to get him somewhere safe. What's his name?" Byron's eyes narrowed. His look communicated everything Mitch needed to know about reconsidering his decision to leave the man behind. He began to pull the door closed.

"They're coming, you know. Church starts at dusk. I'll be out of here in *minutes*, and I'll tell them where you're going. You think you've escaped? All you've done is brought the Lord's wrath down on all your heads. I'll be standing by his right side when—"

As badly as he wanted to go back in and put Byron down for another nap, he closed the door on the man's vitriol and twisted the key in the lock. He tested the door to make sure it was secure, and turned to go. Ahead of him on the stairs, the others from the Parents' Ministry stood waiting. As if he had a plan.

• • •

He leaned against the long bar and the door popped open without setting off any alarms—at least none Mitch could hear. He opened the door wide enough to poke his head through. When the weekend warriors had brought him to the Parents' Ministry he'd been disoriented and seeing through blurry eyes. Now, trying to make his best guess where Sophie would be, he couldn't tell the difference between any of the buildings except for the chapel at the center. The campus seemed peaceful, almost tranquil. Nothing stood out as an obvious choice.

He ducked back inside. "It looks pretty clear out there, but I don't know where to go."

Amye pointed at a clock on the wall above them and said, "It's almost time for the late service. On a night like tonight, everybody will be at the Grace Amphitheater."

"Is that what it sounds like? Big outdoor thing?"

Amye nodded. "The outdoor sermons are the big ones that end a retreat. There's always lights and music and stuff in the normal chapel, but this one is more, like, I don't know. Tribal, I guess. There's bonfires and stuff."

"Where's that?" he asked. Amye pointed over his shoulder. He understood what direction she meant, but without being able to see through walls, it didn't mean much to him. "How about our kids? Do you know where they are?" She shook her head. "That guy, Roper, mentioned something called the 'safe room,'" he said.

"My husband and me have been in pretty much every building in the retreat, but I've never heard of a safe room."

"Anyone else?" They all shook their heads. Mitch rubbed at his temples. He didn't want to go downstairs to get Byron. The guy wasn't about to help them, and even if they tried to force him to cooperate, they had no assurance he wouldn't lead them right into the lion's jaws. No. He was no help. They had to do this themselves.

Nick stepped forward. He tried to talk, but his words were strangled. He cleared his throat and tried again. "We tried to leave yesterday because Alexa overheard someone talking about... what was it, dear?"

She had been nearly catatonic locked inside the room, but on the other side of the locked door, she appeared to be coming back to life. "The Children's Crusade. They said that Pastor Roper was going to 'lead the children to salvation,' whatever that means. I didn't like the way they said it, like it was some kind of euphemism for something else. And, you know, the actual Children's Crusade ended up with all the children either dead or enslaved."

"That story is apocryphal," Nick said. "The 'children' were likely impoverished adults, and not actually children."

"Do you think it matters to them whether traditional and modern accounts are reconcilable with historiography?" Mitch hadn't asked Nick and Alexa what they did for a living, but he was getting the impression these two were teachers or historians or something. Their banter was cute, but there was no time for it.

"I don't get it," he said. "You think they're taking the kids where?" Nick shrugged again. Mitch was getting the idea that if he spent enough time with the man he might be able to detect differences in the gesture that would reveal some kind of shoulder hunching sign language.

Alexa said, "If it's a public spectacle, my guess is they'll all end up at the amphitheater, if they aren't there already."

"I guess it's worth a look."

Amye objected. "I don't think we should go. What if they find us? They have guns. We should get away and call the police."

Mitch understood where she was coming from. The thought of the police coming made him imagine a Waco-style standoff. The image wasn't entirely objectionable, at least not in part. The part where the whole damn compound went up in flames while Mitch and the others watched from a safe distance with their kids. "I'm all for calling the cops. Afterwards. But I'm not stepping foot outside this compound without Sophie."

"Us either," Izzy said. "We're not leaving Michelle here for another motherfucking minute." Steve stood behind his wife and put a hand on her shoulder. He didn't have to say anything.

"Amye," Mitch began, "No one is going to force you to do anything. If you want to go try to bring the police back, I'm not stopping you. If we find the kids, we'll take Brendan with us." Amye's eyes welled up at the mention of her son. Looking at her body language, it was clear enough that she wanted to run as fast as she could away from Pastor Roper and his congregation of apocalyptic nuts. She was forcing herself to stand there with them. Even if she was terrified, she had heart.

"I'll help you."

Mitch hugged her. It was awkward, but she hugged him back tightly and breathed a long shuddering sigh into his chest. He said, "Thank you. You know this place best. We need you."

"I'll try not to let you down."

Mitch let go. "It's time to move."

37

The sun was setting behind the chapel. Orange light colored the wispy clouds and reflected through the glass and steel dome crowning the building, making it glow like a jeweled censer. The entire compound was beautiful, elegant. Mitch felt a surge of frustration at its opulence. He'd spent the last year managing food stamps, rent vouchers, and heating assistance, all while working to pay for day care, eking out just enough to occasionally buy a pizza, Sophie a pair of shoes and a coat from a consignment store, or a toy for her birthday. He had to *save up* to go out on a date, and here he stood in front of a building that looked like it cost more than he'd see in a hundred lifetimes. *Hidden* in the woods, in the middle of nowhere. What could have been bought with the millions it took to build a small village around a chapel that resembled a crystalline Vatican? How much of that money had been funneled away from the people who gathered inside who could have used it to pay for heat in the winter or food all year 'round? It made him angry and unfocused. He tried to concentrate on the task ahead. Money didn't matter. All that mattered was moving forward. Finding Sophie and the other kids.

He crept toward the edge of the building and peered around. He couldn't see anyone. The place seemed deserted. In the distance, he heard a swell of music and an amplified voice. He couldn't tell what the speaker was saying, but he could tell from the response of the crowd, it was something they understood clearly and appreciated. "Church starts at dusk," the gatekeeper had said. No one had returned for them yet, but he took the guards at their word when they said they'd be back. The Parents' Ministry prisoners had to move, even if it meant exposing themselves. He looked back one last time to make sure everyone was accounted for before signaling them out into the open. The others were all hunched over, trying to hide in a shadow that didn't exist. He realized what they looked like: people escaping.

He forced himself to stand up straight. "Everybody, get up," he said. "Stand up straight."

Nick, immediately behind him, replied, "Excuse me?"

"Have you ever wandered into a neighborhood you shouldn't have?" Nick nodded his head. "Then you know if you walk around looking lost or confused, you stand out more than if you look like you belong, even when you don't. We need to stand up and look like we know where we're going."

Nick's brow furrowed, but he got it. He straightened his back and encouraged Alexa to do the same. Amye still hunched over a little, but she eventually relaxed. Steve and Izzy stood up. At his full height, Steve towered maybe a foot and a half higher than his wife. Mitch hadn't noticed before. He seemed to be always hunching near her, trying to be closer.

"Better," Mitch said.

"So where are we going?" Nick asked.

Mitch pointed toward a building catty-corner across the quad from them. Another man in black with a pistol on his hip stood in front of it. "There," he said.

"But there's a guy there."

"Yeah, there is. Looks like he's guarding something, right? Maybe the kids. Anyone know what that building is?" Blank faces stared back at him. "Amye, you said you and your husband have been up here a lot. Any help?" She hunched her shoulders.

Mitch held up a finger telling the others to wait, and stepped out onto the sidewalk, headed away from the guard. He moved as quietly and carefully as he could without looking like he was doing something shifty. He circled around to the side of the other building and reversed direction, slowly walking along the length of it until he was close to the guard. He paused. As soon as he emerged from the shrubs beside the wall, the guy would spot him, and with his bloodied face, he wasn't passing for a New Life parishioner, no matter how straight his spine.

"Excuse me, can you—"

The guard fumbled the phone in his hand, spinning around with red-faced surprise. His eyes widened at the sudden appearance of the blood-smeared man lurching toward him. He tried to reach for the pistol, but Mitch clocked him hard, straight on the chin. The man crumpled without uttering a sound. Only the serial popping of the vertebrae in his neck and the sound of his body hitting the concrete walk like a soft bag of meat accompanied his fall. Mitch began rifling through the guard's pockets. Aside from a wallet and the gun on his hip, he wasn't carrying anything else. Mitch found the phone the guy dropped and silently thanked the girl who'd sent a picture of her pleasingly shaped bare ass and the message, "When can I see u again?" He silenced the device and stuffed it in his pocket. Looking more out of curiosity than a belief he would find anything of help, he opened the wallet, certain the big-ass girl behind the text message would not be in any of the family photos inside. He found a little money and credit cards, AAA and NRA membership cards, and a picture of a pair of gap-toothed kids, but not their mother. Behind the photo, he discovered the scrap of folded paper. On it was scribbled a four-digit number: 9221. Resisting the urge to take the cash, he folded the wallet closed and put it back in the guard's pocket. He waved the others over. They trotted over, looking exactly like a group of people up to something and trying not to look like it.

Slipping the pistol out of the unconscious man's holster, he handed the gun to the person nearest him. "I'm not allowed to have one of these things," he said.

Alexa reflexively accepted it with a trembling hand. Staring at the gun, her expression read like she was contemplating the kind of gift a cat would give, something dead. She said, "I think we'd give you a pass tonight," and held it out for him to take back.

"Thanks anyway." He nodded at Nick. "Give it to him if you don't want it." She handed the gun to her husband who handled it like an ancient mystery carved out of a piece of Aztec jade, trying to figure out which end was the top. Mitch gently pushed the barrel toward the ground and returned to the door. He punched the numbers from the slip of paper into the keypad and waited for the red light to change to green. It didn't. Mitch's resolve faltered. Maybe they *should* just make a run for it and call the police.

Nick said, "No luck?"

No. None in the world. He double checked the number on the scrap of paper to make sure he hadn't misread it. He tried again, but the red beacon remained constant. *Maybe it's his debit card PIN and not a door code.*

"What's that mean?" Izzy asked. She pointed to a line under the numbers that Mitch assumed was merely a flourish. Her finger drew his eye to the barb at the left end of the line. *An arrow?* He reentered the number in reverse: 1229. The red light turned green and a mechanical *chuck* sounded behind it as the electric strike switch released. *Merry Christmas!* He pulled the door open before the lock could defy him and reset, and peered through looking for anyone who might be trouble. He saw no one inside. Not in the lobby anyway.

"Help me get him out of sight."

Nick took hold of the door while Mitch and Steve dragged the softly groaning man in. The others followed and Nick pulled the door shut behind them. Mitch grabbed a lamp off of a low table against the wall and pulled the unconscious guard's hands behind his back. He tied the man's wrists with the electrical cord as best he could, leaving the heavy lamp attached at the end. Alexa opened a door and peeked in. "How about in here?" she said. She stood in front of a suitably large coat closet, gesturing into it like a game show hostess. *Door Number One it is!* Steve helped Mitch stuff the guy inside. He was tempted to jam the guest chair up under the door handle, but decided not to do anything that might draw attention to what he'd done. He felt mostly secure in the knot he'd tied in the lamp cord.

Relieved of his burden, Mitch flexed his hand, trying to dispel the growing soreness in his bones. He was pretty sure he'd broken the guy's jaw, and probably his own second knuckle. His hand was already swelling. Soon, if he didn't get something to knock down the inflammation and the pain, he wouldn't be able to use it at all. There wasn't time to contemplate his future as a sleight of hand magician, though. He turned, trying to fathom the layout of the building and guess where in it they could keep a half-dozen kids captive.

They were standing in a reception area. Instead of the Bible verse banners hung in the Parents' Ministry, pictures of Pastor Roper's book covers adorned these walls. Beside the closet in which they'd stashed the guard was a small private office and a tiny bathroom in the corner. Mitch listened at the door at the back of the reception room. Hearing nothing, he pushed the door open and poked his head inside, half expecting to be bashed in the skull the same way he'd incapacitated their jailer. No blow fell. He stepped the rest of the way through and surveyed the room. Inside was a warehouse of self-help and inspirational books, CDs, and DVDs whose covers adorned the front office. An angry urge to tip the shelves and watch them topple over like dominoes boiled up in Mitch's belly. They were wasting time and he'd led them into the wrong building. Made another bad choice. The children weren't here, and he had no better idea where they might be, other than that there were now *two* buildings out of the eight he'd counted where they definitely weren't. They couldn't keep blindly guessing and expect to remain unnoticed and unchallenged.

Mitch stalked out of the room and yanked open the door to the closet. The man inside flinched; a look of contempt flashed across his face. "Where are they?" Mitch demanded. The guard opened his mouth to speak and winced with pain. Mitch had seen fighters with broken jaws before, and knew it had to kill the guy to try to move it. He didn't care. "Where are the kids?" he asked again. "Why are you even guarding this building if they aren't here?"

"Huarding?" The man winced at the word. "I'm nod... huarding nothin'."

"If you weren't standing watch, then what were you doing out front?"

He shook his head. "Shecking my messages."

Mitch held up the phone he'd taken from the man. He woke it and selected the IM thread the man had been reading before he got ambushed. He scrolled up and read the messages above the round ass. Since taking the phone, the girl had sent two more messages asking where he went. But the time stamp on the image message confirmed the guy's story. He'd sneaked away from the service to read some sexy messages from his girlfriend. He was telling the truth; he wasn't guarding shit. Mitch turned the phone toward the guy. "*This* is all you were doing?"

The man blushed and looked away. "Noh fug yourselv."

While Mitch debated whether a less than affectionate pat on the cheek would focus his attention, Nick shouted from the warehouse. "Hey boss! You want to come see this!" Mitch slammed the door on the stranger and rushed to the storeroom. Inside, Alexa pointed through the stacks toward the back. He slipped between the shelves, finding Nicholas standing halfway up a spiral staircase he couldn't see from the entrance. Nicholas waved. "Up here," he said. Mitch followed him up, taking the wedge-shaped steps as fast as he dared. At the top, he felt a little dizzy, and steadied himself on the doorjamb. They stood staring at another keypad lock. Mitch tried the code from the guard's wallet again. Nothing. He tried it in reverse, as it was written and still the red light remained unchanged. Whatever was behind this door rated an entirely different code. Mitch needed to see inside, but the way was closed.

"Stand back," he said. The second the words exited his mouth he regretted uttering them. Mitch was as far from an action hero as a person could get, yet he was speaking in blockbuster clichés. *Stand back! Let me handle this. Let the girl go.* But then, Nicholas didn't seem to take note of the melodramatic absurdity; he stepped out of the way.

Mitch looked over his shoulder at the floor below them. It wasn't a long drop, not deadly by itself, but if he fell on his neck, or bashed his spine on the rail below as he fell... He couldn't be this timid. He didn't have the luxury of playing things safely. He lashed out with his foot. The stomp did nothing but send reverberations of pain up through his leg into his hip. He kicked again without effect. An image of the black tendrils of corruption snaking out of Sophie's finger, rusting and rotting the deadbolt lock on their own front door came to mind. *Where do you lock up kids who can do that? How do you contain that?* If this lock was in place, he knew she wasn't in the room. Still, he felt the need to kick it in. If only because it meant breaking something, and he needed to break something more significant than a single jaw, though he wasn't doing a very good job of it. He sighed and leaned against the rail. Nicholas held up a finger and stepped around to his right. Mitch lined up next to him. He nodded and said, "One, two, three!" The both of them kicked together, and the sound of the door splintering was only slightly louder than their feet banging off the still shut door. Another coordinated kick and the jamb split free, letting the door swing wide and bang into the other side of the wall.

The doorway led into an opulent office appointed in mahogany and glass. There were no Bible verse posters or book covers hanging on these walls. Instead, the space was decorated with original contemporary art. A pair of sculpted marble Russian greyhounds flanked the dark behemoth of a desk at the far end. Above that hung a large portrait of Pastor Roper. Near the door were a leather sofa and coffee table facing a LCD television mounted to the wall. The screen was black and reflected the desk and portrait behind, giving the illusion of another darker dimension to the office, one in which Roper was waiting for them as Mitch and Nicholas invaded his private space. Mitch turned away from it. Given that the spiral staircase appeared to be the only way up, he marveled at the idea that they were able to get any of these things up here. But Pastor Roper was a man of miracles, wasn't he?

Nicholas trotted over to the desk and started searching through the drawers. Mitch's heart sank. Whether or not standing in this room was a symbolic usurpation of Roper's sanctum sanctorum and a defiance of his authority, Sophie wasn't here. She sure as hell wasn't in a desk drawer. "What are you looking for?" he asked, ready to leave.

Nicholas shrugged. "I don't know. I'm hoping I know if I find it, though."

Mitch moved to the windows. It seemed like every light in the place was on, as if a conspicuous consumption of energy was part of the Pastor's outward display of heavenly-deigned prosperity. Roper didn't care about electric bills; he wanted to see. Mitch went to pull the long drapes closed so Nicholas could perform his search with privacy. Outside, he caught a glimpse of movement in the growing shadows. He stumbled around behind the curtains, holding out a hand for Nicholas to get down. He squinted, trying to get a better look at the people stalking across the center courtyard.

"What the fuck?"

He sprinted toward the door. Nicholas called after him, but he was leaping down the spiral staircase and racing toward the front door before the man could finish asking what he'd seen.

Mitch burst out through the front doors, trying to catch the figures before they disappeared again. If he'd seen them at all.

38

Impulses to both run away and stand and fight competed in Liana's mind and muscles when the man burst out of the building to her left. Instead, her body obeyed its third instinct, to freeze. She stood motionless in the courtyard, heart pounding, hand death-gripping the night black bat, hoping she'd have the strength to swing it when the figure reached her. At the moment, though, her arms refused to do anything but stay rigid and still. She looked for the silhouette of a rifle like the thugs at the gate had brandished, but this man's hands were empty. Mike brushed past her, holding his pen out as if it were actually a sword. The man was undeterred by either of their displays, and continued rushing toward them. It wasn't until he called her name that her eyes cleared and his face emerged from the gloom. Her muscles relaxed; the stress of fear left her feeling used up and she fell into his arms.

He spoke with hushed urgency. "Li? What in hell are you doing here? How did you even..."

She kissed him hard on the mouth, swallowing his words and tasting his lips with her tongue. Her vision dimmed with actual breathlessness. She pulled away reluctantly and barraged him with questions. "Why are you here? What is this place? What's going on?"

In the background, an amplified voice boomed throughout the compound, echoing off the buildings surrounding them. The speaker worked the crowd with the kind of cadence she used to hear Sunday mornings—an inflection unique to preachers, politicians, and salesmen. *All conmen*, she thought. A cheer went up. She couldn't hear everything, but clear words floated above the din like ominous storm clouds on the horizon. "THE COMING OF OUR LORD!" A thundering "Amen" followed.

"What is that?" Mike asked. He looked around for a sign that they weren't alone in this section of the courtyard.

"It's the sundown service," Mitch said. "Everyone's there. Almost."

"CAST OUT THESE DEMONS!" A loud jeer.

Mike stared at the archway entrance to the amphitheater and gripped his pen tightly. "Service? It sounds like an exorcism."

Mitch grabbed Liana's hand and turned toward the warehouse. "We need to find Sophie and get the fuck out of here." She resisted, pointing between the chapel and the warehouse toward the cool light of the outdoor amphitheater.

"Sophie's that way," she said.

Her lover cocked his head, fear painting his expression dark. He shook his head. "No. Not there." His voice cracked and Liana heard the tone of defeat that had infected him after his girl died return to his voice, as if the part of him that had come back to life along with her was dying all over again. Whatever was going on beyond the archway was something he knew was too late to stop. The crowd cheered again. From the sound of it, the three of them would pose no threat to whatever it was they were doing.

She pushed closer and extended her hand again so her finger was pointing along *his* eye line. "Not there. *There*." She pointed to the right of the shining blue archway entrance at another building. Beside the arch, a windowless three story block stood, carved with an ornate fresco of swirling patterns surrounding a cross that became a sword at the bottom, stabbing into the earth. It too was illuminated with blue light that made it stand out from the other buildings lit with white and amber spots. The amphitheater arch resembled the gateway to Heaven as she'd imagined it as a child. Like a welcoming clear sky. The building next to it, by contrast, looked like a monolithic block of arctic ice carved out of some frozen expanse where its strange eternal contents waited for the thaw to free it to lay waste. She shivered in the heat.

"How do you know that?" Mitch asked.

"Same way I knew how to get here. I can feel her." She pointed to her chest. "She's in here." She pointed to the distant building. "She's in there."

"SEND THE DEVIL'S SPAWN BACK TO HELL!" A crashing "hallelujah."

Mike interjected. "Maybe we should get moving, huh? Instead of just standing here in the open, you know, waiting to get shot at."

Mitch looked back at the building he'd come rushing out of. Liana's eyes followed, and she saw the people gathered to stare at them from both the doorway and a window in the second story. She yipped with surprise and took a step back, raising her bat. Mitch put a reassuring hand on her arm. "They're... with me, I guess. They're other parents whose kids have been taken. Sophie's not the only one being held captive here."

"Other... kids?" Liana said. A greater tinge of fear filled her. She'd come to terms with the piece of her life force, or whatever it was, that Sophie had taken, but the thought of being around other kids who could do the same thing—other children with no emotional ties to her who could take as much or as little of her as they wanted—was terrifying. Her hand floated up to her hair, as if she could feel the new white strands replacing the dark that remained. She took a step away. Resistance tugged at her heart and gut in response to her backward movement. The pull forward was there no matter how badly she wanted to retreat. The breathlessness and fear of the dark was in her. She could breathe, but a part of her was suffocating. The part of her in Sophie.

Liana chose to step forward despite her rekindled fear.

Mitch squeezed her hand again, and led her toward the others.

From the amphitheater, two more words rang out with perfect clarity. Liana heard the faint echo of them, and a faint ring like a church bell after a thunderclap followed along. "SPIRITUAL WARFARE!" the preacher called out. And the gathered congregation screamed, "IÄ! IÄ!" in reply.

39

They marched along the campus quadrangle, silent and trying to look like they belonged. Their silence put the lie to their belonging, however. Everyone else in the compound was taken with the spirit of Pastor Roper's sermon and met his every call for praise with ready volume. Among them, only the Parents' Ministry was silent. Though most of the parents had been quick to accept Liana and Mike into their band without hesitation, once Mitch vouched for them, Amye seemed reticent. He reckoned that as the one former true-believing member of Roper's congregation among them, she had to struggle against what she had been taught in fireside sermons like the one growing louder as they crept toward it. He sympathized. For years after losing his faith, he still feared the idea of Hell. Childhood warnings of eternal damnation and a wrathful God had seeped into the deepest parts of his mind. While the tree might wither and die, the roots remained, deep in the ground, making it hard to dig and plant anything new in the same soil. Even now, as he heard Roper cry out about demons wearing the skins of children to deceive humanity, he felt a pang of that old fear. This time it was amplified by the response of the crowd. People howling for the blood of a child. His child. Screaming, "OUR GOD IS A CONSUMING FIRE!"

He peered to his left through the archway and saw the backs of several parishioners, hands raised in exaltation of Roper's words. In front of them, a golden flickering light. Like a bonfire. He forced himself to face ahead and continue on.

There was no door in the arctic block on the courtyard side. The front of the building faced away from the center of the compound toward the archway. A floating deck platform extended out from the north side of the thing. To reach the door they had to pass close to the assembly. He whispered over his shoulder at Liana, asking if she was really sure. She said she was. He guided them around. The front of the building was clear glass, three stories up. A pair of doors in the middle opened into a bright lobby, where a central statue similar to the one standing guard near the entrance to the campus stood. On either side of it staircases wound up to the second and third floor landings. The sun had set more, and now it was brighter inside than out. Once they penetrated the ice, there was no more hiding; they'd be lit and on display like curios in a cabinet.

"Shouldn't we look for an entrance in the back?" Nicholas asked. Alexa beside him nodded.

Amye said, "This is the only way in I know."

"What is this place?" Mitch asked.

"It's the theater. He shows movies here. They do plays sometimes."

As she said it, the shape of the building changed in Mitch's eyes. It went from a block of prehistoric ice to a grand luxurious cinema on Hollywood Boulevard. The Deco-style elven archway of the outdoor amphitheater reflected in the great glass façade of the indoor theater, and he saw how tied together they were in both appearance and purpose. This part of the campus, Roper's stages, were the way to salvation—the gates to Paradise. If the outdoor setting was unavailable due to rain or snow, the great glass theater stood in as its second.

The floating deck ahead of them was thigh high, too high to climb with just a casual step up. They'd either have to scramble over the side, or walk around in between the two entrances and ascend the stairs in the center. Walking around front was less conspicuous than scrambling up like a kid climbing a counter to get at the cookie jar. As Mitch led them around he felt naked and exposed. All it would take for them to be seen and stopped was a single parishioner getting bored, or deciding like the warehouse "guard" to sneak off to check his sexts. He reached back and Liana's hand slipped into his, warm and dry. They held on to each other as they climbed the landing. Mitch turned to count heads. Mike, Izzy and Steve, Nicholas and Alexa, Kristin and Amye were all behind him. Behind them, he could see the pulpit stage at the end of the amphitheater. Tall wooden beams rose on either side, mimicking the trees that once occupied the clearing in which the compound had been built. To one side stood a tall cross draped in white, in the middle an altar, and at the end opposite the cross, instead of a baptismal font or a choir riser, there was the flickering light of a fire beyond. The light from the flames glinted and reflected off the clear glass walls of the sanctuary like fireflies. And in the middle of it all stood Pastor Roper, hands raised, crying out into the microphone extending from his ear-piece, his voice booming and echoing. Without a building between them, Mitch heard his every word. The preacher's eyes were closed as he called to the heavens for help banishing the demon from the body of a child. "Already come home Lord to you, but whose remains are an unwitting vessel for Lucifer's evil! The Sun of Righteousness is risen. The Lord, our God, has promised a fire for the wicked, and we shall trample the ashes of the evildoers under our feet!"

"IÄ! IÄ!" the congregation shouted.

"Who then commends this abomination to the fire?"

Roper opened his eyes and seemed to look directly at Mitch. His guts churned as he waited for the preacher to stop calling out to his god, and start calling out to the armed men among them to stop him from invading the theater. Instead, the preacher took a breath, measured for dramatic effect, and continued on. *Spotlights,* Mitch realized. *He's standing in spotlights and can't see past the first row.*

He rushed to the door and punched in the code. 1229. The red light turned green. Mitch couldn't hear the latch click over the sermon, but with his hand on the handle, he felt it. He held open the door and ushered the others in as fast as they would go. He followed Amye through, pulling the door shut behind them.

Inside, it was almost quiet. The walls shut out most of the sound, but the droning baritone of Roper's voice still vibrated the tempered glass, surrounding them in a resonant hum. Above them loomed a three-story statue of the now familiar faceless god seated on a throne. He wore a diadem of stars and held a long scepter topped with an orb and cross. Instead of the symbol of salvation sitting in authority atop the globus cruciger though, the sword end of his warrior's cross pierced the world. He pointed accusingly at them with his free hand. It reminded Mitch of the fire and brimstone religious tracts he used to find as a kid stuffed in the horror novels at the library. The ones that made it clear in no uncertain terms, *everyone* was going to Hell. D&D players, metalheads, kids who went trick-or-treating or read *Harry Potter*. All condemned by a jealous, vengeful god who brooked only adulation and supplication. He remembered the deity depicted in those comics had been faceless too. The thing looming over them was gilt in gold leaf, reflecting the dancing light outside, looking like *it* was made of fire.

Liana pointed toward a door in the back of the hall off to one side. Mitch was all too happy to make a direct line for it. Anything that got him out of the blind-eyed sights of Roper and his gargantuan Crusader god. All the rest followed, except Amye, who stood staring up at the accusing stone finger pointing at her. Her face was wet. Mitch turned around and went back for her. "Come on," he said, grabbing hold of her hand.

"Are we... Are we doing the right thing? How will we be judged for this?"

Mitch gently turned her face toward him. "Your child needs you, Amye. How would the loving God you know judge you for abandoning Brendan to a mob and a bonfire?" She looked at him blank-faced and blinked at his question, processing it. He gestured toward the others waiting at the door. Mitch wanted her to come along freely, because they couldn't let her leave the other way. Not when they were so close.

Kristin came over and took Amye's other arm, whispering, "Come on. It'll be all right." Amye took a faltering step toward the others. And then another. And then she was running to them. While the Parents' Ministry embraced her, Mitch circled around them and grabbed ahold of the theater door. He held a finger to his lips and pulled.

• • •

The dark theater possessed a kind of primal obscurity, like a Platonic space in which shadows were paraded on the wall while captive viewers uncritically accepted them as reality. The impression gained strength by the appearance of the dark shapes of solid forms on the stage ahead of them—a looming row of black rectangular silhouettes like tablet stone grave markers. As Mitch's eyes adjusted to the darkness, the forms resolved into clarity. They weren't tombstones. It was a row of gun lockers.

The "safe room" was a cruel pun.

An unseen figure in the seats resolved out of the gloom, turning to face them. With the jovial voice of one ready to serve, it asked, "Which one you ready for next?" The man scowled at the sight of them and his tone quickly changed from deference to hostility. "Who the hell are you?" As he started to stand, Mitch caught sight of the pistol hanging under his arm in a cross draw holster. He launched himself at the threat. The man leaned away from Mitch's swing and he missed. Over-extended and off balance on the downward sloping theater floor, he stumbled over the row of seats ahead of him. He caught himself on the folding seat in the row in front of his target and fell over the rigid chair back, leaving him breathless and vulnerable. He scrambled to right himself before the guy had a chance to jam a shiv under his ear a half-dozen times—or, more likely shoot him in the back of the head. Instead, he heard the man grunt and the sounds of a struggle. He pushed himself off the seats and twisted around to see Izzy, Steve, and Nicholas grappling with the man, keeping him from drawing his weapon. The man punched Izzy in the nose, and she staggered away, blood gushing from between her fingers, black in the darkened room. Steve's face flushed with rage. He hauled the man up off his feet by his throat and slammed him into the hard floor. Steve was on him, kneeling on his arms and laying into his face like a berserk mixed martial arts fighter doing a ground and pound. Mitch heard something snap, and the man screamed, only to be silenced by the thud of another heavy fist in his face. Nicholas and Mike pulled Steve away while Kristin ducked into the fray and disarmed the man. Steve shook off the others holding him, and went to help Izzy up from where she'd landed on the floor. She pulled her hands away from her broken nose, appearing ready to take over for her husband, ready to do worse than he'd done. Steve held her back, asking if she was okay. She snorted loudly and spit a red wad onto the floor in reply.

Liana turned to Mike and said, "*This* is why I can't breathe." She took a deep gasping breath. "Sophie isn't buried; she's locked in one of those."

Kristin rushed up to one of the safes and began spinning the handle trying to open it. The wheel turned freely, but the door didn't budge. "What's the combination?" she shouted at the man. "What's the god damn combination?" Mitch climbed the stage and tried entering the building door code into the keypad of the box she'd picked. Nothing happened. He stared at the door for a moment, as if he was trying to see through. On the surface, the boxes appeared new and untouched. Again, he imagined the decayed lock on his apartment door, and pictured the children inside trying to rot their way out. *This* was how you kept children who could decompose things with a touch from getting away. Whatever it took to get them in there, once inside the doors were too thick, and no matter how much corruption was inside, none of them were strong enough to break out. The logo "DeepWater" was engraved in silver filigree script on the front. He read them again and again trying to find meaning, as if there were secrets that could be understood by solving the riddle of the brand name. But, there were no secret incantations other than a string of numbers that would open the door.

Liana touched a safe two over from his right. "This one," she said breathlessly. "She's in this one." Mitch ran over and tried the code again. A red light flashed on the keypad. He spun the wheel and pulled. It remained shut tight. A fresh panic made his heart beat faster.

"Hang on, Sophie!" he called into the box. "It's Yunka! I'm going to get you out!" He turned, scanning the stage for anything that could help him get the box open—an ax, a crowbar, something. But he knew these containers were built to be impenetrable. The only things on the stage other than the safes themselves were a couple pair of welding gloves and a small collection of empty sterile injection bottles and needles. He realized how they got the kids in, but that didn't help the parents get them out again. There was only a single way he could imagine to open the doors: the combination. No matter how close they were to success, without the codes, the boxes might as well have been on the other side of the Earth. "Bring him here," he called down to Nicholas and Steven.

They lifted the woozy man by his armpits and dragged him up the stairs at the house right side of the stage apron before dropping him roughly on the boards in front of Mitch. He knelt, cradling his right arm hanging limply at his side. *That was the snap*, Mitch guessed. *Steve breaking his arm when he landed on him. Good.* Nicholas prodded at the man's shoulder. He flinched and rocked forward before regaining his balance, but didn't say anything. He looked up at Mitch with his swelling, bruised face and smirked. It was a horrific expression to behold. "What's the combination?" Mitch said.

The man spat on Mitch's shoe.

Mitch gritted his teeth. "It doesn't have to be like this. All we want is the fucking combination so we can take our kids and go."

"You can go to the Devil, right behind your hellspawn." The man rocked back on his heels and tried to stand. Mitch slapped him hard across the face, open handed. The crack echoed in the quiet theater. Amye yipped a little. The man dropped back to his knees. Mitch stepped forward and slapped him a second time before shoving down on the back of his neck until his face was pressed against the shoe he'd spit on. He squeezed the back of the man's neck until a couple of his knuckles audibly popped from the effort. The top of the balding man's head turned bright red as he struggled to sit up, but with only one arm to push, he couldn't move. Liana laid a soft hand on Mitch's back, encouraging him to let go. Mitch gave a last shove before he let go and stepped back, breathing heavy and wide eyed. He looked at Steve and said, "Just fuckin' shoot him."

Steve pulled back the slide on his gun to check if a round was in the chamber.

"What?" the man hollered. He rocked up, raising his good arm in front of his face. "You can't kill me."

"You've made it clear there's no point in talking to you. If you're not going to tell us anything, there's no point to leaving you alive either. I can't have you putting us in danger, trying to get the others' attention. So, fuck you!" Mitch nodded at Steve, who put the gun to the back of the man's head.

"Five-five-six-four-five!" the man shouted, his voice cracking.

Mitch raised a hand to hold off his execution. He held his breath an extra second, unsure Steve actually would wait. When the gun didn't fire, he returned to the safe Liana said Sophie was trapped inside. He turned to look at the man and said, "If that code does anything other than spring this door wide open, you're a dead man. Understand? I'll kill you myself."

Steve shoved at the back of the man's skull with the barrel of the gun. He nodded. He was breathing heavy. However tough he had been with a pistol in his shoulder holster, he was ready to piss in his pants with one pressed to his skull. "The combination is the same for all of them. Five-five-six-four-five. Jesus forgive you."

"You better pray someone other than Jesus shows you some mercy, motherfucker," Izzy said.

Mitch entered the numbers into the lock. Nothing happened. He tried again, slower, pushing the buttons on the keypad as carefully as his trembling hand would allow. He hadn't realized he'd been holding his breath until the light turned green and he gasped with surprise at the sound of the tumblers inside the door moving. He spun the handle and pulled open the door. The heavy door swung smoothly and silently on its hinges. Sophie fell out and Mitch dropped to his knees to catch her. She weighed so little in his arms, he thought he'd missed her. Her skin was pale as paper and he could feel the bones of her ribs move under his fingers as she took in a slow, deep breath. Her face was drawn and she looked up at him with cataract-shaded eyes. They seemed blind, but still beheld him with relief. She wrapped her arms around his neck and hugged him. Her fingers were so cold against his skin. He squeezed back, terrified he would break her if he held on too hard. His vision blurred with tears as he cradled her. Diminished as she was, being reunited with her made him understand what wholeness felt like. Liana knelt down next to them. Mitch pulled her closer. Sophie reached over with an arm to hug them both, and there they stayed, crying together and happy for a perfect, ecstatic moment.

Kristin typed the numbers into the keypad on the next safe in the line and opened the door. Alexa shouted, "Jack!" She and Nicholas dashed forward to claim their boy from his prison. Kristin moved down the line, opening the remaining safes, one after another, freeing the rest of the children until she found her daughter in the second to last locker. Cassie's body fell out, still and limp. She sobbed, repeating her name again and again, trying to get her to sit up or even just look up, and demonstrate that there was life still in her. "Look at Mommy, Cassie. *Cassandra*, please wake up and look at Mommy. *Please*," she sobbed. The child lay in Kristin's lap, dead again. "She was doing better. She was almost all better," she cried. Her wail pierced through Mitch, breaking him out of his reverie.

He gently passed Sophie to Liana. The girl resisted at first, clinging to his neck. Liana shushed and told her it was okay. The child came away and Mitch took the bat from Liana in exchange. He stood and looked at the parents reunited with their children. Nicholas and Alexa smoothed down their son's hair and kissed his face. They'd mentioned a second child—the neighbor's kid. By the count, she wasn't here with these children. *Is she the one in the fire?* Izzy and Steve released their daughter, Michelle, from the last safe, clinging tight to her as she crawled into their arms. She was diminished and weak, but moving. Next to them, Amye cradled her son. He was the oldest looking of the children, tall and lanky, maybe nine or ten. Where his shirt had pulled up, Mitch could see a roadmap of purple veins and large lividity bruising on his back. Inside each safe was a spider web of blackened and rusted steel. The interior of Brendan's prison looked the worst. A stinking metallic pile of black rust spilled out from it onto the floor. Mitch's intuition was right: all of them had tried to get out, but none had the strength to rot through six inches of steel completely. And for their efforts, every one of the kids had given up a piece of themselves trying to be free. Some more than others... Cassie had given all apparently, and if there was any life left in her, she didn't show it. He wondered if kids who were closest to being fully restored to life—and Kristen had said she was almost better—were most vulnerable. The air in her tomb didn't go as far as it did in Brendan's or Sophie's. And only his niece had a piece of someone else with her inside, and was able to call out for help beyond her confinement. Because of her, they had their kids back—plus one more: Byron's unnamed son, lying still on the stage floor in front of his safe, suffocated back to death like Cassie. No one cradled or mourned him. No one claimed him. He lay there, an example of what awaited them all if they let this reunion linger too long.

"What do we do now?" Steve said. "We can't take them out the front doors. We're lucky nobody saw us come in that way."

Mike said, "There's got to be an emergency exit." He slipped through the curtains at the back of the stage and disappeared.

Mitch walked up to the kneeling man. Unlike the other parishioners in their God Warrior shirts, he wore a golf shirt with an emblem over his heart depicting an eagle perched on top of two crossed rifles. Below that, it read "LOUIE'S FIREARMS AND SPORT." Mitch wondered if he was in here watching the safes because he'd been the one to supply them. His knuckles were white from clutching the bat, and his arms trembled with the desire to swing it and swing it and swing again. "What's your name?"

"What does it matter to you?"

"It doesn't, I guess." Mitch glanced back at Liana. She looked at him with a transformed face framed by salt and pepper gray hair and fresh crow's feet. Sophie's touch had aged Liana, but given them a bond stronger than that shared by any "natural" mother and child. He recalled the woman in the cemetery, broken by the loss of her daughter, who'd reached out for Sophie and got a withered arm in return. He had an idea what Sophie could do if she had nothing holding her back. She could form a physical bond of love that transcended all obstacles, or she could cripple a person with her rejection and judgment. Rebirth had given her the power of a parent. What had the detective said to him? *Children begin by loving their parents, then they judge them.* No one asked to be small and weak in a world that favored the big and strong. And when they needed devotion and fierce protection, some of them learned exactly how hard the world was. Sophie, Michelle, Jack, Cassie, and Brendan all had the ability to really hold them accountable. They had the kind of power to love or harm, typically the exclusive privilege of adults. And as comforting as Mitch found that thought, he could see the man kneeling in front of him was terrified by it. He was terrified of being judged. This place—the entire compound—was devoted to it. A sprawling palatial estate dedicated to a fierce parent meting out punishment. Mitch understood why the man was frightened.

He didn't want to be vulnerable. Like a child.

He raised the bat. The man shook his head and sweat flew off his face. "I did what you said. I gave you the combination! Have you *seen* what they can do? Do you *know* what they are? They're monsters! Demons!"

"I know what they are. I know what you are." Mitch reared back.

The man flinched, raising his unbroken arm again to protect his face. "No! Don't! My name is David Louie! My wife's name is Paula. We have kids," he said.

"So do we!" Mitch swung low under Louie's upraised elbow. The meaty thud echoed with a loud cracking of the man's ribs snapping. His arm immediately dropped to protect his side and he doubled over, exposing the back of his skull. Mitch already knew what kind of sound that was going to make.

"Stop!" Amye shouted. Mitch turned to look at the parents gathered behind him. They stared back with a mixture of tacit approval and seeming horror at Mitch embracing the work he intended to do. The bat in his hands suddenly felt too heavy to swing again. He let his arm fall to his side. Liana beckoned him with an open hand to step away from the man.

"Come back to us," she pleaded.

He took a step away. Amye pushed past him, carrying her son in an embrace, his heavy head on her shoulder, limp arms dangling at his sides. She knelt down in front of the gasping man. "What are you doing?" he asked. She didn't answer. She knelt in front of David Louie, and with her free hand, touched the side of his face, guiding his head up to look at her. The dead boy reached out in a mirror of his mother's gesture and placed his hand on the other side of the man's head. He leaned forward and opened his mouth, breathing in. The bright red flush in David Louie's skin went pale. His mouth dropped open and no sound came out other than a low long breath. He wrinkled and dark blotches grew and spread on his skin. *Liver spots.* The boy's cheeks filled out, becoming less gaunt. His skin pinked and his thin lips, which had pulled back, eased down over his teeth again until his red lips met. David Louie toppled over and shuddered. With a sigh, his body relaxed and the smell of his bowels and bladder releasing floated up into the room. The boy threw his arm back around his mother's neck and embraced her. He looked over Amye's shoulder at the others. His cornflower blue eyes, the same as hers. She stood and turned. Tears spilled over her cheeks, but she was smiling the same wide smile her boy wore when she set him down on steady feet. Alive, he looked just like her.

Liana cried out, clutching Sophie tighter. Wide eyed, Nicholas and Alexa whispered their horror, while Steve and Izzy didn't say a word at all. Mitch felt his stomach knot at the sight of the man's body beside Amye and her restored boy. An animal reaction to watching a man die.

In the lobby, the sounds of Roper's sermonizing and the crowd cheering swelled in volume for a moment, and then died down, muffled again by the lobby doors. They were coming for them.

Mike reappeared through the curtains. "I found the exit," he said. "Let's go!" He pulled back the drape and nodded for them to follow him through. Izzy and Steve ran through the gap clutching their child, followed by Alexa and her family. Amye, her healthy son Brendan beside her, holding her hand like they were racing to catch a bus to school went next.

"Come on!" Liana hissed. She held out an arm for Mitch.

Kristin remained sitting on the floor. Mitch waved for her to join them, but she stayed put, softly singing to her child. She caressed Cassie's hair, trying to smooth it down. Mitch skidded over to her and tried to pull her to her feet. "You have to get up," he said. "We have to go."

She looked up at him and shook her head. "No. You go."

"We can't just leave you."

The door to the theater opened and a man called out from the shadows under the mezzanine. "Hey, Louie! We're ready to see what's behind Door Number Two." Another man with him laughed.

"Please, go." Kristin shoved at Mitch and pulled David Louie's gun from her waistband. She aimed it at the approaching men who hadn't seen them yet and were still joking with each other.

Mitch ran. Liana grabbed his hand tightly and pulled him along, refusing to let go.

"Hey you! Where are yo—"

Kristin fired.

The rest was Hell.

40

The bang of the emergency exit door slamming shut contained more finality than the gunshots it muffled. There was no handle or latch on the outside, just a flat circular plate and a keyhole for which they had no key. In the theater, he heard Kristin wail and empty her pistol while the men who'd come to claim their next sacrifice fired back, shouting in confused rage. The muted chaos tore at Mitch's guts. As badly as he wanted to rush back in, there was nothing he could do to help. The door was shut. Liana pulled him away from it. Together, they ran along a cobblestone walkway leading toward an asphalt lot behind a neighboring building to escape. On the other side of it a pair of tour busses were parked at an angle to the sidewalk. Beyond them was a large parking lot half-filled with cars and pickup trucks. Liana jerked at his arm, pulling him in a different direction, away from the lot. He skidded to a stop and pointed toward the others. "What about them?"

Liana watched the rest of The Parents' Ministry prisoners run for the lot without looking back. "I think we're on our own," she said.

Mike's eyes widened at the sight of the assembled congregants flooding out of the amphitheater, howling with something far different than the religious ecstasy they'd enjoyed only moments ago. He turned to flee across toward the courtyard. Liana let go of Mitch and barely caught hold of his shirt collar, stopping him. "Not that way." She nodded toward the tree line on the other side of the road running behind the compound.

Mike protested. "But the car is that way."

"You want to run through the *middle* of this place?" Mike shook his head and reversed direction.

Mitch took Sophie from Liana and hefted the child up in his left arm. He handed the bat back to Liana so he could get a better grip on Sophie. She wrapped her arms and legs around him as tightly as she could, but he could feel how depleted she was. His thoughts flashed to Brandon and the man in the theater. One of his therapist's mantras intruded in his mind: *His name is David. He is a living person.* Was. *Fuck him! He wanted to kill us.* He looked back and saw his first glimpse of a dark pursuer in the gloaming. His heart beat faster.

Around them, the amplified sound of Roper's voice shouting, "FIND THEM!" echoed through the compound. It pushed them into motion better than any pep talk or starter's pistol. It took away Mitch's breath and his last shred of hope that they could slip away unseen. They made a direct line for the woods. He hazarded a look back just as they shoved through the tree line. People were fanning out over the courtyard. The tall sidewalk lights were coming on, glinting off of rifles and guns. A few parishioners jogged out into the street they'd just left, pausing to squint and stare into the trees. He saw Junior among them, face contorted with rage. He shoved on, hoping they hadn't been spotted. The sound of the shot registered at the same moment he saw a cloud of maroon mist erupt from Mike's back. Mitch skidded to a stop and doubled back. He dropped to his haunches and grabbed at Mike's shirt with his free hand to drag him behind cover.

"Li! Help!" Whatever concern he'd had for giving away their position was gone; it was known. More shouting rose from the street. And then more shots. Pieces of bark peppered his face as a bullet impacted in the tree next to him. He couldn't help Mike with only a single hand. He couldn't put Sophie down. Another bullet, this one in the dirt, kicking up grit and pieces of rock. He worked to hold on to both of them, and accomplished little until Liana appeared, grabbing Mike under his arms. She and Mitch dragged him behind a tree with a thick trunk. There wasn't room for all four of them behind it, so Mitch scrambled on to the next one. He felt a bullet whip by his face as he darted for cover. At least he thought it was a bullet. It was hot and fast and felt like death and inevitability. For a second, he regretted not taking at least one of the guns he'd had in his hands along the way. But then, he'd rather die holding hands than a weapon. He'd never dreamed of being a soldier and had no desire to die in a proverbial pile of brass. Still, if he could return fire, the people shooting at them might feel compelled to also take cover. There was none in the road, and that would mean moving farther away. But wishing for a gun he didn't have was useless.

"Is he...?" he called out to Liana.

"There's blood everywhere!"

"Imma kill you MEEE-SHELLL!" Junior screamed. Gunfire punctuated his threat.

The screeching tires and the sound of bodies thudding against metal and breaking glass interrupted the shouting and shooting. Mitch hazarded a peek out from behind cover and saw the moment the silver minivan careened to the side of the road, mounted the curb, and smashed into the side of one of the sword-engraved obelisks near the bonfire pit. As it hit the standing stone, the driver over-corrected and the minivan yawed wide, tipping up onto two tires and rolling over. It flipped once, coming to rest on its side after a short, screeching slide. The clatter of breaking glass and a revving engine sounded for a few seconds after the vehicle stopped moving. And then there was a short moment of terrifying silence punctuated by the lone wail of a child. The sound made Mitch feel like crying out, joining it with his own wail of terror and desperation. He forced his mouth and lips shut, clenching his jaw and holding back the need to scream at the madness of it all.

Aside from the child's wail, there was a lull in the noise, as if the parishioners couldn't believe what they were witnessing.

The gunshots had ceased. Mitch couldn't see or hear Junior anymore. And then it began anew. "Over here!" someone called out. A crowd of people gathered around the minivan. Their bellows blending together in an incomprehensible cloud of anger that swelled and ebbed and swelled again into a terrifying crescendo. One man climbed the roof rack and peered into the window. A single shot cracked and he fell back, landing heavily on the road, dead. The wind of rage became a storm beating at the sides of the vehicle.

Another group of people appeared to help the shooters struck in the road. They knelt around their fallen friends and tended them. The woods into which they'd been firing forgotten in the moment. Mitch tried to get a better look at one of the shadowy lumps, wanting to make sure Junior was dead, but he couldn't see any of them well enough to tell. Mitch heard another car motor revving up and tires screeching. The helpers in the road popped up, looking like meerkats searching for a predator. The car left the parking lot headed in the opposite direction around the roadway circle. A couple of parishioners stood and ran toward the sound, snatching up their fallen comrades' guns as they went. The others that remained dragged the broken bodies out of the road, into the grass.

Mitch crept over to Liana and Mike and whispered, "Can he move?"

She pressed her hands against Mike's shoulder. He gritted his teeth and looked like he was suppressing a scream. Tears streaked her face. "We have to get him to a hospital."

"Mike? Can you get up?" Mitch said.

Mike gritted his teeth and nodded. He tried to stand, failed, and fell back against the tree, yelping in pain. Mitch's head whipped around. No one looked their way. No one heard. They were focused on the chaos out in the open. Whoever had been driving the van had saved them, whether or not they intended to. Liana helped Mike to his feet again and they began making their way through the woods, away from the commotion.

Disregarding the tales he'd heard of people turning back for a last look and regretting it, a love falling into Hades or turning to salt, he looked behind them one last time. The crowd was pulling someone out of the minivan through a smashed window. Steve struggled and they dropped him on his back on the asphalt. The crowd closed about him with violent undulations. A moment later, they dragged Izzy out the same window. She lashed out and screamed, kicking one man down. Another jumped forward and struck her in the gut with the butt of a rifle, driving her from the others' hands into the ground where she landed with a flat thud and a strangled groan as all the air in her lungs was forced out. The crowd stepped back instead of stomping her. She rolled over on her side and got up onto her hands and knees. Gasping and coughing, she put a foot on the ground to stand. The man she'd kicked shoved her back down while the other one leveled his rifle at her.

Mitch hadn't turned to salt, but he did get a glimpse of Hell and regretted looking back all the same. He turned away, hunching over and cupping a hand on the back of Sophie's head to hold her closer to his shoulder and avert her eyes. In the distance, he heard Izzy's voice carry up over the din. "Go fuck yo—"

BANG.

A cheer.

The world went dark for a moment. Steve and Izzy had saved them, and he'd done nothing. *There was nothing you could have done. Go!* "Where is it?" he asked.

Liana turned. "I don't know. I was following Sophie when we came in. I wasn't really paying attention." She pointed toward a rise on the other side of the parking lot. "That way, I think." She pointed at the statue at the end of the courtyard. "Yeah, that way!" They circled around, staying in the concealment of the trees.

More screeching tires and rifle fire echoed in the dark. They heard the loud crack of something snapping, followed by a howling engine that grew fainter as it moved farther away.

Mitch pictured Nicholas, Alexa and Jack getting away. He hoped Amye and Brendan were with them. He hoped they'd be following behind soon.

Mike stumbled over a root. Liana tried to keep him upright, but he fell. He opened his mouth in a breathless groan of agony. Mitch took a moment to crouch and scan for a sign that anyone was following them. He couldn't see anyone in the trees, though the sounds of the frenzy continued to echo through them. He heard a loud *whump* and saw an orange light glowing in the growing night. A faint "amen" followed. The minivan burned brightly in the distance. He doubted anyone had lifted Michelle out of that car before setting it on fire. They cheered while a child burned. He closed his eyes and listened for her screams. All he heard was Sophie breathing next to him. *She is a living person. She is a living person. She is a living fucking person!*

"What are they doing?" Liana asked.

"You *know* what they're doing. We gotta get him up. They're coming for us next." He helped her right their friend and they moved on. They stepped carefully. There was no one left to come screaming out of the parking lot to distract the worshipers of the New Life Church. The four of them had been left behind.

41

Disorientation and the deepening dark led them to the gatehouse instead of Liana's car. A group of parishioners had gathered, spiritedly discussing the smashed sentry arm that lay in pieces in the road framed by the tire marks of a vehicle that had *almost* lost control. Through the trees, Mitch could see Pastor Roper at the head of the group. They were too far away to hear what he was saying, but that Roper was furious was clear. His voice carried over the sounds of dwindling chaos in the compound, though the meaning of his words were lost in the rustle of wind in the trees. He pointed down the road in the direction of the skid marks before turning his finger back toward one of the gate guards, jabbing it in his chest.

A pair of cars pulled up to the gates, and Roper waived them through, shoving at the guard standing in their way. Instead of a line of dieselpunk-style war machines with enraged albino madmen dangling off the sides, a pair of suburban soccer mom SUVs pulled through, slowing down enough to safely pass by the crowd, before taking off. There was no shouting or honking, no sense that anyone was giving spirited chase, other than the gravel kicked up by spinning tires.

While he wanted to hide and wait for the rest of Roper's congregation to quietly disperse and head home, Mike was still bleeding heavily, and every minute they spent sitting still put all of them in more danger. He turned up his palms. *Where now?* She nodded over her shoulder, got a better grip under Mike's good arm, and turned them as quietly as she could away from the compound entrance. Mitch hefted Sophie up in his left arm and followed. This time he didn't look back. He couldn't bear the thought of it.

Ahead of them, everything looked the same. The trees were all identical in their patternless anonymity, and there were no paths to follow. To make matters worse, it was dark and getting darker and their surroundings were becoming more confounding by the minute; details that might have stood out in the daylight, became invisible at night.

Mike's legs folded twice more as they fled. The first time, Liana staggered, wrenching her back around, and letting out a short, sharp cry of pain, but saving him from falling. The second time, the cumulative fatigue of their efforts growing to be too much, they toppled together, collapsing in the bracken and dry underbrush. Mitch dropped next to them, waiting for the shouts of men to be turned in their direction. Still, they seemed to be evading detection. He tried to set Sophie down, but she clung to his neck and puled at him not to let go. He whispered to the girl, "I need you to help me help Li, okay?" She looked at Liana, who was gently rolling Mike up into a sitting position so she could try to get under his arm again. His head lolled and his eyes rolled once before closing. His face was as wan as a nighttime cloud. Sophie let go of Mitch's neck, took his hand instead, and they went to help Liana. "Let me," he said. Taking Mike's arm from her, he crouched down on one knee and pulled the man over his shoulders in an attempt at a fireman's carry. Although Mike was shorter and weighed less than any of them but Sophie, he was dead weight, and Mitch couldn't get the leverage or exert enough brute force to stand from his crouch with him slumped over his shoulders. Liana helped pull him to his feet. In the still moment before he could get a foot forward, Mitch heard the patter of Mike's blood trickling onto the leaves underfoot. More frightening than the congregation's chants, or the gunfire, the soft *pat pat pat pat* was as terrifying a sound as he'd ever heard.

Liana lifted Sophie and they moved on. Mitch's footsteps were heavy and irregular, but he kept his head down and watched where he stepped. Eventually, they found the car. The road was quiet. As they laid Mike in the back seat, Mitch peered through the window into the woods they'd just emerged from, the feeling of being watched prickling his skin. He looked for a sign that someone was staring out at them, lining up a rifle shot. He saw nothing but trees. It didn't feel like a some*one* to him though. More like a some*thing*. Some malign creature lingering just beyond his sight, unseen and vicious, was deranging the congregation and calling Hell down on them. An antlered beast of chaos and violence that demanded blood as a sacrament and offered death as its blessing. *Nonsense!* There were no monsters. None like that, anyway. Then again, he'd never believed the dead could come back to life. The proof of *that* was clinging in his girlfriend's arms. So who was he to say some inhuman horror wasn't lurking at the threshold of his perception, waiting for him to turn his back or let down his guard?

He backed out of the car and took Sophie from Liana. He set her on the front seat, and climbed in after her. Liana slid behind the wheel while he buckled Sophie into the middle. Again, he felt the pangs of guilt at not having her strapped safely in a car seat in the back. But circumstances wouldn't make exceptions for them. He had to cope with what he had.

Liana peeled out of the pullover, her open-throated car tearing off down the road with a roar. "Where do I go?" she shouted over the engine and road noise.

"Sophie and I got here in the trunk of a car," Mitch replied. "I don't even know what state we're in."

"New Hampshire." Liana leaned over and popped open the jockey box. Her smart phone slid out and dropped into Mitch's hands. He woke it up and opened her maps app, typing "HOSPITAL" into the search box.

"There's a medical center a half an hour from here," he said. Keene felt too close, too dangerous. "Should I find a different one?"

Liana angled the rearview mirror down. "I don't think we have time to take him anywhere else."

Mitch undid his seatbelt and got up on his knees, leaning backward over the seat. He tried not to topple over when Liana took a corner faster than she should've, and then another. He felt Sophie's hand on his hip, as if she could steady him. Still, the gesture meant something. She was right. If they drove an hour or more into Massachusetts, Mike would definitely bleed to death. Hell, he might do that before they even got as far as Keene. They hadn't had time to even make an attempt at dressing Mike's wounds. He was pale and his head was rolling back and forth with the motion of the car. Mitch pulled off his shirt and wadded it up. Leaning over the seatback, he steadied himself with one hand and pressed the fabric into the exit wound in Mike's chest with the other. Mike groaned and moved his head, but didn't wake up. That was good; groaning meant he was alive. Mitch kept applying pressure. He had no idea if he was helping. All he was doing was plugging up an exit wound; the entrance in Mike's back was still bleeding freely. He hoped that the pressure against the seat might help slow the flow of blood out of that end of the wound if he couldn't.

Liana pushed the car faster and faster, tires screeching and engine roaring. More than once, Mitch's downward pressure on Mike's wound was what prevented him from falling over as she barely kept the car on the road. He hoped he wasn't hurting him too much. But at this point, pain was an inevitability. With or without him leaning on his chest, Mike was suffering.

The rural road gave way to town highways, and eventually the city. Traffic thickened, but they made it to the hospital in a little less than the time the phone had predicted it would take. The shirt stuck to Mitch's hands as he let go. He knelt back in the seat, staring at his stained hands, maroon and tacky. Not the fresh red wet of newly shed blood. Mike lay in the backseat still and silent as Liana pulled into the parking lot.

An ambulance blocked the pull-through under the canopy in front of the ER doors. Mitch pointed toward an empty parking spot nearby. She pulled into the space and jumped out of the car, wrenching forward the driver's seat. She leaned in, begging

Mike to wake up, tapping his face. "Open your eyes, god damn it. We're here. Mike! Wake up!" Tears dropped from her eyes onto his pallid face and ran down his cheeks. Tears he couldn't cry for himself. Mitch leaned back over the seat and felt at his neck for a pulse. His inexpert fingers couldn't find one. He wasn't a doctor or even a nurse, and knew he could be wrong.

He wanted so badly to be wrong.

"Wait here; I'll get help." He turned to Sophie. "Stay here, honey. Stay out of sight, okay? Can you do that?" She nodded, unclipped her seatbelt and climbed down into the footwell. He scrambled out of the car and ran across the parking lot toward the emergency room doors under the bright fluorescent lights. Toward help—trauma teams and blood transfusions. He ran toward hope.

Hope died as he rounded the ambulance parked in the bay and caught sight of a familiar figure that stopped him dead. A man in a God's Warrior shirt stood near the doors smoking a cigarette with a policeman beside him, listening and taking notes. The only thing the parishioner was missing was a rifle slung over his shoulder. Mitch ducked back behind the emergency van, heart pounding. He listened.

"Can you describe them?"

"Yup. Three of 'em. A man, a woman, and one of them dead kids. They came smashing through the parkin' gate in a red RAV4 or a CRV—I don't know. It was red. Anyways, they tore around the retreat shouting their hate. Deadophiles shouting about how 'cadaver lives matter' or whatnot. We've been telling you for months that they send us threats on Facebook and the e-mail all the damn time. It was just a matter of time before one of 'em followed through. Never seen anything like it. They came blasting through just as we were lettin' out service and people were tryin' to get to the parking lot to go home. It's like they planned it that way—when everyone was feeling good and walking across the street. They plowed right through Tim Standish, Junior Williams, and Dave Hutchens. Then they blew up their car like them chickenshit terrorists in Eye-raq. They're

Satanic, man. These people. They won't rest until it's Hell on Earth."

The cop asked another question, but Mitch's heart was beating too hard to focus on what he said. His muscles were frozen and he couldn't find the strength to pull himself away from the side of the ambulance. He looked around for another entrance into the hospital, but there wasn't one he could see from his vantage. What he did spot were the two SUVs he'd seen leaving the compound through the front gate. Parked side by side just across from the ambulance bay, both sported white oval stickers on the back with the letters "NLC" inside, as if the New Life Church was its own country. In the rear windows were big sword-crosses with the familiar slogan surrounding them. The cars he'd seen leaving were carrying their wounded—people who'd survived being run down by Steve and Izzy, who were now being counted among the victims. *The people who had been shooting at us, who shot Mike and wanted to throw Sophie in a fucking bonfire, are pinning the blame for everything on us!* Mitch imagined himself going back to prison, only this time in New Hampshire, where they had the death penalty. He forced himself to move, knowing that if he didn't, the cop or an EMT would come walking around and find him standing there, shirtless, bloody, and paralyzed. And then it'd be this upstanding church-going man's word against his. He pushed off the van and ran back to the car, his conscience burning with shame for his cowardice.

Liana stood with her back turned to the open car door and her face in her hands. Her bent back hitched with a sob. As Mitch approached without help in tow, she looked up at him with red eyes and said, "He's gone." She fell into his arms. He held tight, not knowing what else to do. He looked over her shoulder into the car at the man who had saved her life once a long time ago, and now had given his to help her save Mitch and Sophie's too. Sacrificing everything for people he barely knew. "What do we do now?" she asked. Mitch didn't know how to repay a debt like the one he now owed to Mike and Liana. And he didn't have time to figure it out. He heard the ambulance engine turn over and the siren wind up.

He helped Liana into the passenger seat. Sophie climbed up onto the seat next to her and snuggled tight against her. Liana latched the girl in and held her. He got behind the wheel and started the car. The ambulance pulled away, leaving him an unobstructed view of the holy warrior telling his lies to the cop. "The police aren't going to help us," he said. "No one is going to help us."

"Tony will," she said.

Mitch didn't want to go to the funeral home. He didn't want to put another innocent person in danger just to help him. But he didn't know what other choice they had. Everything that wasn't already lost, was leaving. He put the car in gear and pulled out of the parking lot, aiming them toward home.

Interlude: Scenes from an Apocalypse

42

The news anchor stared into the camera lens as he read from the teleprompter beside it. His expression and inflection betrayed none of his own beliefs or leanings as he said, "Five state governors have pledged today to sign into law emergency bills passed by their legislatures exempting reanimate children from coverage under existing child protection laws while strengthening the rights of providers ranging from medical personnel—including pediatricians—to state licensed day care operators to refuse services to formerly deceased children without penalty. This, after two other state legislatures, New Hampshire and Maine, passed laws just last week enacting serious legal repercussions for people harboring those children without notifying authorities. The governors of both states signed those bills into law immediately. The so-called 'Anti-Deadophile' laws are expanding in the wake of a coordinated terrorist attack on a religious retreat in New Hampshire three weeks ago that left ten people dead including shooter, Kristin Freeborn, and the drivers of a car bomb, identified as Steven and Isabella Leigh, and their reanimate daughter, Michelle. Six other people, all members of the church, were injured in that attack, but survived the blast.

"Opponents of these bills say that they unfairly target families and children who have done nothing wrong, and whose only offense is to have been given a second chance at life. However, alarming reports involving reanimate children have been reported from around the globe. And international tensions are rising as riots continue for the second week in Athens and Istanbul, and seem ready to spread. France, Belgium, the Netherlands and Switzerland have all agreed to accept European refugee families with reanimate children. In the Americas, however, only Canada has opened its borders to people seeking asylum. United States Secretary of State Lorena Rivera said in a press conference last evening that the U.S. government was looking at the situation, but was not at present considering lifting its travel ban prohibiting people with reanimate children from either entering or leaving the country."

In his earpiece, he heard direction from the producer and followed along seamlessly, turning to face camera B without dropping the pretense that his delivery of the news was conversational, not scripted. As the light on top of the camera blinked to life he introduced the guest at his glass table in the wide shot. "Sitting with me now is Pastor Gideon Roper of the New Life Church in New Hampshire, the scene of last month's vicious shooting and car bomb attack that seems to have galvanized a frightened nation into action. Thank you for joining us, Pastor Roper."

Roper leaned forward in his chair seeming to expect the anchor to shake his hand, but not reaching across the desk. "Thank you for having me, Les. Let me begin by saying that the New Life Church categorically opposes violence, even as it is brought right to our doorstep, to our places of worship. What we seek is not violence, but a reaffirmation of God's law and love and an understanding of his infinite mercy."

"Some are claiming, Pastor, that the reanimation of these children *is* a miracle from God. You disagree."

"Oh yes, we do. As it says in Hebrews 9:27, 'It is appointed for man to die *once*, and *after* that comes *judgment*.' The Lord tells us the dead are truly dead—not yet even in Heaven or Hell. They are asleep until the *last* day. Anyone who says that after you die, you are not really dead, or can come back, is trying to turn you from your Father, straight toward Hell. We stand opposed to all the works of Lucifer's agents on Earth."

The news anchor continued his interview without ever admitting that his own reanimate son was at home with his mother.

Part Five: Sophie's Forgiveness

November

43

The flashing light in the sconce beside the French doors made Mitch freeze in the middle of the line he was quietly reading aloud to Sophie. He held his breath waiting for the next two flashes, the ones that signaled the all-clear. The view through the windows of the French doors separating the apartment upstairs from the stairway down to the funeral home lobby was blocked with blackout curtains hanging on a tension rod. Mitch couldn't see who was at the door when Tony flicked the light switch, but if there was only one more flash instead of three, he had sixty seconds to grab Sophie and the bug-out bag behind the sofa, and start down the fire escape. When the next three flashes came after a short pause, he let out his breath. Things were safe. For the moment anyway. He finished reading the sentence he'd begun in *The Fantastic Flying Books of Mr. Morris Lessmore.* Sophie had a half-dozen storybooks Tony had bought for her online, but this was the one she asked Mitch to read more than any other. It was her favorite, even though half the time he read it, the story made him tear up a little. It was melancholy for a children's book. But she loved it, and he loved her, so he read it as often as she asked for it. And he promised her he'd read it over and over again until he couldn't anymore.

Tony pushed through the doors into the room. In the short time Mitch had known him, he seemed like he'd aged ten years. He looked tired; his beard had grown longer and wilder, and the gray in both it and on top of his head seemed to be spreading like ash in a fireplace. It seemed an impossible transformation in only a few months, but then, the whole world was changing every bit as rapidly. Maybe more so. It made Mitch feel afraid to look in a mirror. After escaping the compound, he'd shaved his head in an attempt to change his appearance, but when no one seemed to be looking for him, he let both his hair and beard start to grow out again. The media had picked up and run with the narrative that Steve, Izzy and Kristin were a terrorist cell of reanimate sympathizers. There were speculations they hadn't acted alone—that others had conspired with them—other sleepers waiting to attack. People's fears were elevated by the belief that churches weren't off limits to violence any more. No more sanctuary. Another piece of America's innocence lost, the pundits said. Mitch knew differently. If they only could see what the New Life Church, leading the way, was really like, with its apocalyptic banners and guns. He thought people should be able to see through Gideon Roper's bullshit charade, but then, people believed things unquestioningly when they were scared. He figured that was how Roper and his congregation were managing him and Liana, Nicholas and Alexa, and Amye—if she'd escaped too—from a distance. As long as they were looking for the unnamed others who'd helped orchestrate the "New Life Assault," none of them could publicly challenge Roper's version of events. Panicked, terrified people would have Mitch strung up from a crane arm before he could say that it was Roper's people who'd blown up the car, who'd started shooting first. Even if they listened to him, he didn't want to be the face of the opposition. He wasn't a revolutionary, or even political. And whether or not anyone believed they hadn't *planned* the attack, he was still a "deadophile." How he hated that portmanteau. He hated its given meaning as well as the heavy unspoken implication of it. But once branded with the word—

and there was no way he could avoid it, not with Sophie in his arms—you were one of *them*. Mitch just wanted to stay out of trouble. Since going into hiding, however, he'd missed a meeting with his parole officer. Thus, "out of trouble" wasn't on the menu any longer. Keeping his head down was his only remaining choice. That, and running away.

"Who was it?"

"Those detectives," Tony said. "They don't believe me when I say I haven't seen you. I think they talked to Dr. Downum at the morgue. I don't know that for sure, but Miranda's not answering my calls, so it'd be my guess. They said the next time they come back, they'll have a warrant to search upstairs. I don't know what they're waiting for, to be honest." He didn't need to say it was time for Mitch and Sophie to move on; they all knew it.

"You've done way more for us than I should have ever asked you to." Mitch closed the book. Sophie muttered a quiet objection. Mitch scooted her off the sofa onto the floor where a couple of stuffed animals lay, momentarily neglected. She sat, staring at the adults as if, given a conversational opportunity, she'd chime in with the answer to all their problems. Mitch spoke instead. "I have a line on a safe house in Vermont where we can hole up for a few days. From there, I know some people in Peterborough, Ontario, willing to let us stay with them, if we can get across the border to their place. Li sent me a SteamText this morning. She's already there." He glanced at his prepaid smartphone. Like the name suggested, Liana's message had already evaporated into the digital atmosphere.

"How are you going to get into Canada?"

Mitch shrugged. He had an idea, but he'd put off trying to implement it. It went against his head down philosophy. The time had passed, though, to stop doing time, and make the most of it instead. "I need to get something from our old place... Our passports, if they're still there. Then we're headed out of town."

Tony nodded and started toward the curtained window at the far end of the living room. "I need to show you something," he said. As he walked by, Sophie reached out and hugged his leg, making him pause for a moment. He leaned over and reached down to tussle her hair. She closed her eyes and leaned her face closer to him. Mitch gently peeled her off Tony's leg and picked her up. Since spending a day locked in a safe, she didn't like to be too far from any familiar person she could cling to. He was happy to hold her as much as she wanted.

Tony led them to the window and pulled back the curtain, pointing into the parking lot below. Mitch ducked out of the way at first, then approached the window at an oblique angle to see what his friend was trying to show him. Parked near the wrought iron gate in the back was a small, sun-faded blue car. Tony said, "There's a booster seat in the back and a full tank of gas."

"I can't... I don't have the money to..."

"This wouldn't be a very good stop on an underground railroad if I made you pay for the way out."

"But a car is exp—"

Tony held up a hand. "It was a donation from a sympathetic client who lost her daughter a while ago. It was supposed to be a sixteenth birthday present. Instead, she wants Sophie to have it. So she can have a sixteenth birthday, and hopefully a lot more after that."

Mitch hugged his friend.

"You do know how to drive, right?"

"I think I remember."

44

Mitch parked around the corner and sat in the darkened car for a while, looking into the rearview mirror and waiting. He had no idea how to identify a "tail" and didn't possess the skills to lose one if he could've picked out someone following him. He had a driver's license, but it had always been cheaper to take the T than own a car. He couldn't afford insurance and upkeep. His skill behind the wheel extended to not running off the road and not hitting any other cars on it. *All you gotta do is miss,* he told himself. Liana's motto. The car he was sitting in was likely as temporary as his continuing U.S. citizenship. Either that or his freedom.

After enough time had passed that he felt somewhat less vulnerable, he got out and opened the back door. Sophie hadn't wanted to sit in the car seat, but reluctantly let him strap her into it. She could tell how badly he wanted her to be safe, and so she let him have this thing. She'd sent a tendril of rot through one of the arm rests, though. "Hon," he said. "This seat has got to last. You can't—"

"Sorry," she said. Her voice was so thin, so ethereal, he wasn't sure he heard her as much as imagined what she said. Her bottom lip quivered and he dropped the subject. All the chair had to do was keep her safe until they got near the border. He expected they'd either be walking across it, or riding in a trunk again. They certainly weren't driving through a customs checkpoint, not unless something about them both changed. Though Tony had accepted his lie about passports without challenging him, Mitch didn't believe for a second that he'd fooled his friend. An ex-con with an off-the-books adopted—now abducted—child didn't have a passport any more than he had a third eye that saw into the future. He pulled her out of the car and locked it up with the keys instead of the remote fob. It was a Toyota and there was no way to lock or unlock the thing from a distance without the lights flashing and horn beeping. Even the quiet clack of the locks sliding into place with the key was more noise than he wanted to make.

Together, they walked up the block toward their old apartment. He heard a faint screeching and looked up. Perched at the top of the lamppost in front of the house, a hawk tore at the body of a pigeon. Downy feathers fell to the concrete below, blowing along the gutter in the light nighttime breeze like snow. He focused back on the dark block and headed home.

Their house had been picked apart as badly as the bird. The front windows were smashed and someone had spray-painted *DEADOPHILE!!!* in two-foot-high red letters beside the boarded- up door. Mitch doubted the back entrance was in any better shape. If the doors were nailed shut, that meant the upstairs neighbors had left... or were forced to leave. He'd once liked this neighborhood. It wasn't swanky, by any stretch, but the people were friendly enough. They waved when they saw each other on the street and would say "hi" at the bus stop; the rest of the time—most of the time—they minded their own business and expected the same from everyone else. At least they had once. Times changed.

He thought about atrocities he'd seen on the television in war torn parts of the world, how dehumanization of other people gave license to folks claiming righteousness to turn against their neighbors and behave as badly as the human species was capable. Torture and beheadings, rape as a weapon of war, mass murder and "ethnic cleansing" were all the natural result of reducing one's neighbors to something less than human. If you can look in the eyes of a person and ignore everything about them that resides in you, then there are no limits to the evil you can do. If they're apes, rats, cockroaches, or viruses, then anything responsible human beings can do to keep their filth from spreading is justified. Isn't it? What's lower than a virus?

A corpse.

Don't speak ill of the dead. Show some respect for the dead. These platitudes were trotted out when a family member "passed away" and their body was out of sight and not a problem, being handled by guys like Tony Tremblay who took on the responsibility of sanitizing death, preparing the living to see a false, made up version of it in a chapel, in a box, in a hole in the ground. But a cadaver in a hospital bed or in the street is rotting meat, and the potential for more disease and death. Getting rid of a corpse—cleansing the places they've infected—these are things people must do to ensure their survival. Especially if the dead are intruding upon the places normally owned by the living.

Deadophile.

Hell, if that's what he was, he'd wear the name with pride. He had a responsibility he'd taken on even before Violette left. When he'd come out of prison she introduced him to his niece, the living legacy of the man he hadn't had the heart to murder. She told him that although she loved Sophie, every day she looked at her, the girl reminded her of her father. She looked so like him. Mitch didn't see it—she looked like herself to him. Maybe a mix of the two of them in the right light, or when she turned this way or that. But that didn't matter and Sophie spent an increasing amount of time with him until finally he was all she had when Violette ran away. And then Faye killed her, robbing him of his chance at redemption. But the universe, or some mysterious science, had given him another chance to get it right—and he was going to take it.

He glanced over at Faye's boyfriend's car parked out front of their house and heard the music thumping inside. Laughter and shouting carried through the closed windows like they were playing a game or having a celebration. The detectives had explained it to him already: *corpus delicti*. No body, no crime, no accountability. Faye and Meghan had their alibis, the evidence of her crime had walked out of the morgue, and for all they knew was long gone. They were free to get on with their lives without paying any price for Sophie's death. Free to lift a few drinks and celebrate having gotten away with it.

His neighbors.

The people who killed Sophie.

He walked up to the steps of their old apartment, and knowing what his niece needed wasn't inside, took her around the back of the house instead. He lifted Sophie over the low chain link fence separating their backyard from Faye's before climbing over after her. She waited patiently, quietly, while he stumbled over and rattled the fence loudly. He didn't have to shush her or try to distract her. She was a natural predator. Silent as the grave.

The music was so loud he figured he could kick in the back door without anyone hearing. Hell, he could have thrown a grenade through their window and no one in the neighborhood would have known any different. Instead, he crept around to the cellar window that had been broken as long as he'd lived next door—probably longer. It popped right open when he kicked at it. He got onto his hands and knees and backed into the opening, hanging down and feeling with his feet for the floor or a shelf or a washer and dryer. Anything. It wasn't a bottomless pit, he knew. If he just shimmied in and dropped, he'd land on something solid after another foot or two. Still, it felt like dangling over the edge of a cliff. He let go and dropped down. Once he had his feet under him, he held the window open for Sophie. She slipped in on her bottom and he pulled her free of the window, letting it close behind them with a muted bang.

The cellar was dark, but a little light spilling in from the street lamp at the corner helped him make out the shapes of the things stored there. Piles of boxes and old junk. A bicycle leaned against the far wall, gears rusted and tires flat from disuse. A stinking heating oil tank stood at the far end of the room, next to an old refrigerator near it in the corner. Above them, loud music and stomping, elephantine footsteps rattled the boards over their heads. Without any insulation between the first floor and the cellar, he could hear everything above as clearly as if he were up there sharing a beer with his neighbors. Steven Tyler sang about walkin' the dog, while Faye laughed at a story her boyfriend told about getting in a fight in a bar with someone named Fitzie. Mitch climbed the stairs to the door leading out of the cellar into the kitchen. He turned the knob carefully and the door opened a fraction before catching on a hook latch. He could undo that easily enough with a finger. He closed the door and returned to the cellar to wait. *Let them finish the bottle and pass out. Then we'll go up.*

He tried to pull the girl close to him to wait out the revelers' celebration, but she wouldn't budge. Instead, she wanted to inspect a corner of the basement near a pile of boxes. Mitch followed her over. "What is it, hon?" he whispered. She didn't answer. She let out a groaning sigh and pointed at the ground beneath the stack. The checkered vinyl flooring was torn, exposing the two-toned concrete beneath. There was a clear, jagged line where it appeared new concrete had been inexpertly poured and spread to patch an older portion. Sophie knelt and ran her hands over the rough, lighter-colored cement. She looked at Mitch, pleading silently.

"What? I don't get it."

She held his wrist and pulled him down to the ground next to her. With her other hand, she touched the cement and said, "Here," in her thin dream voice.

"I don't understand, hon. We just have to wait for a while and then we can go upst—" She slapped at his forearm in the petulant way she'd done when she was still alive and wasn't getting her way. He tried to imagine what it was she wanted, but couldn't.

She pointed at the floor and pleaded again before caressing the cement some more. "Here," she insisted.

He stood up and began moving boxes out of the way, not sure what she was looking for. He imagined he wouldn't be surprised if he uncovered a door in the floor leading down into... what? A sub-basement? But once the stack was shifted away, he found nothing but the light patch surrounded by the darker, older concrete. "It's just the ground, baby. There's nothing there."

Sophie flattened a hand out on the lighter colored patch of floor and the black veins snaked out from her hands. She grew more pallid and her skin tightened around bone until she looked nearly skeletal. Mitch tried to pull her away from the spot, but he couldn't move her. The concrete darkened and broke under her palms, loud cracks echoing around them. He held his breath waiting for the sounds of the heavy footfalls above to move toward the basement door and come clomping down the stairs. The party overhead continued unabated, however. Sophie kept rotting the floor, spreading her decrepitude out until it had consumed a section maybe four feet across. She sat back up, wobbly and weak. Her face was sunken in and her skin seemed as thin and translucent as onionskin. Mitch felt a sharp pain of desperation stab at him. This wasn't what he'd come here to do. She was almost all gone. If he asked her to rot a lock or a doorknob, he wasn't sure there'd be anything left of her but a sack of bones.

"You have to stop, baby! You have to keep something for yourself until we can get upstairs." She shook her head and pointed at the ruined concrete. "What's down there, hon?" He wanted to say, *don't make me dig. Please don't make me dig it up, whatever it is.* But he didn't. Instead, he set her gently aside, letting her lean against a crate full of old kitchen junk, and began to carefully pull away the cracked and loosened cement chunks with his hands. Shoving them up against the wall, he uncovered damp earth below. He didn't need to look at his niece to know she wanted him to go deeper. So he did. Shoving his fingers in, he pulled back at the dirt, two, three times, before finding what it was she was after.

He pulled the dead boy up out of the ground by his jumper. It was hard to tell, but Mitch figured he was maybe two or three years old. His overalls had Thomas the Tank Engine on the bib. His skin was patchy and rotted away and what remained was black with decay. He smelled like earth, and for that Mitch was thankful. When the boy opened his shriveled eyes, Mitch wanted to drop him and run away. Instead, he pulled him the rest of the way out of the ground and sat back with the child in his lap.

Lips thin and pulled back from tiny teeth, his sockets barely filled with the shriveled remains of what had once likely been big bright eyes, the child moved its face in a horrendous mockery of a toddler waking from a nap. It reached up with skeletal hands and rubbed at what was left of its eyes. The kid barely looked human. Mitch tried to contain his horror. His body wanted to run, to climb back out that little window and into the night, and never look back. But he couldn't. Not until he got Sophie what she needed. Not until both of them got their second chance. But now this. This boy. The corpse in his arms wriggled and reached up for him. Mitch felt a chill on his face like an arctic blast. Sophie crawled over and touched the child. He turned his head toward her and they studied each other for a moment. The cold receded.

Mitch's eyes filled with tears and a fresh rage gripped at his heart. He'd just pulled the body of a boy out of a shallow grave in his neighbor's basement. Buried in the cellar like some dirty secret Faye could just cover up and pretend was never there. Just like she'd treated Sophie. Put in her crib and covered with a blanket like nothing at all was wrong.

Non-accidental trauma.

BANG!

Anger.

BANG!

Shame.

BANG!

Rage.

He looked to his niece for some kind of direction. She knelt in front of him, quietly studying the child in his arms, and gave him no guidance. Whatever she'd come back knowing or feeling, she was still just a child with a child's way of telling him what she wanted.

He thought about the people upstairs. What if *two aren't enough. What if Faye and her boyfriend won't heal both these kids. So what do I do with* him? Sophie took the boy's hand and pulled. Mitch placed the tiny thing gently in her lap. She smoothed the remains of the hair on the boy's skeletal head gently like she'd once done with her dollies and cooed at him. The boy opened his mouth to groan in response but no sound emerged. Not even a breath. He just opened and closed his rictus in a decrepit pantomime of speech and wiggled his shriveled little eyes. Mitch wondered if they shared some kind of connection, like a psychic link. *She'd known he was under the concrete after all. Maybe it's not as strong as that. We know our own, don't we? I bet you can just tell when someone like you is near, huh?* He'd once been at a party with a friend of a friend who had been recently discharged from the Marines. The guy shook Mitch's hand and asked where he'd seen combat. Mitch told him that he'd never served and the guy just nodded and gave him a look that said he knew he wasn't in the forces but that there was more than one kind of war zone. They spent most of the evening talking about other things: sports and the weather, the hosts, the quality of the beer. Just a couple of broken men sitting around talking about anything but being broken. *Some of us can just find each other, can't we. The bungled and the botched can feel each other from* miles *away.*

He sat behind his niece, wrapping his arms around her while she tended to the dead boy. Fatigue started to set in. He forced himself to stay awake. Forced himself to keep listening to what was going on above them. After a while, the diminishing sounds from upstairs suggested the partiers had celebrated enough for the night. He checked his watch and blearily noted the hour. Half past two. *Give it another half an hour. We'll still have enough time for Sophie to take what she needs and for us to get on the road before sunrise. We can get to a motel and I can catch some sleep before we head the rest of the way.*

And what about the boy? What do I do about him? He tried to think, to conceive a plan where he brought his niece back to life and was still able to do something right by the boy. *He's not my responsibility. I don't owe him a thing.* Except he didn't believe that at all. Everyone else had failed the kid, and they'd buried him like a dirty secret. He'd pulled him out of the dirt to do what? Shove him *back* in the ground and pretend he'd never seen him? He couldn't bury all of his problems. He wasn't any good at covering things over and walking away.

Mitch recollected the conversation he'd had with the detectives on his front porch. Although the boy was suffering from months of decomposition, he could tell the child didn't resemble either Faye or her adopted daughter. Re-homing. "You're not Faye's. Whose son are you?" The child couldn't answer.

The silence deepened. He checked his watch again, and whispered, "Time to go." Standing, he held out a hand for Sophie. She refused to move. "Come on. It's time." She pulled the boy closer, nestling him against her shoulder like Mitch did with her. He knelt down and caressed her gray face and wept. "I can't help him. I can't." Her brow furrowed and she scowled at him. "I can't save every kid in the world, Sophie. I just want to save you." She didn't move. He sighed and held out his arms. He had to do something. "Okay." She smiled and allowed Mitch to take the boy from her arms. Together they stood and headed for the stairs.

45

Faye lay in bed, sprawled out and dead to the world. Next to her, the boyfriend was also unconscious. His pants were bunched around his knees and her skirt shoved up over her hips, but neither had gotten as far as taking their underwear off and actually getting it on before passing out. Mitch thought about shielding Sophie's eyes and covering the couple up before letting her at them. But given what she was about to do, seeing a pair of losers in an embarrassing state of semi-undress wasn't going to scar her.

He led her to the side of the bed and stepped back, waiting. She didn't reach out for the couple the way he'd seen Amye's son, Brandon, do. Instead, she turned and pointed to the child in Mitch's arms. It squirmed uncomfortably trying to find a comfortable position, but jutting, exposed bones meant no matter how the boy shifted, one of the two of them was repositioning. Mitch shook his head at her and said, "No. You go first." She shook her head and pointed at the boy.

Mitch sighed and stepped up to the bed. He crouched in front of Sophie and implored her, "Please, honey. He can go second. Just leave enough behind for him. Please, do this for me." She shook her head and reached for the child. Mitch helped her hold the boy in front of Faye's face. His small jaws opened and closed, tiny brown teeth clicking softly. Sophie gently nudged them forward until the dead child was close enough. Mitch felt his ribcage expand in his hands as the boy took in a breath much too deep for a child his size.

Faye's unfocused eyes popped open and she struggled to sit up. Mitch shoved a hand down on her head, forcing her back against the mattress. He looked into her face. It was frightened and full of panic. He knew that look. It was the expression of every person whose life had just taken a turn they couldn't control as it spun out from under them like a swift current propelling them toward the falls. It was the look his mother wore as his father popped her for "mouthing off," his sister when she embarrassed her boyfriend in front of his crew, Junior Wilson on the wrong side of a hammering, and a fresh fish on the block staring at his cell door. It was the look of having your self-determination and dignity taken from you by force. As he held her head down on the mattress, moving his palm up to the side of her overtanned, wrinkled face, Faye pleaded with him with wet, wide eyes begging for a mercy that wouldn't be reciprocal if circumstances were reversed. Mitch stared in Faye's face and denied her grace.

The boy continued to inhale, stealing her breath, and Mitch felt her skin growing cold beneath his fingers. The chill crept up into his hand; he kept his hold firm and let the boy take what he needed from her. He let the child hold her accountable for the things she'd done, knowing that when he'd stared up at her with that same look, she'd turned him down. When Sophie had begged for compassion, Meghan shook her until her little brains were bruised, and she died in her crib while Mitch and Liana slept in the next room unaware the entire world had been shaken.

Sophie grabbed Mitch's shoulder and pulled at him. He let go of the woman and let her lead him away. Settling on the floor next to his niece, they watched the rotten flesh on the back of the boy's head begin to fill in and darken with pink life. Faye's skin was thinning and wrinkling, fat blue veins protruded as liver spots grew and spread like drops of ink on paper. The boy was taking her future away from her, reclaiming every day she'd denied him. The kid stepped back, teetering on unsteady feet. He looked better, but still dead. Patches of flesh filled in with fresh, thin skin, pale and delicate. His eyes were full and brown beneath the fading cataracts. Faye lay on her stomach, gasping shallowly and shivering.

Fucking hell! He left her alive.

Faye was still conscious of what was happening, and couldn't do a thing for herself even though Mitch wasn't holding her down anymore. Despite his horror at the realization, he tried to push Sophie forward to take the boyfriend. Instead, she led the boy around like an older sister and grabbed the man's hand, trying to drag him closer to the edge of the bed. When she couldn't move him, she let out a frustrated groan and knitted her eyebrows, asking Mitch for help. He stood and shifted the drunk man over so his head hung off the edge of the bed. The boy breathed him in. Mitch turned away, not wanting to watch Sophie's last chance at restoration slipping away. Given away by a girl who'd always been generous and eager to share what little she had, no matter how little.

He felt her hand slip into his and he dropped back down to the floor, pulling her in for a hug. Mitch couldn't control himself any longer. All her life, he'd been trying to do the right thing and never coming quite close enough. Nothing he did fixed the problem. He made things worse, broke promises and people, and failed at every attempt to make anything better. His attempts always resulted in him being left with fewer options than when he started, and this time was no different. Every single act of justice he'd attempted in his life left him feeling empty and alone. "I'm so sorry for everything."

"Don' cry," she said. She wiped away his tears with tiny fingers. When she smiled again, a touch of life sparkled in her eyes and he though he caught a glimpse of the girl she'd been before he'd let everything slip away. The girl who laughed when he blew on her belly. Who giggled uncontrollably when he pretended to stub a toe and hopped around the playground on one foot. The girl sitting on the floor asking the woman he was infatuated with to crouch down and build her a pyramid. Like the child she'd been in the best moments of his life.

It was only a few seconds long and gone in an instant.

Nothing good can last.

He looked at the boy. The child had finished with the lover and was sitting on the floor against the wall. His cheeks flush and toddler fat, hazel brown eyes unblemished and clear. He glanced at Mitch and his face screwed up in a tortured expression. Feeling the pangs of a living body for the first time in who knew how long, the boy responded in the way that toddlers do when they feel any kind of need like nourishment, warmth, or love. He began to cry. The high keening noise rose in the quiet night, drowning out the labored breathing of the half-corpses on the bed. It filled the room and spilled out into the hall. And Mitch felt the pull at his gut. The drive to heed the cry and answer the call with whatever the child needed. A blanket, a dry diaper, a meal.

The boy pushed himself up from the floor and tottered over to him and Sophie. He was so small, so fragile. Someone had to miss him. *Someone had to wonder what had happened to their little boy, didn't they?*

"Shut that fackin' baby up!" a drunken voice called out from down the hall.

Meghan, he realized. He'd forgotten about Meghan.

At the sound of her voice, Sophie latched tighter to him and cried, "No shakes! No shakes!" He realized then why she hadn't wanted to take from Faye and her beau. It was Meghan who'd shaken her to death. Meghan who owed her life. Faye had come over afterward and relieved her daughter, sending her out into the night to establish an alibi, knowing that it would be their word against hers. Knowing what to do, because she'd done it before.

The boy cried. The woman shouted.

"I said..."

Mitch heard heavy footsteps thumping toward the bedroom. Sophie clutched at him and the boy cried harder. The steps hesitated. Mitch imagined Meghan trying to work out why there would be a baby crying in their house, but having trouble making sense of it through the fog of drink and whatever else was pulling at her consciousness. He set Sophie down and stalked toward the door. It swung open before he could get his hand on it, the knob punching him in the gut and his forehead smacking the door. He staggered back, seeing stars. Meghan stared at her mother, a nascent scream trapped in her throat. Faye had been a fifty that looked seventy and acted fifteen. Now she looked like a thousand-year-old mummy.

Meghan turned and saw Mitch as he lurched toward her. She sidestepped him and stumbled drunkenly along the edge of the bed. He was dizzy from the knock against the door and overshot, but righted himself quickly. Turning to face her, he wondered why she'd run into the corner where she couldn't get away. *She's still wasted. She has no idea what she's doi—*

The sight of the gun from the nightstand cut his thoughts short and he was reduced to an animal recognition of peril staring him in the face. The hair on his arms stood on end as his skin pimpled up and his breathing increased. He launched himself at the girl as she pulled the trigger. The flash from the muzzle in the dark blinded him, but he still found his mark and tackled Meghan into the wall. The rush of breath out of her body stank of booze and bile as she vomited down his back. She pulled the trigger again, somehow missing him a second time. His ears rang and the sound of the world around him dulled. All he could hear clearly was the throb of his pulse pounding in his skull. He drove an uppercut as hard as he could into Meghan's stomach, unconcerned that he was laying into a girl half his size.

She had the equalizer.

He punched her again and again, feeling her muscles convulse and go slack until he realized that his body was the only thing keeping her on her feet. Mitch stepped away and let the girl fall to the floor, convulsing and dry heaving. The gun was lost. He turned. His world came apart.

Sophie lay slumped against the wall next to ragged holes where the two rounds that had gone all the way through her had embedded behind her. *She was never aiming at me!*

He rushed to his girl, dropped to the floor, and lifted her into his lap. He cradled her ruined head, gently trying not to hurt a child who couldn't feel a thing. "Sophie! Don't leave me! Sophie!" The boy's cries faded back into the world as Mitch's dulled hearing slowly repaired itself and the sounds of the room returned to life. Behind him, he heard Meghan groaning and a heavy thump as she tried to pull herself back to her feet and failed.

Not like this. Please, not like this. I can't take it again. "Do you hear me?" he shouted. "She can't die again!" He howled into the dark. He cried and cursed and damned everything that had led to this moment. He blamed himself and Meghan and God and everyone real or imagined that he couldn't hold to account. He cursed everything and prayed for the world to end in a blast of cleansing fire. Without her, nothing!

Without her, *nothing!*

No cleansing spark ignited in the night. No light came to show him the way. He knelt on the floor clutching a dead child and wished for another chance.

But wishes are worth less than the time it takes to make them.

46

Bill Dixon closed the door on Meghan Cantrell and slapped his palm twice on the roof of the car. The patrolman turned on the lights and drove away from the curb, leaving the detective standing on the sidewalk at the far end of the lawn in front of the house. His partner was supervising the medical examiner's team loading the body of the dead girl into the back of a transfer van while her uncle sat on the stoop, wrapped in a gray wool blanket, staring blankly into a cold cup of coffee. His eyes were puffy and swollen from crying. His face looked like that sad sack boxer suckered with promises of a shot at the title and a big purse to come after you win this one fight. But that guy never had an honest shot at the title. The best he got was a good mention by some retired, punch-drunk pugilist on HBO if he had the stones to stand toe-to-toe with the fate predestined to him by the odds fixers. Still, some take their lumps hoping that the gods might be fixing the other guy's odds instead. Hope dies last.

Life is a sucker's bet the minute they put you on the scale.

The ME's van pulled out of the driveway, leaving Braddock standing alone by the kitchen door around the side of the house. Dixon shrugged. Braddock nodded once before they converged on Mitch.

"Time to go," Dixon said as he approached the steps. "We've got some more questions for you." Mitch had told him that he and the girl had needed a place to crash after their own house was ransacked. He said he thought the neighbors were still staying down at the boyfriend's place in Revere. When Faye and her beau came home, he and Sophie retreated to the basement. That's when they found the dead boy and things started to go south.

The story was *almost* plausible. Until he got to the part where he and Sophie fell asleep waiting for the party upstairs to die down.

"When I woke up, the boy was gone. Everything was quiet and so I went upstairs to find him. I was going to take Sophie and him and leave. That's when I found them all in the bedroom like that." His delivery was sincere. The details were simple and not too great in number. The guy was a damned good liar. But Dixon ferreted out lies for a living. People fed him a line of bullshit every hour of every day and if he couldn't see through it, he never would have made it to lieutenant detective. He wasn't perfect, though. Fortunately, everything he missed, Braddock caught. Today, they both agreed: Mitch LeRoux was convincing, but he was also full of shit.

Dixon extended a hand to help the man off the steps. Mitch refused it and stood up on his own. Braddock gestured to their car; Mitch shuffled toward it like an old man. Both detectives had seen a lot of people prematurely aged in the last few weeks. Their bodies wasted by the appetites of the dead kids, but their minds left solid and clear. Prisoners locked in meat-cells that would probably live for decades, if cared for. Even if those people had no one to tend to their needs, the Commonwealth would step up. It'd work to keep them alive. And that was what most of them deserved. Going through the records, as they had, none of the kids who'd come back had died of things like leukemia or other acts of God. He almost laughed at the thought of an act of God. It had seemed like that at first. A lot of people had gone on about divine mercy and the meek being blessed. And then the kids got hungry and Hell broke loose. It wasn't long before they found the first adult victims of God's mercy drained and left for dead in a kitchen, a bedroom, a church cafeteria. You only had to open your eyes to see it wasn't mercy that brought the dead kids back from the grave. But Mitch wasn't one of those. Instead of having his soul sucked, he'd been aged by experience, disappointment, and despair. All the things that build up and kill people slowly—the precursors to a bullet in the mouth or leap off a bridge into freezing water. Mitch wasn't a dead man, but he was dying inside and unless something intervened, it wouldn't be long before his despair metastasized.

Dixon helped him into the back seat with a hand lightly atop his head before closing the door with more care than he'd shown Meghan Cantrell. Braddock waited on the other side of the vehicle. They'd worked this out while they waited for the social worker to come for the boy. He was two years old and looked healthy, but there was no telling how long he'd been in that basement—in the grave Mitch had failed to mention in his confession, but Dixon found anyway. Who knew how long the kid had been in the ground? It complicated things. He might have gone off the grid years ago. Who knew where to go looking for a missing boy who'd been essentially transported through time? Two and a half years old when he died, two more until he came back, how many years later. He tried not to think about it. They were homicide detectives, not missing persons or special victims. No *living* child was supposed to be their problem.

"So, what do you think?" Braddock asked.

Dixon checked his watch. "Day's early. We're good."

The partners climbed into the car. Braddock turned over the engine and pulled out into the light mid-morning traffic. Dixon turned around in the seat and said, "We've been looking for you for a while, Michel."

• • •

For hours, Mitch sat in the interrogation room, shivering, waiting for the detectives to come in to pick apart his story, confront him with the inconsistencies and holes in his tale and get him to confess to what he'd plotted in Faye's house. They hadn't done that. Instead, they left him in the bright box with a soft plastic bottle of "purified" tap water and a chocolate chip granola bar from a vending machine.

My last meal.

So he waited. He waited for them to come haul him back to jail to await trial. Although he had no illusions about what he'd do if freed, he didn't allow himself the fantasy of what life would be like on the run, heading to Canada to hide out. There was no point to it. He couldn't imagine a scenario where a judge would grant him bail. He was officially a recidivist and a flight risk. Instead, he sat and worked out his confession. A true one.

When Dixon and Braddock returned, they didn't bother with the routine they'd run him through last time—questions and threatening posture. The bigger one just held open the door while his partner said, "Let's go." Mitch stood and followed them.

He hadn't been able to see the road during the ride to New Hampshire a month ago, but he still felt a sense of *déjà vu* riding in the back of the detectives' car. Wherever they were taking him, it wasn't jail. They were on their way out of town. According to the late afternoon sun, they were headed northeast this time. Toward Revere, he guessed. Maybe Arkham. Beyond that, it was hard to get his bearings. He tried to orient himself with the scenery passing by. The majority of it, however, was so uniformly commercial—cell phone merchant, pawn shop, shuttered video store, Dunkin' Donuts—that he couldn't tell anything about the neighborhood by looking at the landmarks, except that he wasn't being taken on a sightseeing tour of historic Miskatonic River Valley mansions. After a while, the city congestion lessened and the highways through thickly-settled neighborhoods began to thin to the urban blight of office parks and old factory buildings that populated the borders between contiguous towns. If you missed the signs, there was no way to tell when you left one municipality and entered another. They'd left Kingsport far behind, that much was certain.

Eventually, the car slowed. His hope that the world might show him some mercy diminished. Braddock pulled off of the highway and into the lot behind an abandoned-looking industrial building. The air smelled of caramelized sugar and machine oil. Mitch leaned over to see if the blocky building still boasted a sign for whatever concern had once occupied its rooms. Painted on the weathered brick wall between the third and fourth floor windows was a long, faded banner that read "MANTOOTH AND ROWE CANDY CO." Beyond the far wall, a dark river flowed.

That's where they'll find my body. If they find my body.

Without his niece to save him, he knew this to be his final stop. He figured it was time for deep blue justice and wondered how long the end of his life was about to last, and how badly it was going to hurt. Although there were no other cars parked in the lot that he could see, he figured there was a line of policemen inside each waiting to take a strip of his hide to tie to the lamp posts like memorial ribbons.

Braddock pulled up next to a yellow school bus and shut off the engine. Both men climbed out of the car. Dixon opened the rear door and Mitch flinched waiting for the cop to seize his bicep and drag him from the back seat. Instead, Dixon stepped aside and gestured as though he were inviting him to step out onto a red carpet. Mitch slid over and crawled out. "Where are we?"

"Welcome to Aylesbury," Dixon said.

Braddock walked ahead of them, saying, "Let's get this over with," over his shoulder. Mitch wanted to feel like his feet were rooted to the spot. It was surprisingly easy to move in the direction of his doom, though. He fell in behind the bigger man, trailed by his partner, as they walked into the factory through a pair of solid metal doors that screeched from years of rusted neglect as they opened.

It took Mitch's eyes a moment to adjust to the dimness inside. Shapes to the left and right began to emerge from the gloom, floating by like half-realized symbols in a dream. They passed giant tarnished vats with dusty electrical control boxes standing guard in front, three-tiered industrial grinders, and metal link belts stretching along long tables. The austere functionality and cool efficiency of it all reminded him of Dr. Downum's autopsy theater.

They led him up two flights of stairs. "In here," Braddock said, pulling back an opaque plastic strip curtain. Mitch stepped through into a long room with dusty wooden floors and thick support beams rising up to metal pulley wheels like some steampunk forest. The windows at the far end of the room practically glowed white with the bright sun beaming through years of built up dust and sugar residue that made it hard to see. He walked toward them, thinking maybe he could leap through one to get away. If he was lucky, he might catch his carotid on the way through and bleed out peacefully in the gravel outside, if the fall was insufficient to kill him.

The room stank of sweat and fear and shit and rot. It was what he imagined an abattoir must smell like. There was no remnant of confectionery labor in this chamber. As his eyes adjusted, he saw them. Four bodies, laid head to toe in a line in the dark along the far wall. Three men and one woman. A miasma of copper and ammonia hung in the stale unmoving air. *Dixon and Braddock are settling scores. The whole world has gone mad and this is what it looks like. Lines of bodies in candy factories converted into secret execution chambers. Who are these people? Parents of returned kids? Killed for what? Doing the wrong things for the right reasons?* He took a step toward them, ready to take his place at the end of the line. *Room for one more.*

Dixon laid a hand on his shoulder, redirecting him toward the far wall. "That's none of your business," he said.

"In here," Braddock said, holding open an office door. Mitch stopped, trying not to imagine what special Hell they had awaiting him in the next room. Though he'd led himself through the corral chute up to this point, he couldn't force himself to take another step forward into the all-too-brief future. He couldn't run to face the pneumatic bolt. Dixon took Mitch's arm gently and guided him the last few steps.

"What is this?"

Dixon exchanged a glance with his partner and said, "Your last bite at the apple. Make it a good one."

That sense of having been somewhere before swirled in his head, threatening to uproot him from the present. He walked into the room, unmoored from reality like a man waking from a dream. Feeling like he was stepping back in time, walking into the medical examiner's office weeks earlier, looking at his niece propped up in a chair and thinking, *there is no word for someone who's lost a child because it's too horrible a thing to name.* When Sophie slipped off the worn old office chair and ran toward him, he doubted his sanity. *They've already killed me. They killed me and I didn't even know it. And where am I? The things I've done, this isn't Heaven.* He dropped to his knees and the girl wrapped her arms around his neck, exclaiming, "Papa!" He cried and hugged the ghost and waited for everything to slip away into hard reality again. This reunion, a quantum memory before the rope tied to the Owl Creek Bridge snapped his neck. A dead man's dream of a life he wished he could have.

But she persisted. Squeezing him, the scents of sweat and dirt and unwashed child. He pulled back to look in her face. The places where her skull had been torn away by Meghan's bullet were covered in fresh pink flesh that looked tender, like newborn skin. One of her eyes was brighter than the other, but both were clear and blue. Her hair was uneven, only stubble over the new skin and bone, but the rest of it was as he remembered once upon a time. Dark and brown, not gray.

"Why you crying?" she asked. She reached up and wiped away his tears with brown-stained fingers. She tasted his tears the way he'd always joked when she cried. *Mmm. Baby tears. So sweet, like syrup.* It had always made her laugh in the midst of crying and soothed her. This time, *she* said the words, pulling him from his daze and grounding him in the present. Bringing him back to the dirty, dark office in an abandoned candy factory. A Hell of Heaven on Earth.

"I'm just so happy to see you," he said, trying to explain his tears. "You make me so happy."

He turned to Dixon and Braddock. The men stood in the doorway of the room watching. A smile played around the edges of Dixon's mouth, his crooked, boxer's jaw jutting a little sideways. Braddock's face remained as it always did, bearing the inscrutable expression of a man caught for posterity in an antique photo. Mitch wouldn't have been surprised if the world from the other side of his eyes appeared sepia. "What did you do? Who are those people out there?"

Braddock said, "They're not your problem."

Mitch pulled Sophie closer, realizing what made their reunion possible. His niece was not dead, as she'd been before, but fully alive. He knew that meant one thing. "What's going to happen to Meghan?" he asked.

"Forget about her. She's not your responsibility," Braddock told him. "*That* girl is."

"Why are you doing this?"

Dixon stepped forward and crouched down. He pulled a picture of a reanimate child out of his pocket. "This kid crawled out of the basement belonging to a guy who told the Sex Offender Registry Board that he was living at his mother's house. Turns out he was living on the other side of town near the public library and an elementary school. Four other kids crawled out behind him. The guy greased himself before any of them could... take back what they lost. So we have five missing children whose parents never gave up... until their kids came home. We got the kid you brought back, but we can't find his people. He got traded like some baseball card and who knows where he really came from. Romania, Poland, Utah. It's all the same. There's no one to take him. You follow me?"

Mitch nodded.

"Those... humans out in the hall are like the rapist, murdering coward who ate his bullet: scumbag liars who should have been one place and weren't. Guys who weren't sorry for anything they did, just sorry they got caught. Don't you dare feel bad for them. Nobody's going to miss a single one of 'em."

"Meghan?"

"Nobody's going to miss her either." Braddock said, tilting his head toward the hallway.

Dixon smoothed down part of Sophie's uneven hair. "We weren't planning on doing things like this, but once we got her back the way she belonged, the only thing she'd say was, 'I want my Papa.'"

Mitch sighed. "I'm only her uncle. Her father—"

Braddock stepped forward. "You're not an uncle any more. You hear me, *Papa*? You're getting a second chance at a second chance, Mitch. It's more than most people get. It's probably more than you deserve. Tough thing is, she *wants* you, and we can see you need her. So here we all are."

"Thank you."

"Don't thank us. Do the right thing by her. Take this fresh start and do it right. My guess is, she needs more than you can give her all by yourself. You're already behind the eight ball, it being just the two of you."

He thought of Liana waiting for them in Canada. "Three. We're three."

Dixon reached in his other pocket and pulled out an envelope. "There's nothing left for you at your house or Faye's. You copy? Stay away from there. Use this and get that fresh start."

Mitch allowed himself the brief fantasy he'd banished in the interrogation room. His friends Brett and Sandra in Ontario had a big place. Liana was there, waiting for them. "We will." He stood up, holding Sophie to his chest. She lay her head on his shoulder the way she did when she was too tired to walk home from the library or day care. Her head fitting just right into the space between his neck and shoulder. The way that made him feel like they were made to be together. Puzzle pieces that fit into each other and formed the big picture.

He walked toward the door to leave. Braddock held out a set of keys. "Your car's parked around back. You got a full tank and a free State Police pass out of Massachusetts. After that, you're on your own." Mitch took the keys and stepped through the door. "Don't get caught in New Hampshire," the detective called out after him.

He stepped out into the hallway and walked past the bodies lined up against the wall. He walked out of the factory without looking back.

It all finally felt right.

Epilogue: Scenes from a Beginning

They sat on the same side of the booth toward the rear of the diner. The place was starting to get busy, and Mitch cut Sophie's hot dog into pieces hoping it would cool faster and they could get back on the road before long. The waitress came by and asked if everything was all right. They hadn't had a chance to have a bite yet, but he said, "Yup. Everything's great." Sophie took an exaggerated breath of air and blew as hard as she could on the hotdog, missing most of her plate and sending a paper napkin sailing off the other end of the table. The server lingered. He liked the image of eggs and bacon arranged like a skull and crossbones over her heart. Mitch was about to ask if they sold copies of the T-shirt when she cut him off with her own question.

"I'm sorry if this is rude, but can I ask...?" She gestured in front of her chest, as if she wanted to point to her face, but couldn't bring herself to do it.

Mitch slipped a twenty-dollar bill out of his pocket, keeping it hidden in his palm for the moment. In the last couple of days, he'd mentally prepared himself to drop money on a table for a meal they hadn't had time to eat just so they could leave quickly. He hadn't yet had to do it, but up until this moment, there had been only stares, no questions. Along with the cash, he prepared his lie, silently repeating it before speaking aloud. He cleared his throat and said, "It's okay. We can talk about it now. A faulty night light started a fire in our house. We all got out alive, but she got burned a little. If you've got kids, do *not* buy those little plug-in star projectors from the drug store." He turned to Sophie and fed her the line they'd rehearsed. "You're all better now, though. Aren't you?"

She nodded and smiled at the waitress. "Like my punk rock?" she said. She rubbed a hand over the shorter portion of her hair, misspeaking her line, but nailing the delivery.

The server smiled back and said, "Oh, I'm so sorry. You look great, sweetie." She slipped the order pad that she'd been nervously fumbling into the pocket in the front of her apron. Leaning down, she whispered to Mitch, "You let me know when you're done, and if it's okay, she can have some i-c-e c-r-e-a-m for dessert." Before he could protest, she added, "On me." Mitch smiled and said that'd be great. He didn't want the woman to pay for Sophie's dessert, but then, she hadn't had any ice cream in a very long time. Not in *this* lifetime. A customer at another table waved the server over and she left to see what he wanted.

Sophie stabbed a piece of hotdog and smeared it around in a pool of mustard Mitch had squirted into the corner of the paper lining the plastic basket it had come in. He sweated a little just thinking about how much mustard she had on the dog, but she didn't seem to mind. She chewed it eagerly with her mouth open, smacking loudly. He picked up his own dog and took a big bite. Mustard only; no ketchup.

The television against the opposite wall caught Mitch's attention. It was set to the local mid-day broadcast, and he'd been ignoring it. The news from Burlington didn't interest him. He didn't intend to stay long enough for anything that happened in the town to matter to them. But then the local news ended. And regular programming resumed.

Pastor Roper's wolf smile filled the big screen and the camera panned out to show him sitting next to a talk show host Mitch didn't recognize. He tried to tune his ear to the broadcast, but the growing restaurant noise drowned out half of what they were saying.

"Today on The Wendy... religious leader and... Gideon Roper... New Life... Welcome!"

"Thank you, Wendy... to be here."

Mitch put down his lunch and tried to breathe deeply and slow his heartbeat. He tried to convince himself that he couldn't have a panic attack every single time he saw Roper on the television. But seeing the man brought back all the sights and sounds of the compound. The cheering "amens" and the distant crackle of a bonfire. He heard gunshots and screaming. The sound of an explosion and the smell of burning gasoline—and something else—overtook the aroma of the diner. He felt the weight of Mike's body across his shoulders and the despairing defeat of pulling into a closed weigh station on the way home, to move him from the backseat of the car into the trunk, just in case they got pulled over. The quiet rustle of his ashes slipping out of an urn into the Charles River in a secret memorial in the middle of the night, and Liana's sobs. All of it came rushing back in an overwhelming flood of sense memory that blinded and deafened him.

Sophie laid a hand on his forearm and slowly the world reshaped itself into the Thru-Way Diner. The clinking of knives and forks against plates was louder than the memory of rifle cracks echoing in the woods. "I love you, Papa," she said. She knew him as well as he knew himself. And she always knew when he needed that touch, the spark of life that ignited him.

"I love you too, hon."

"When do we get to see Lia?" She'd given Liana a new nickname, and he liked it. Liana had said on the phone that she did too.

"Soon, sweetie. She's waiting for us." It was another ninety-minute drive to the crossing at Hemmingford, where he understood there was a U.S. border agent with his own reanimate child. More were waking up every day. According to their contact, he'd be working for another five hours. Even though there was time to finish lunch before getting back on the road, Mitch didn't want to cut it too close. If they missed him, they might not have another chance.

"And who is this with... today?"

"*This*, Wendy, is Violette Wilson. Her husband, Junior... injured in the attack on..." Mitch's head whipped around at the sound of Junior's name being spoken on television. *Injured?* Violette sat smiling next to Pastor Roper on the studio sofa. On a large screen behind them in the studio was a picture of a bandaged and badly-bruised Junior lying in a hospital bed. Mitch heard his sister say the words "stable" and "awake" but was too shocked at the sight of the man who'd shot Mike in the back becoming the face of the "tragedy" at the compound to be able to comprehend everything she was saying. When she pressed her hands together and said, "God has blessed us," it was as loud and clear as if she was sitting in the seat across the table from them.

The camera panned out again to show another person on the sofa. Amye's son, Brendan, sat next to Violette. "And who is this?" Wendy Whatsername asked.

Violette pulled the boy close in an awkward embrace. "...our boy, Brendan. Well, our foster son. We... after his mother passed in the terrorist attack..."

The sound of the table cracking snapped Mitch back to reality. A black tendril snaked from the tip of Sophie's finger across the Formica tabletop. She stared at the television with a dark look. He leaned in between her and the TV and said, "Should we go?" She nodded. He dropped the twenty-dollar bill on the table along with another ten from his wallet. It was probably twice the amount of the check, but their server had been nice. He climbed out of the booth, wrapped up his own uneaten dog and fries in the paper basket lining, in case Sophie got hungry in the car, and they slipped out of the restaurant.

As Mitch pulled the car onto the Interstate, the newsreader on the radio declared, "The Reanimate Child Identification and Registration Act is now headed to the Senate after passing overwhelmingly in the House. Sources close to the Oval Office have said that the president intends to sign the bill into law and strongly encourages the Senate to send it to his desk. Elsewhere in the country—" He jabbed the "SCAN" button on the radio and settled on a local NPR station broadcasting bebop jazz. He wasn't really a fan, but it kept his mind off the approaching border better than road noise. After a few miles, he heard Sophie's quiet snoring and he breathed a sigh of relief. She deserved some rest. They both did.

Maybe they'd find some on the other side.

THE END

Afterword

I've been writing fiction for just about as long as I've been able to write complete sentences. I've been writing *horror* almost as long. In the fourth grade, I remember we were given a homework assignment to come up with a Christmas story to read aloud to the class before the holiday break. I wrote a tale about Santa Claus saving a child in a vicious and bloody battle with H.R. Giger's alien from the Ridley Scott film. It was a different time then, and I wasn't expelled and the police weren't called, although my teacher sent a sternly worded note home to my mother and I was discouraged from writing anything like it ever again.

It was my first literary rejection.

But I kept at it, and eventually sold a story around the same time I found out about the Northeastern Writers' Conference, or Necon for short. I wanted to learn more about writing and publishing, and maybe meet a couple of my heroes, so I signed up for it. It was there that I met the organizer and creator of the con, Bob Booth, a.k.a. "Papa Necon." The first time I encountered Bob in person, I owed him an apology for having fucked up my registration payment and inconvenienced him. He smiled at me and said Necon had eventually gotten the money and I had made it there, so what did I have to apologize for? He then invited me to sit down with him and talk. He asked about my work, and I told him I had a single publication to my name, a five-hundred-word story published in a magazine that went out of print and out of business immediately after. He proceeded to treat me like both a professional and a colleague that entire weekend.

That was Bob Booth.

A year later, I was sitting at the same table with Bob at the next Necon and told him that I'd sold my first novel, *Mountain Home*, to a small press in Canada. He reacted with the kind of joy and pride at my accomplishment that people typically only show their own kids. He treated me like a member of his family every single day I knew him thereafter.

That was Papa Necon.

Another year later, and I was sitting with Bob while he was struggling with cancer, and he asked if I'd be interested in writing a novella for a project that he was thinking about. I said of course I would write for him, and began writing a new book the Monday after the conference let out. I wrote as fast as I could, trying to finish in time for Bob to read it, and got about two thirds of the way into the story when he went into hospice care. When he died, I struggled to finish the story, but I felt like the rug had been pulled out from under me, and I limped along at a quarter of the pace I'd written the beginning. I eventually phoned in the last third, hit "save," and closed the file. I let the book sit on my hard drive and didn't let anyone see it or even know it existed. It hurt too much to think about the book I failed to write in time for my friend to read it.

A couple of years later, again at Necon, Brian Keene, with a cigar in one hand and a glass of whiskey in the other, asked me whether I could write and deliver a book to him by the following September for the Maelstrom imprint of Thunderstorm Books. I was stunned by the offer and very nicely buzzed by my fourth or fifth IPA and I think I shouted, "Hell yes, I can!" I didn't have to think about it.

And the book I thought I had buried forever on my hard drive came back to life.

That following Monday, I printed out and began reading *Come to Dust* (which at the time was called *God Loves All the Dead Kids*). I hadn't realized at the time I was writing it that the book was a howl against the pain of losing someone you love. The first time I read it all the way through (the first time I had since Bob died), I cried. And then, I started to mark it up with a red pen. And then I wrote a new outline, and a new middle act and ending that wasn't rushed. And when I wrote "The End," I cried a little again, knowing that Bob would have been proud of this book. It's one of my favorite things I've written.

As I sit here and write this afterword, I still feel the loss of my friend and wish I had one more chance to tell him how much I love him. I wish I could put this book in his hands and personalize it. I would tell Bob how much it meant to a brand new writer to be welcomed the way I had been into the family of Necon writers who had a thirty-year history with each other already. How much it meant to me that he was my friend. In lieu of being able to fulfill that wish directly, I'm writing the following five words, and saying no more:

This is for Papa Necon.

Acknowledgments

First of all, I owe a huge debt of gratitude to Brian Keene. He gave this book the spark of life that brought it back from the dead. Thank you, my friend, for the chance to do right by this story and by our friend Bob. I'd also like to thank Paul Goblirsch for his work at Thunderstorm Books and Maelstrom bringing this project fully to life.

To my influences, colleagues and, best of all, good friends, Christopher Golden, James A. Moore, Paul Tremblay, Jonathan Maberry, Nicholas Kaufmann, John Mantooth, Chet Williamson, John Dixon, Adam Cesare, Thomas Pluck, Errick Nunnally, Christopher Irvin, K.L. Pereira, Jan Kozlowski, Jack Haringa (must die!), Adrian Van Young, Brett Savory, Sandra Kasturi, Michael Rowe, Brendan Deneen, Gabino Iglesias, Rob Hart, Kasey Lansdale, Joe Lansdale, Andrew Vachss, and Dallas Mayr, you all inspire me to work harder and be better at what I do. Thank you.

My son, Lucien, helped me find my way both into and out of the darkest places this book took me. Any truly terrifying moment in here came from the places in my heart and head where I couldn't bear to think of being without him. Thank you, sweetheart.

Lastly, my undying love, respect, and gratitude go to my wife and ideal reader, Heather. True until death!

Bracken MacLeod is the author of the novels *Mountain Home* and *Stranded*. His short fiction has appeared in several magazines and anthologies, including *LampLight*, *ThugLit*, and *Splatterpunk*, and has been collected in *13 Views of the Suicide Woods*. He lives outside of Boston with his wife and son, where he is at work on his next novel.

CPSIA information can be obtained
at www.ICGtesting.com
Printed in the USA
FFOW03n1647270917
40364FF

9 781945 373664